Shonda Ramsey

WITHOUT RESERVATIONS

Roadmap to Romance Series
Book One

SPRINGBORO, OHIO

Without Reservations
Book One of the Roadmap to Romance Series
Published by Authentically Created
PO Box 532
Springboro, Ohio 45066
www.authenticallycreated.com

Authentically Created is a division of Lilian Grace Designs, LLC

ISBN 979-8-9898545-7-8 (paperback)
ISBN 979-8-9898545-8-5 (hard case)
eISBN 979-8-9898545-9-2 (epub)

Library of Congress Control Number: 2026909556

Cover design by Shonda Ramsey

Printed in the United States of America
First Edition 2026

10 9 8 7 6 5 4 3 2 1

05192026

Authentically
CREATED

To Mom and Dad

The greatest example of a lasting love. The two of you have given me a beautiful life filled with creativity, fun, beautiful memories, and a loving family. Your love for each other is beautiful to witness. Thank you for all you've done to enrich my life by taking us on family vacations that still impact and inspire me today.

Hello Friend!

First, let me say thank you! I am so grateful you are reading my book, *Without Reservations*. Much hard work has gone into the making of the *Roadmap to Romance* series that spans across several years. Truth is, I abandoned it twice because I wasn't sure if I could properly tell the stories in a way that honors the characters I've been dreaming up.

There are some things you'll need to know before you continue, to ensure we are a good fit for each other. I am a Christian writer. I have published other books in the Christian Non-Fiction genre prior to publishing this fictional series. Those books have dedicated Biblical teachings that align with their overall messaging.

The *Roadmap to Romance* series is a work of fiction, specifically clean and wholesome romance. Though this series isn't overly preachy in terms of religious content, there is mention of God, prayer, and spiritual growth. You'll likely also discover moments where grace can be found and shared between the characters.

Additionally, within the pages of all seven books in this series, you can rest assured that the content will be free of "spicy" scenes. I am a firm believer that intimacy deserves respect and privacy. My characters are imperfect humans who often make the wrong choices in their lives and have consequences because of their actions.

By writing them in this manner, I feel my characters' stories are more relatable to our own lives and perhaps could even provide a lesson hidden somewhere that we needed to learn.

This book, *Without Reservations*, broaches the sensitive topics of children before marriage, divorce, a car accident, the death of a spouse, forced proximity and shared living spaces before marriage, forgiveness, and second chances. It is clean of explicit language and there is no mention of drugs or alcohol.

It is my hope that you find a welcomed escape among the pages of this book as you travel to a tropical island where you'll get to know more about Teresa and Lucas. Pay close attention, as I have hidden several "Easter eggs" throughout the whole series. Can you find them all?

For more interactive experiences, visit my website to learn more.

With Grace,

Shonda Ramsey
shondaramsey.com

WITHOUT RESERVATIONS

PROLOGUE
SATURDAY, JUNE 3, 1995

It was the summer of 1995. And I was stuck on vacation with my super annoying family, when all I wanted was to be on vacation with my best friend, Elizabeth Reed. This was the first time we'd ever gone to Sanderling Pointe Island. My mom sold it to me as "one of the most fun and pristine beach experiences we'd ever have." I'll admit, the island was pretty, but my cousins were not part of the fun. At 12, Sarah was boy crazy, while Louise was celebrating her first birthday in a few days. As the oldest, I was the built-in babysitter.

Not wanting to endure a day at the beach with the whole family, I had overslept. The impatient voices of my parents drifted up from the kitchen, prompting me to put on my favorite swimsuit and quickly grab everything I could fit into my small denim beach bag. I would rather be anywhere but here, and I hoped that I could escape into someone else's world with the new romance book I checked out of the library for this trip. I haven't had the best of luck with romance, and this book was the closest I could ever come to living out a happily ever after at this point.

"Teresa Rosa," my mom yelled up the stairs, "hurry up, we are all waiting for you."

I bounded down the stairs, uninterested in spending a day sitting on the hot sand while the southern sun scorched my fair skin. I climbed into the back of the van to take my seat between Sarah and Louise. Impatient, my dad pulled away before I sat down. The van lurched forward, causing me to fall onto Sarah's lap.

"Hey! Watch it," she yelled, pushing me away from her.

I stared out the window during the short drive to the beach. The trees here were like none I have ever seen before. They had long, curvy limbs, and moss hanging high from the branches. They definitely weren't like the trees in Ohio.

I noticed a path where people were riding bicycles that stretched from our condo all the way to the beach entrance and wound through areas shaded by the trees. Seeing this path awoke the adventurer in me. Once I got out of the van, I ran up to my mom, suddenly eager to ride a bike on vacation—especially if it meant I could stay out of this van.

"Hey, Mom," I said, out of breath from running, "is it possible to get a bike while we are here? It would be fun to ride the trails we passed on the way to the beach."

"Sure, honey," my mom smiled at me. "We already have them ordered, and they will arrive later today."

For once, I was grateful that my mom had taken the liberty of doing something without asking first. This bike could be my ticket away from my family this summer. I would talk her into letting me explore alone once they came, and because I was nearly 16, I knew she would say yes.

Following my parents down the sandy beach path, I noticed a gentle breeze carrying the smell of coconuts and salt. I squinted at the glare of the sun on the white sands and reached into my bag to retrieve my sunglasses.

As we made our way across the beach, I struggled to walk in my flip-flops on the dense sand. My feet sank further and further. I stumbled, leaving one of my flip-flops in the sand behind me— and landed face-first in a dune. Embarrassed, I quickly got up to brush the sand off, removed my remaining flip-flop while retrieving the one left behind. I rushed barefoot to catch up with my family and stop my feet from burning in the hot sand.

"This spot looks good," my mom said as she spread out her beach towel, and everyone else followed suit.

I sat down on my towel and began pulling contents from my bag—lip gloss, a hair tie, hat, and my new book that I couldn't wait to dive into.

"Teresa, honey, make sure you put some sunscreen on that pale skin of yours," my mom practically yelled for the entire world to hear.

I felt my cheeks flush as I looked up to see if anyone else had heard her. And that's when I noticed *him.*

He was tall and muscular, with dark brown hair that was long on top and short in the back. If I had to guess, he was my age or slightly older, and he was throwing a football with what appeared to be a younger version of himself.

A woman called out to them, and I followed the sound of her voice. She was holding a small boy who was also the spitting image of *him* and had to be about the same age as Louise. What are the odds that there would be three boys the same age as the three of us girls?

My mom broke my thoughts by slathering my back with sunscreen, causing me to jump at the sudden intrusion and sound of the sunscreen bottle's loud spurt.

"Ew, Mom, what are you doooooing," I asked, annoyed by her presence.

"The sun is hotter here than back home, and I don't want you to get a sunburn," she answered me in her usual chipper voice as she continued lathering up my back.

"Please, Mom, just hurry," I whispered, while praying that no one would see.

"Oh look, Teresa, those boys over there look like they are the same age as you and Sarah," my mom said loudly as she pointed at the two boys tossing the football. She waved and yelled loudly, "Yoo-hoo, hi there, boys."

"That's cool," I replied nonchalantly. Perhaps if I didn't show an interest, she would leave it alone.

After she walked away, Sarah leaned in closer to me. "Tess, the one my age is handsome; he's just so dreamy! Do you think he has a girlfriend? I bet he does." Her smile twisted into a frown.

"Don't get ahead of yourself there, Sarah," I said, patting her arm. "They likely don't even know we exist."

I picked up my book and began reading while lying on my stomach. Unable to focus, I couldn't help myself and peered over the top of the pages to catch glimpses of the curve of his arms as he flexed when he'd catch the ball. The breeze picked up, and his hair fell into his eyes. He reached up and smoothed his hair back into place and turned his head slightly towards me, meeting my eyes with his.

I quickly shifted my gaze back to my book, hoping he didn't see me staring at him. But suddenly, there was sand all over me and my book as the football came to rest in front of my face after bouncing a few times. I sat my book down, grabbed the ball, and stood up to face him as he jogged my way.

"Hey, sorry about that," he said as he approached. "My brother overshot that throw and I couldn't catch it."

I smiled. "No prob," I said while trying to keep my cool. "Do you play a lot?"

"Yeah, I'm the captain of our football team for my senior year. We start training camp when we get back from vacation," he answered, with a smile that filled my stomach with butterflies.

"That's awesome," I practically gushed and knew I needed to tone it down a bit. "I'm Teresa Wright, by the way."

"Nice to meet you Teresa Wright, I'm Lucas Miller," he replied, before being interrupted by his little brother.

"Luke, hurry and get the ball," his brother yelled from across the beach.

I held up the football and grinned. "Can I throw it back to him?"

"Sure, let's see what you can do," he said.

I shifted the ball in my hand with the laces up and gripped tightly. I threw the ball and watched as it sailed through the air, a perfect spiral as the ball revolved over and over before floating down and being caught by Lucas's brother.

"Wow," Lucas said as he looked at me, "I did not expect that at all. That was a perfect throw."

"Great throw, Teresa—just like I showed you," my dad yelled from behind me.

I smiled and looked down at my feet. "My dad is the pee-wee coach for our district. He taught me how to throw so I could help from time to time."

"Lucas, we are leaving. Let's go," his mom yelled.

"Cool," he replied. "Well, it was nice meeting you. I'd better get going. Hope to see you around," he said as he turned and jogged towards his mom.

"Lucas, did you see that throw?!? Also, did you get the name of the girl with her?" his brother screeched.

Once settled back on my beach towel, I picked up my book to read again—but I found it difficult to concentrate. The way he said my name was on repeat in my mind. I was grateful when my mom declared it was time to head back to the condo for lunch and swimming. I could definitely use a dip in the pool to cool off after that encounter. I wondered if our paths would ever cross again.

It's the last night of our vacation, and I snuck out one final time to meet Tess in the pool while our families slept. The last week was a whirlwind of time—simultaneously moving ridiculously slowly and speeding up. When I was with family, time would drag on as I counted down the minutes until I could meet up with Tess again. Yet, when I was with her, time flew by so fast we were saying our goodbyes as quickly as we said hello.

I knew that this likely was nothing more than a summer romance, and the distance that separated us would keep us apart.

But deep down inside, part of me hoped I would see her again. I quietly closed the door behind me. As I opened the gate to the pool, I saw her sitting on the edge.

She was looking down, her feet dangling in the water while the moon glistened on her blonde hair. She was wearing the same swimsuit she wore every time we were together. It was white with blue stripes and bows tied delicately at the top of her shoulders. It framed her petite body perfectly. Her skin was no longer as pale as when I first met her, with a nice golden tan in its place from a week in the sun.

She was so lost in thought she hadn't realized I was standing there watching her. A tear slid down her face, sending ripples in the pool as it hit the water below. I needed to make her smile, so I did the only logical thing. After I tossed my towel onto the closest chair, I ran toward the pool and jumped in right in front of her. For maximum effect, I tucked my knees into my chest as I sailed toward the water with a huge splash that I was certain drenched her.

I came up out of the water to see her mouth wide open in shock, her hair wet and plastered to her face.

"Luuuuuuuke!" she said louder than she should have.

"Shhhhhh," I said with a finger over my lips as I stifled a laugh. "We don't want to wake up the whole neighborhood."

"You are impossible, you know that?! I suppose I better get in, now that I'm already wet," she replied as she slid herself into the water.

"Just get it over with Tess! Go all in—it helps," I told her as I watched her shiver in the cool water.

She quickly went under water and came up, her hair smoothed back across her head, the water reflecting the moonlight all around her. I felt my heart skip a beat at the sight of her. Is it possible that I fell for a stranger while on vacation?

We swam over to the edge of the pool, floating as we leaned against the pool wall. My hand brushed hers and rested there, our fingers barely overlapping. We sat this way in silence for what felt like forever, but really was only a couple of minutes.

"Luke," she asked, "does this week really have to end?"

Like her, I too didn't want this week to end. "Unfortunately," was all I could say in that moment.

The weight of this new relationship coming to an abrupt end was so heavy, I felt like I couldn't keep my head above water. I stood up and waded over to her, scooped her up, and carried her out to the middle of the pool like I had done every night this week.

She wrapped her arms around my neck and laid her head on my chest as I swayed back and forth, allowing the water to splash up on us both. Her laughter was a welcomed sound, taking sadness out of the evening. We spent some time floating next to each other and staring up at the stars in the sky. We held hands in the water before finally standing up and shivering as the cool night air blew across our wet bodies. We climbed out of the pool and began drying off in silence. A million thoughts were racing through my mind.

I had overheard my mom telling my dad that there was a plan to come back to this same condo next year at this time, and they had asked the Wrights, Tess's family, to join them. I wasn't sure if that would happen, and I wondered if she knew about it.

I cleared my throat. "Do you think you guys will come back here next year?"

She looked up at me. Her blue eyes brought butterflies into my stomach instantly. "I am not sure, but my mom said they were hoping to come back during the same time and stay here again. I just don't want to get my hopes up," her voice trailed away as she looked away from me.

In the short time that I have gotten to know Tess, she confided in me that her family had a way of over-promising and under-delivering. Her dad frequently traveled for work during the week, so he was always in a rush on the weekends when it was football season. She spent most of her time alone, either reading or drawing.

I reached over and put my hand on her chin, moving her gaze back to me. "Hey, it's okay, I have an idea. Let's exchange telephone numbers and addresses so we can keep in touch. We may not get to talk every single day, but it could be fun to write letters back and forth."

If my parents would let me, I am fairly certain I would call her every day. But I also knew my dad hated paying for long-distance calls. Though I'm not a big writer, something tells me that Tess is worth it. I'll do it for her…for us.

"You'd do that?" she asked. "You would write me letters and mail them?"

"For you—yes, I would." I said, smiling back at her.

She looked hopeful as she replied, "Can you draw me some funny pictures too, like you did on the napkins at dinner the other night?"

I laughed at the memory. "Oh, you know I'll draw pictures that will be hil-ar-ious!"

"A year feels so far away. I don't want to forget about you," she said sadly.

"A year will go by faster than we realize, and we can promise each other that we will meet here again exactly one year from now."

Realistically, I knew it was a stretch. But I hoped my words to her would be true, especially with graduation next year and college prep during the summer. My grandma always said, "If it's meant to be, it will find a way."

We spent the rest of our night sitting in the chairs by the pool so we could dry off before going back inside our respective condos. We talked about our hopes and our dreams for the upcoming school year, and what colleges we wanted to attend.

"I haven't yet decided on my college major and was hoping to either become a lawyer or an art teacher," she said with passion behind her voice. "What about you?" she asked.

"Go pro football," I told her with a grin, "but I am considering majoring in finance because I am a numbers guy and the odds of going pro are astronomically small."

She giggled, "I wouldn't have pegged you to be a math nerd. The first time I met you, you came across more as the jock type."

I smiled back at her. "I've always been good with numbers. It just comes naturally to me. To be honest, I just want to go with whatever will have the biggest payout."

"Biggest payout, huh," she teased while poking me in the side.

"Yeah, I mean, who doesn't want a rich husband when they get older?" I joked back.

She smiled at me softly. "For what it's worth, money doesn't matter to me. I just want a husband who supports me and my big dreams."

"You have great dreams," I said as I winked at her.

I glanced at my watch and saw that it was midnight. "Ugh, it's time to go in."

Tears filled her eyes. "I don't want to go yet, Luke," she said as we stood up.

I reached out to her and held both of her hands in mine while we said our goodbyes, neither of us wanting to let go. I pulled her close to me and wrapped my arms around her as she sobbed against my chest. She smelled of coconuts and chlorine—a smell I'll always associate with Tess, despite it being a traditional summer scent.

"Don't cry, Tess, it will all be okay," I heard my voice catch in my throat as I swallowed down the emotions that threatened to come out.

I leaned down and kissed her on top of her head. "If anything, we'll always have this summer romance."

TWENTY SEVEN
YEARS LATER

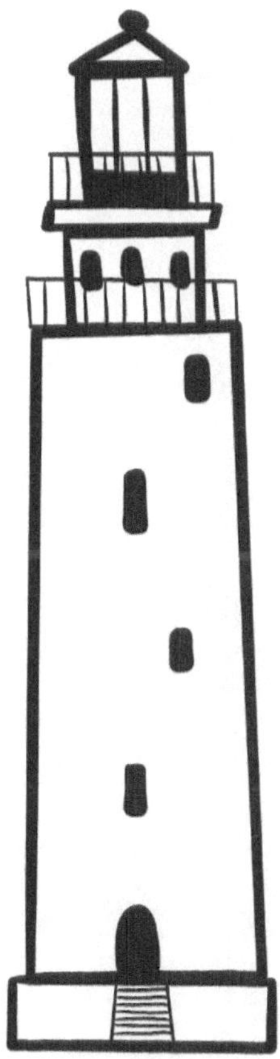

ONE

Lucas Miller

After a late start, I nervously checked my watch as the plane took off. By my calculations, we would land at the layover airport in approximately one hour and 45 minutes, arriving at 9:00 p.m.—which meant I was behind schedule by exactly two hours. Delays at the airport are often unavoidable, and I usually try to allow for that, but it was still nerve-wracking. Rarely do they inform you of the cause of the delay and whether it could be a bigger problem than you realize.

I'm not one to freak out. But—if I'm being honest with myself, I'm a little on edge with this trip. It had been a very long time since I had gone back to Sanderling Pointe Island, primarily because the last time I was there, I had my first real heartbreak.

What brought me back to the island 25 years later was a great opportunity with a close friend of mine, William. He moved to the island six years ago to set down roots and buy investment properties. A hurricane hit the same year he opened up, and it left the island in pretty terrible shape. For a while, he practically bled money in repairs and lost out on tourists with the island shut down to rebuild.

Now, the island was not only bouncing back; it was thriving, and William decided it was the best time to sell, as new investors were arriving frequently. And that is where I come in. Once the sales go through, he looks to make improved investments on the island and needs a risk assessment done to ensure he chooses the best option.

"Attention passengers of Flight 267 to Savannah, we are now approaching the Richmond Airport," the flight attendant announced. "Please fasten your seatbelts and prepare for landing."

Once the plane landed, I grabbed my bag from overhead, headed out to collect my luggage, and checked my connecting flight number on the board. With the delay, I knew it was cutting it close. I located my flight number, only to discover the board showed the status of my flight as departed. Frustrated, I walked up to the nearest desk with an attendant.

"How can I help you, sir?" the attendant behind the desk asked, while chewing her gum loudly.

"I missed my connecting flight because of the delay of Flight 267 to Savannah," I replied as calmly as I could, while handing her my phone to show her my boarding pass.

"You have two options: you can transfer your ticket to a flight going out first thing in the morning to an airport that is a 45 minute drive to the Savannah airport, or you can get a direct flight to Savannah leaving tomorrow evening," the attendant replied, emotionless.

My heart began pounding loudly—I knew I had to decide quickly. "I'll take the flight going out in the morning."

She pecked at the keyboard with her fingers at a painstakingly slow pace. "Oh, wait, so sorry, it just booked up fully, there are no more seats."

The growing line behind me groaned and grumbled at me to hurry while I tried to keep my cool. "Okay, fine, let's go with the flight going out tomorrow evening."

She smirked while still chomping her gum. "Excellent choice, Mr. Miller. Here is your new boarding pass for tomorrow's flight. Is there anything else I can help you with?"

I took a deep breath. "Actually, yes, do you have any information on nearby hotels that you can give me?" I replied rather curtly, my frustration getting the best of me.

She looked annoyed with me. "No, I'm sorry, we don't have that information here. Best of luck! Next!"

I stepped off to the side and headed towards the only open place to grab something to eat. I had skipped dinner because of the delay, and my stomach reminded me that it needed food. After I ordered, I took out my phone to search for a place to stay until my flight tomorrow.

One by one, I struck out with hotels, as it seemed all the closest hotels had no vacancies because of a convention in town. Just my luck. I would likely be stuck here overnight, which would make for a long and uncomfortable evening.

"Here's your grilled chicken with asparagus and steamed rice," the waiter said as he placed my food in front of me.

I figured I should give it one more shot before accepting this as my fate. "By chance, do you know of any hotels nearby that may be available tonight despite the conference in town?"

He stood and thought for a minute. "No, actually, I don't think so. They all usually book up really quickly for the medical conference. The moment the date is announced, doctors and nurses from all over usually book."

"Thanks, man, I appreciate it," I replied as I picked up my fork to eat.

I was hungrier than I realized and finished my dinner quickly, paid my bill, and headed back out to the terminal in search of an unoccupied place to sleep for the night. On my way, I noticed a semi-dark first-class lounge with the door open and only one other person inside with their luggage. I headed in and took a spot as far away from the other person as possible. Once settled in, I picked up my cellphone to give William a call to check in.

He picked up on the second ring. "Hey man, how were your flights?"

I sighed, "Delayed and then missed. That was why I wanted to call you real quick. I missed my connecting flight and am stuck at the layover airport until tomorrow evening. Looks like I won't make it to the island until late tomorrow night."

William chuckled. "Tough break, man. Look, why don't we skip dinner tomorrow night and plan to connect once you get settled in on the island? Would that help you out?"

I was relieved that I didn't have to ask to change plans. "Yes, that's great, actually. I know I'm not technically starting for a week, but I like to get in and get up to speed beforehand so I can come up with a game plan."

"Sounds great. I'll email you the details of the investments tomorrow. Take your time going over them, and reach out once you are ready to get together. Get some rest," William said before hanging up.

I noticed my battery was getting low on my phone and fished out my charger to plug it into the outlet next to me. Because it was June, I mostly packed summer clothes, and the lounge was colder than I liked. I went through my carry-on bag to grab my athletic jacket.

Luckily, because I was one of the first two people who arrived in this space, I could secure one of the few couches here. I was grateful that I had paid extra for the first-class ticket. This is the first time I've ever had to use any of the added perks of being a ticket holder.

I secured all of my valuables to myself before laying down on the couch and pulling my knees up to fit as best as possible on the short sofa. With my jacket covering my arms, I rested my head on my neck pillow. I must have been tired, because I fell asleep fairly quickly despite being at an airport.

The next day dragged on as I painstakingly waited for evening to arrive so I could get out of this noisy airport. When the alarm on my phone finally went off, I quickly made my way to catch my flight out.

The Savannah airport was so packed, there wasn't much elbow room as I made my way to the baggage claim. I pulled my cellphone out of my pocket to turn off airplane mode and check any messages that had come in during my flight.

A woman bumped into me, causing me to drop my cellphone, while someone else kicked it across the floor. I rushed to rescue it from further damage, checking it over. I was relieved to discover no major damage, just a few scuffs on my case.

In my inspection, I noticed I had several notifications of missed calls and texts—far more than I would have guessed. I quickly scanned the baggage carousel and didn't see my luggage, which gave me time to check the messages. My daughter, Emily, had sent me 20 texts, and there were six missed calls from her. To prepare myself, I quickly scrolled through the text messages before calling her back to understand the situation.

She picked up on the first ring. "Dad! Where have you been? I need you right now! There is an issue in the master bathroom. The toilet is overflowing. I cannot get it to stop. What do I do?!!"

Remaining calm, I replied, "Look behind the toilet. Do you see a knob? Turn it off. That will shut off the water to the toilet, which should help it stop overflowing."

She grunted as she did as I instructed. "Okay, there, it's off, but water is still coming out."

Because she was always impatient, I paused, then asked, "How about now?"

She let out a squeal. "Yay! Thanks, Dad. It stopped, but now what? There is clearly a problem here."

It is really hard to troubleshoot a plumbing issue when you aren't there to see it in person, but this house is now her problem and not mine. I signed the house over to Emily last week, so I am no longer the owner. But I am not homeless. I have a condo reserved for a month, as my next move is undecided.

Trying to be a supportive father, I answered, "My best guess without looking at it is that you likely have a clog in the pipes. If you have flushed anything other than toilet paper down there that doesn't dissolve properly, it will do that in those old pipes. I'll text you the number of the plumber I used there; he can get you squared away. For now, use one of the other bathrooms."

She sighed. "Great, thanks, Dad. I have a feeling I know what caused this. Brandon has been using wipes lately, and I told him not to flush them. But I bet he is!"

I chuckled. "Well, tell Brandon this one is on him, and he can fix it! The house is, after all, both of yours now."

She groaned loudly, clearly annoyed, "I get it, really I do, but you kind of dropped it on us right before you left! And I have never owned a house before, we don't know what we are doing, and we really need your help. When will you be back?"

I spotted my luggage as it was coming down the chute. I knew I had to act fast. "Not for a month at the very least. Look, hun, I have to get going. I'm at the airport, and my luggage just came around."

"Okay, Dad, call me back later. I love you," she replied.

"Okay, I'll call you later. I love you too," I said as I hung up.

I nearly missed grabbing my luggage before it went back around. I rushed to pull it all off the conveyor and haphazardly tossed it at my feet. Once I retrieved all my bags off the belt, I started arranging it so I could easily pull the load behind me. I had two large rolling suitcases, two bags that attached to the handle of each of the rolling suitcases, and my carry-on bag, which was flung over my shoulder.

As I bent down and picked up one of the rolling suitcases, my carry-on bag dumped its contents out onto the floor because in my haste, I hadn't fully zipped it. Annoyed with myself, I grabbed everything and shoved it back into the bag, this time securing the zipper fully before I headed over towards the car-rental desk. Honestly, could this trip get any worse?

TWO

Teresa Wright

The sound of screeching tires and shattered glass sent adrenaline pumping through my heart, as my car skidded to a violent stop. Stunned, it took me a moment to survey my surroundings as I breathed out a prayer of thanks that I was still alive. Carefully, I opened the door and stepped out onto the side of the highway.

Instantly, I was relieved to see just how lucky I was in that moment. The front end of my SUV was mangled so much that the wheel was completely shoved into the front fender. Had the other car hit me merely inches farther back, it would have been a direct impact to the driver's side door.

The other driver stumbled over to where I stood, tears streaming down her face. "I'm so sorry. I took my eyes off the road for a quick second to check my phone."

"Are you hurt?" I asked the young woman.

She patted her arms and chest, checking for injuries. "No, I think I'm okay."

"I'll call for help," I said as I reached into my pocket to get my cellphone.

After waiting for half an hour, I finally rode along with the tow truck driver as he drove to a repair shop in Savannah. It would be a bit out of my way, but was the best option for repairs while I was here. After the driver dropped my SUV and me off, one of the associates gave me a ride to the Savannah airport where I could get a car rental to drive to Sanderling Pointe Island.

In no time, I had the keys to my temporary vehicle and climbed in behind the wheel. Not letting the accident stop me from my plans, I took a deep breath before starting my rental car, a cherry red convertible. What are the odds that I would get an upgraded car rental because of a no show.

The drive took about 45 minutes to reach the bridge to the island. Nervous energy filled me as I inched closer. The last time I had been on the island was one of the happiest times of my life. Though I was young, undoubtedly I had found my soulmate. It's such a shame it had ended abruptly the way it did.

Once I was on the island, I had a short drive to Serenity Sands. Despite the condo being on the complete opposite side of the island entrance, it took less than ten minutes to reach. As I turned down Spanish Moss Lane, I put the top down on my convertible to breathe in the salty ocean air as I drove past the beach entrance to make my way to the condo.

It felt so good to be back on Sanderling Pointe after what felt like a lifetime ago. I have never been one for spontaneity, but after my split, I needed a change of scenery and pace to help get me out of the creative rut I was in. With my house on the market and almost everything I owned in storage, I decided a long road trip was exactly what I needed. I was giving myself one month to secure a new place to live and potentially open up an art gallery here on the island.

When I drove down Spanish Moss Lane, I noticed that there were still a lot of repairs happening after the last hurricane. They have rebuilt a lot already, but some of the more mature trees were clearly missing. Little baby palm trees are now in their place, waiting to grow strong and tall.

I flashed my pass and drove through the gated area after being waved through by the attendant. I loved this area of the island. The area had many homes and condos, all within the same neutral color palette. Tall live oak trees with gently swaying Spanish moss hanging from their branches sheltered each home.

The condo I selected for this trip was at the end of the street, and as I pulled into the parking spot in front, it looked simple upon first glance. I jumped out of my car, grabbed a suitcase and a bag from my trunk, and headed up the walkway to the front door entry.

I sat everything down so I could pull my phone out of my pocket in search of the code to get into the door, quickly punching in the numbers. Excitement filled me, as I couldn't wait to see what was on the inside. If it was anything like the online pictures, I knew I was in for a retreat of sorts.

I pushed open the door and rolled my suitcase in next to the table by the door. It was a one bedroom, one bath condo with a living room, an eat-in kitchen, and a washer and dryer just off of the kitchen. It was simple, but the best part wasn't inside. It was just outside the back doors.

I opened the double doors that led onto the patio, and as the warm, salty air hit my face, my breath caught as the view came into sight. It was more stunning than I remembered. The waves crashed onto the sand while the seagulls flew overhead, laughing. There was a private pool just off the patio with lounge chairs lined down the side and a fire ring just beyond the pool in the sand. I couldn't believe I had this place all to myself for a month.

In a split second, the memory of Luke and me in a pool during my last visit surfaced. Just thinking about him filled me with immense guilt about how I ended our relationship. He deserved so much more than I could have given him back then. I shook my head and let out a deep exhale. What are the odds he would be here anyway? There is no way I would ever see him again.

Not wanting to waste any more time on fairytale dreams that never come true, I went back out to my car to get the rest of my items to bring in. My friends would arrive later, and we were having a girls' night in tomorrow, which meant I had to go out in search of provisions for the party. I reached into one of my bags and grabbed a notebook to make a list of supplies I needed to pick up.

My phone rang. It was my realtor back home. "Hi Ted, I hope you have good news for me."

He sighed, "Unfortunately, I do not. Your inspection revealed some damage in the attic caused by squirrels, the buyers are requesting you cover the costs for the needed repairs."

"How does that even happen?!?! What are the needed repairs and how much is this going to cost me?" I grumbled.

He took a deep breath in. "It's fairly common, actually. Unfortunately, they did a lot of damage not just to the attic, but to your wood siding as well. They chewed several holes in many areas, all of which will need repaired. Feces completely covers the insulation in the attic, so it also needs to be removed and new insulation installed. For that alone, the quote came in at $11,000. And we have a recommendation for the siding to be replaced, which we are awaiting a quote for."

I really didn't want to spend that kind of money on a house I was selling. "Can we just pull from the buyer and sell it to the next bidder with an as-is offer?"

He paused for a moment. "I don't think that's a good idea. You could lose out on both and still have to do the work."

It sounds like I don't have many options. "Would it be okay for me to take some time to collect my thoughts? I promise to call you back before the end of the day."

He quickly replied, "Take all the time you need and get back to me when you are ready."

I hung up the phone, tossed it in my purse, grabbed my party planning list, and went to the Driftwood Deli and Grocery to get food and party supplies. My mind needed a distraction from the news I had received. I couldn't let this slow down my plan to move here, and I had to get the house sold so I could buy a place on the island.

On my way to the store, I took the long and scenic route as I cleared my mind. This change in route led me past the lighthouse to the parking lot of the only art gallery on the island. Sanderling Pointe Gallery and Gifts was in a strip mall nestled behind a row of loblolly pine trees that lined the highway. The strip had several buildings in a row, each slightly different from the others. The art gallery was the most unique of them all.

The gallery was on the corner and had large windows along the side and front of the building on both floors. Ivory-colored faux shiplap adorned the building's exterior, and black modern letters spelled out the gallery name. The staff kept the outside very well manicured, which created a welcoming space. Just sitting outside of the gallery filled me with excitement as I considered the possibilities that awaited me.

I got out of my rental car to go inside when I noticed the for sale sign in front of the building. This wasn't a surprise to me, because I already had my eye on this beauty. And I was dying to see the inside.

I walked up to the door, opening it with anticipation and excitement. A chiming bell announced my entry, and I was surprised to see how open and airy the space was.

A stunning older black woman walked towards me with a smile. She had short hair that was a natural blend of gray and brown, with curls that came halfway down her face. She wore an elegant black jumpsuit with a chunky belt at her waist with simple silver jewelry.

"Hello, and welcome to Sanderling Pointe Gallery and Gifts. I'm Eloise Freedman. How may I assist you today?" She reached out her hand to shake mine.

I clasped my hand in hers. "Eloise, so nice to meet you. I'm Teresa Wright. I spoke to you on the phone last week about the gallery."

She let go of my hand and smiled. "Ah, yes, Teresa, welcome to the gallery. I would be happy to show you around if you'd like?"

I could not wait to see the rest of the gallery. "Yes, of course, I would like that very much."

Eloise led me through the space. I hung on to every word she said about each piece of art and its artist. Her extreme passion for the gallery was clear, making her decision to close it confusing.

I didn't want to come across as too harsh. "Eloise, may I ask why you are closing the gallery?"

She took a quick breath in. "Well, my dear, the time has come for me to retire. For two years, I've sought an art enthusiast to take it on, but my time is up. Because I don't own this building, and the owner wants to sell it, I decided now was the chance to move on."

I smiled softly at her. "I love it more now that I have seen it in person than I did when I viewed it online. Do you know whether the owner has received any offers?"

She thought for a moment before replying, "No, I don't think anyone has formally offered yet, but there have been several interested parties coming through."

Not having made an appointment, I knew I shouldn't take up any more of Eloise's time. "Thank you for taking time out of your day to show me the gallery. I have really enjoyed my time with you, but I must be on my way."

She smiled. "You are welcome to come by anytime. I am not closing for at least another month and plan to remain open until I move everything out."

I turned and walked out of the front door, heading back to my car. I couldn't stop thinking about how much I needed to sell my house so I could buy this building for my art gallery. I have wanted to open a gallery to showcase my art for many years, but I put my family's needs ahead of my own. But now—it was my time.

I picked up my phone and called Ted back. "Hey Ted, I decided to move forward with the repairs. Whatever it takes, get it done, and I'll cover the cost."

He enthusiastically replied, "Excellent! I'll get everything taken care of and work on negotiations for the costs, too. After that, I'll get the final documents ready for your signature."

I wanted to make sure we were still on the same page. "I can still do this sale while out of town, correct? Could you possibly move the closing date up since I need this sale to go through quickly? By adding the cost of the repairs into the sale, they can schedule them on their own after the sale is final."

He didn't seem to be fazed by my demands. "Absolutely, I will make sure it happens. Also, I will send the documents overnight for your signature before the closing date, and I will arrange for their return shipment to me."

I was relieved that I was one step closer to potentially closing this chapter of my life for good. Once I no longer had the house hanging over my head, I would be free to do whatever I wanted to do for the first time in my life.

I started up my car and pulled back out onto the highway toward the grocery store. As I drove, I couldn't help but dream about the possibility of opening my gallery in that beautiful location. I aspired to share my art with the world instead of hiding it away behind closed doors.

I could visualize exactly how I would lay everything out. The existing gallery would only need a few minor changes to turn the upstairs area into a classroom. I have always wanted to be an art teacher and having the space to teach would be incredible.

Downstairs, in addition to my gallery viewing area, I could section off areas for local artists to rent gallery space to showcase and sell their work. This would truly make the gallery feel like a permanent part of the community. We could even host events that honor the artists and give them much needed exposure to strengthen their career.

I was so lost in my dream that I missed my turn and had to backtrack to get to the store. Once I parked in the lot of the Driftwood Deli and Grocery, I paused for a moment to allow myself time to finish dreaming about what my future might now hold.

Unfortunately, when I closed my eyes, the only thing I could see was Lucas Miller smiling at me. Annoyed, I opened my eyes and collected my purse from the front seat. I will not let my past define my fresh start on this island. Lucas Miller is ancient history. Some things are better left in the past.

THREE

Lucas Miller

Pushing my way through the congestion of the crowd, I arrived at the car rental counter, luggage in tow, to check in and pick up the keys to my convertible. I was glad to be closer to my final destination, and though I had a 45-minute drive ahead of me, it felt good to be this close to some much needed down time. After tossing and turning all night on the too-small airport sofa and spending the day at the airport, I smelled of stale coffee and cheese puffs—and desperately needed a shower.

I walked up to the associate. "Hi, I'm checking in for Lucas Miller, here to pick up a convertible."

The attendant typed my name into the computer. "I'm sorry, sir, you were scheduled for pickup yesterday. And since you didn't make the pickup time, that vehicle went to a customer who came in first."

I realize now that I probably should have called them to reschedule my pickup time, but unfortunately, that didn't cross my mind last night when I was desperately trying to find a place to stay.

Through gritted teeth, I replied, "That's on me. Do you have another one available or something similar?"

The attendant searched through the keys on the board behind her. "It looks like we have only one vehicle remaining, a van. It's bigger than the car you initially requested. Will that be okay?"

I really didn't want a van, but if that was my only option, what choice did I have other than to take it?

I sighed louder than I had intended to. "I suppose if that's my only choice, I'll take it. Is there any way to trade it for the convertible when it returns? I'll be in the area for a month."

"Actually, yes, I can put a note on your account that will trigger a flag to call you when the convertible returns," she replied.

Relieved and ready to get on the road, I replied, "Great, thanks! Let's do that so I can get going now."

After signing all the paperwork, she handed the keys over to me and directed me where I could find the van on the lot. I immediately spotted it—it was actually really hard to miss. I shook my head and chuckled as I unlocked the door and climbed inside. Of course, it had to be this van. It was almost exactly like the one we used to get when we'd come on vacation here every year—right down to the same color of blue. I was instantly thrown back into the nineties, but now I sat where my dad always sat, in the driver's seat.

I started the van and pulled out of the lot on my way to Sanderling Pointe Island. I likely wouldn't get there as fast or stylishly as I would in a convertible, but at least I was in a reliable vehicle that I knew would get me there. What are the odds that I would get this vehicle, out of all the ones there could be? I was estimating it would be about one in a hundred, which either makes me very lucky or extremely unlucky—depending on how you look at it.

As I drove, I couldn't help but think about Tess and wonder if I would run into her on the island while I was there. I knew the chance of that happening would be about as likely as landing in this rental van, but just the thought of her sent a prickle of dread through me. In a perfect world, Tess wouldn't have ghosted me. But I also wouldn't change any part of my life for anything.

The drive went by quicker than I thought it would, and I stopped for a bite to eat before heading to my condo. I had no desire to come back out again later. I stopped at The British Isles Pub, which had become one of my favorites when vacationing with family.

With all the delays and lack of sleep, I thought some good food, followed by a nice shower and an early bedtime, was exactly what I needed. Settled into the booth, I placed an order for their famous fish and chips with extra tartar sauce and a side of lemon. My mouth practically watered at the thought of eating this dish. It was something I was looking forward to and planned on eating more than once while I was here on business.

My dinner arrived piping hot, and despite burning my tongue on the first bite, I continued to shovel it in. I would have to put in extra gym time this week for this meal, but I reminded myself it was okay because I was on vacation.

Now that my belly was full, I noticed that exhaustion was setting in as the threat of a food coma was imminent. I hurried to the van, put the condo address into the GPS, and headed back out on the road. It was right around dusk. The sky was growing darker, and I knew I needed to hurry. The island didn't have streetlights, and once the sun set fully, it was almost impossible to navigate the dark streets.

I turned down the road to the condo and pulled up to my location, only to discover that most of the parking spots were full. Luckily, someone was pulling out when I got close, so I took their spot for the van. I looked up at the condo numbers to confirm I was in the correct location and double-checked the condo number on my reservation email to make sure I had everything I needed to get inside. It looked like the lights were on in my unit—they must have been left on for my arrival yesterday.

As I got out of the van, loud music instantly greeted me. Someone was certainly having a good time. I hoped it would end soon so I could get some sleep. I grabbed one of my suitcases, walked up to the front door to punch the code into the door, and walked into what appeared to be a party going on in my condo. The music was playing at a deafening level while women were dancing and drinking from gold plastic cups. I put my suitcase next to the table by the door. At that moment, I was officially out of patience.

One by one, I quickly escorted the women out of the condo and told them that the party was over. Everyone was gone except for one woman. She was beautiful, with long blonde hair, a petite and fit frame, and dressed elegantly in a black summer dress. My eyes caught hers. They were as blue as the water just beyond her, something eerily familiar about them.

She walked up to me. "I'm so sorry. The music was loud, wasn't it? I told Lynn it was too loud and to turn it down, but, classic Lynn, she did her own thing."

Annoyed with the beautiful intruder, I snapped back, "What are you doing in my condo?"

Confusion filled her face. "This is my condo. I just got here yesterday and am staying in it until the end of the month."

Now it was my turn to be confused. "That is impossible! I reserved this condo for a month."

Grabbing my phone, I checked my reservations to confirm the condo booking. "I booked it on a discount site about a month ago. I have the confirmation email, the code to the lock, and the dates from June 4, 2022, to July 1, 2022."

She smirked. "Yeah, well, I too have a confirmation email, the code to the lock, and the dates from June 4, 2022, to July 1, 2022. It sounds like the only difference is that I booked it directly with the condo resort three months ago."

She held her phone to show me. And she was, in fact, correct. She did all the right things. Chances were the site I booked from didn't update after her reservation, and now, here we are—double booked. Admitting defeat at this point was not an option. I needed this condo, and I would do anything to stay here.

Perhaps I could try buying her out of the rental. I just wanted to take a shower and go to sleep after the struggle I had to get here—but I didn't want her to see my desperation. Being blunt seemed the right way to go to get my way.

I pulled out my wallet. "How about I give you some cash to go get a hotel room, and we talk about this tomorrow?"

She was clearly annoyed by this suggestion and responded, "How about no!"

I pulled out a few more bills. "Okay, what if I also buy out your rental here for the month so you can go find somewhere else to stay?"

Fire flashed in her eyes. "Are you serious right now?! Again, no! I'm not leaving. Besides, I'm already unpacked."

We went back and forth a few times, neither of us willing to budge. This woman was certainly very stubborn. I had run out of ideas, and she was wearing me down quickly.

I checked my watch. "Look, it's too late to call the owner of the condo because the office is closed. What do you suggest we do from here?"

Anger crawled across her face and tinted her cheeks pink with heat. "The obvious answer is that you need to go find somewhere else to stay since I booked first."

I had a feeling she would say that. Perhaps being forceful was the incorrect approach; maybe it was time to turn up the charm to try to win her over.

I flashed my million dollar smile her way, my gaze locked to hers. "I'm sorry, I think we've gotten off on the wrong foot. Truly, I'm really sorry for running off your guests. What are you doing here for a month?"

She softened a bit. "I am opening up a business and moving here. How about you?"

I could work with this. She was speaking my language now. "Small world. I am here on business and am considering opening a satellite office here."

She smiled softly. "What kind of business do you have, if you don't mind my asking?"

I relaxed more and fell into easy conversation with her. "I work in finance. I'm a numbers guy, always have been, and I am helping a client with his investments."

She seemed to have frozen. "Oh, that's nice," she said quietly.

Have I said something wrong? Did she not like math nerds or something? I thought this conversation was going better, and now I wasn't so sure that was the case. Realizing I was making her uncomfortable, I didn't know how else to turn it around. We are, after all, strangers.

I extended my hand to her. "I'm Lucas Miller, and you are?"

A look of shock filled her face. "I know who you are! I had a feeling it was you earlier, and then I thought there was no way. I cannot believe it's you."

Confused about how she knew me, I had to ask, "I'm sorry, do I know you?"

Her face immediately went scarlet, and suddenly—I knew *exactly* who she was. My stomach dropped and my heart skipped a beat. I took a deep breath in. "Teresa?"

She glared at me. "Yes, Teresa, who else would I be?"

Dumbfounded, I opened my mouth to speak, and then quickly shut it. What are the odds of Teresa not only being here, but also double booking the same condo? The air around me grew thick as my heart raced and heat began to rise up my face. Worried I might say something I regretted, I did the only logical thing I could think of doing. I turned around and ran right out the front door towards my car. I had to get out of there, and fast.

FOUR

SUNDAY, JUNE 5, 2022

Teresa Wright

What the *actual heck* just happened? I reached out and put my hand on the nearest table to steady myself, taking a few breaths in and out. The sound of the door slamming jolted me back to reality. Adrenaline kicked in, and I couldn't stop myself from running out the front door after him.

What was he doing here?

His face went ghostly white when he realized who I was—and turned quite red just as quickly. Before I could say another word, he was out the door and gone. After all these years, I finally had a chance to…what exactly? Start over with Lucas? The idea is preposterous.

But yet, somehow, there was now a glimmer of hope to undo all that had been done and start over again.

I stood on the sidewalk and watched as a vehicle backed out and drove away, wondering if maybe he would come to his senses and turn around and come back. I often thought about what it would be like to see him again. Would he rush to wrap his arms around me, holding me tightly as he professed his undying love for me, even after all these years? In some ways, I had hoped we could just pick up where we left off. But this—this was not the fairytale reunion I had always hoped for.

After a few minutes, I realized he wasn't coming back and went inside. As I shut the door, I noticed his suitcase sitting there. Panic went through me. This meant that I would have to talk to him again—and I didn't know if I was ready to do it a second time—especially not after I fumbled that one, big time. I could have been nicer to the poor guy, but I had to fight him tooth and nail to keep this condo. How hard would it have been to just let him have it and go stay with Lynn?

I looked at myself in the mirror above the entryway table. "Smooth move, Tess. Real smooth. If he didn't hate you before, he definitely hates you now."

I looked down at his suitcase and noticed a luggage tag hanging from the zipper. I reached down and looked for a contact number. Unsurprisingly, the tag included a meticulously written contact number and the words *reward if found*.

I paced back and forth, debating whether to call or text him. Would he even pick up if I called? What would I say when he answered? I practiced out loud, but decided I sounded ridiculous— so I chickened out and sent a text instead.

> Hey, it's Tess. You left your luggage here. You may want to come back and get it.

I quickly hit send before I could change my mind, and sat my phone on the table. As soon as I sat the phone down, it started ringing. *Was he calling me right now? What would I say?* I grabbed my phone and saw on the screen that it was Lynn, not Lucas.

Disappointment filled me, but I picked up the phone anyway. "Hey Lynn, what's up?"

She was clearly worked up. "What's up? I just got shooed out of your condo and all you have to say is what's up? Who was that, Tess?"

I had forgotten the part where Lucas had kicked everyone out. "Oh, yeah, right, that." I didn't know how to approach this without her freaking out on me.

She practically screamed at me, "Seriously?!?! What is going on? Spill it now!"

I should have known she could read me like a book. "Fine, as always, you win. So…funny story…that was Lucas."

She gasped. "Whaaaaat?!?! As in, *THE Lucas*, Lucas? What is he doing here? Is that his condo or something?"

I chuckled, "Yes, business, and sorta but not really," I answered her questions in order.

She grew silent momentarily before speaking. "Did he kick you out of the condo for the loud music? I feel terrible. You asked me to turn it down. I'm so sorry."

I winced because I realized I had misled her a bit. "No, no, nothing like that. Turns out we both booked this condo. There was a glitch online or something, and we both had confirmations for the same dates and everything. Super weird, Lynn. Like, what are the odds of that?"

Lynn was giddy. "Fate—that is what this is, Tess. It's fate! You two are destined to be together. You always have been. Where is he now? Is he still there?"

I sighed, "It's not that easy, Lynn. I really screwed up. There is no way he will forgive me for how things ended. Besides, he ran out of here as soon as he realized who I was. He couldn't get out quickly enough and left his luggage in the process!"

She sucked in air before replying, "You always do this, Tess. That was a long time ago. You really need to forgive yourself. Besides, it's not like it was totally your fault you didn't make it back to the island that year. The plus side to this that I am hearing is he left his luggage. Is his number on it?"

I groaned, "It's always easier to forgive others than it is to forgive yourself, especially when you betray your heart by listening to the conflicting voices in your head. His number is on the luggage, and I've already texted him. But he hasn't responded. He would likely rather lose his luggage than see me again. Ugh, Lynn, this is such a disaster!"

She grew silent for a moment before finally saying, "What are you going to do about this, Tess?"

I had absolutely no idea. "Can I come stay with you guys? Do you have any extra room in your condo?"

Lynn didn't even wait before responding, "Not a chance, sister, sorry. We are maxed out right now. Louise came after all, and she just took the sofa bed. This is a one bedroom condo, and there's me in the one, and Louise is on the pull-out bed. We are going to be fighting over the single bathroom."

I was frustrated, but I understood. "I'll think of something, I'm sure. I'll catch up with you tomorrow. Get some rest, I love you!"

After I hung up my phone, I immediately checked my messages. There still wasn't a response, but when I looked at the message I sent Lucas, it showed that it had been *read*. This confirmed that he was avoiding me.

My mind replayed our interaction, over-analyzing every word I spoke. I also noticed that his demeanor in our interactions was quite rude, which isn't like him...or wasn't like him. As an adult, I couldn't possibly know who he is now, especially since the last time we had been together, he was eighteen and getting ready to enter his first year in college.

Twenty-six years have passed between us; a whole lifetime of ups and downs on my end, and likely the same on his. I promised myself I wouldn't look him up, no matter how many times I thought about him. But now, here he was—and curiosity was getting the better of me.

I opened the web browser on my phone, typed his name in the search box, and hit enter. There were so many results that came up for his company, which, according to the search, was very successful. Good for him. He said he wanted to do something in finance. But, I was surprised his dad let him major in finance when he pushed Lucas so hard to focus on going pro in football.

A soft knock on the door interrupted my search—and my thoughts. I suddenly felt like I had just been caught doing something I shouldn't be doing, and I nearly dropped my phone. Before getting up, I waited a moment. I walked to the door and opened it, but no one was there. Must have been the wrong door, maybe? I closed the door, locked it, and went back to my seat on the sofa.

I looked around and realized that in everyone's hurry on the way out, plates with half eaten food on them and cups with drinks still in them had been dropped all over the living room. Instead of cleaning, I opened my messages and texted Lynn.

He's still not responding to my text.

Give him time to process, Tess, he'll come around when he's ready. You should get some rest.

I knew she was probably right. He needed time, right? Hopefully, he could find a hotel to get into for the night and catch up with me tomorrow. Maybe then we can both laugh about the strange coincidence that we both ended up here in the exact same place at the exact same time. If anything, it would be great if we could be friends again.

Looking at the mess again, I stood up and decided some fresh air and a moonlit stroll on the beach were exactly what I needed to clear my mind. I opened the patio doors and walked out towards the beach, past the pool. I kicked off my shoes just before stepping onto the sand. The soft, cool touch of the sand was a welcomed feeling on my bare feet. I walked out to the water's edge, letting the waves lap up over my feet as I sank into the wet sand, fixed in place. The sky above me showed stars for miles, and the moon's reflection rippled in the water.

I needed this moment to center myself again. I simply couldn't let this encounter rock my balance. With my eyes closed, I took a deep breath in and let it out many times until I felt at peace. Taking it all in one last time, I looked out across the water where the sky and water met. Walking back inside, I picked up my shoes on the way back in and tossed them by the patio doors. Now to tackle this mess and get ready for bed.

I picked up a plastic cup and tossed it into the garbage can when another soft knock was at my door. I opened the door to see Lucas standing there. His shirt was untucked, his hand running through his hair. He looked frazzled—and I felt like I was to blame for the state he was in.

I smiled softly. "Please come inside," I said while motioning for him to join me.

He stood there motionless, unwilling to move or speak.

I frowned. "Or don't; the choice is yours, but the invitation remains. You are welcome to come inside, Lucas."

He looked away from me. He opened his mouth as if to say something, but nothing came out.

This was becoming awkward. "Lucas, are you okay?"

He looked back at me, sighed, and then stepped inside. We stood closely as I closed the door behind him.

I motioned toward his luggage. "You left your luggage. I thought you might need that."

His gaze followed my motion. He nodded—but still hasn't said a single word.

The only other thing I could think of was to invite him to sit on the sofa. "Would you like to sit with me for a bit?"

He looked over at the sofa and then back at me. With a heavy sigh, he looked down at his feet, hair falling in his face. He reached up and smoothed it back before saying, "Can we talk?"

I don't think I could have prepared myself for the conversation that was certainly about to take place. There was nowhere to run and nowhere to hide. It was time for me to face my past head-on, work through the hurt, and hopefully find my way back to healing.

FIVE

SUNDAY, JUNE 5, 2022

Couldn't I have said something to Tess other than "Can we talk?" It felt like such a weak thing to say—and I was not a weak man. Prior to driving back to her condo, I had driven to the closest hotel, only to be told there were no rooms available. I sat in the parking lot and called every single hotel on the island—23 of them to be exact—each one telling me the same thing as the one before them: no vacancy.

Apparently, there was a golf tournament in town, and since I had arrived on the island without reservations, I had nowhere to go for the night. I was exhausted. My choice was to sleep in my van or to come back here, and because I needed a shower badly, I came back here. I wanted to see if I had any chance whatsoever of convincing her to let me stay here.

I was mad at myself for leaving my luggage behind, followed by relief that I had an excuse to come back. When I first arrived, I knocked, but quickly headed back to the parking lot before she opened the door—I didn't know what to say.

I hid safely behind my van, which happened to be parked next to a cherry red convertible with a Savannah Rentals license plate. Some jerk got my car, and they were here!

Seeing the convertible reminded me of all the challenges I've had getting here. Maybe this was a giant reminder that I shouldn't be here on this cursed island; the proverbial cherry on top, if you will.

My phone buzzed in my pocket, and all I could think was, what now?! I pulled it out to see a text from Emily.

Hey Dad, just making sure you made it to the island okay. I haven't heard from you and was worried.

I felt like a terrible father. I promised her I would call her and then didn't, so I texted back right away.

Sorry, honey, having a little trouble getting into the condo, but I am here safe and sound. Get some rest. I love you.

After I hit send, I noticed a tightening in my chest creeping up. I am guessing it's from sleeping on my side all night on that hard sofa. I took a couple of deep breaths to relax the tension I was holding in my neck and shoulders—but it didn't work.

I knew I shouldn't keep delaying this conversation, so I walked back up to the door and knocked again. Now that I was inside the condo, looking at her, I still didn't know exactly what to say. Panic was setting in.

I cleared my throat before speaking, "So…how've you been?"

Really Luke, is that the best you've got? She probably thinks I'm a weirdo now.

She looked at me and smiled softly. "I've been good. How about you?"

I ran my hand through my hair as I looked away to avoid eye contact with her. "Fine, fine."

Again with the gruff reply. *Who was this version of me?* It's as if being in the same room as Tess has turned my brain into a big pile of mush—I'm stuck in the in-between of being cordial and wanting to interrogate her.

I couldn't take sitting in silence much longer. "What has been happening for the last 26 years?"

I really wished I could punch myself in the face right now. Maybe then it would wake me up and save me from this embarrassing conversation. I would truly rather be anywhere but here right now.

My heart rate quickened as logic and emotion collided within me. If given the chance to ask her why she ghosted me back then—I always told myself I would. Yet, here was the perfect opportunity, and instead of finding out the truth, I was making small talk.

She nervously fidgeted with her hands. "Oh, you know, the usual. College, kids, life. How about you?"

What did that even mean? Was she avoiding this conversation just as much as I was?

I couldn't look her in the eye for fear of crumbling. "About the same, actually."

We sat in silence for what felt like a million years, but in fact, it was less than five minutes. Neither of us wanted to speak, yet both of us had so much to say.

Breaking the silence, I got right to it. "Is there any way you can stay with your friends? I will pay you back for the rent on this place if you can."

She stopped fidgeting and stood up, arms flailing excitedly. "Why do I have to be the one to leave? Why didn't you just get a hotel room to stay in?"

I watched her in silence as she started collecting the plastic gold cups and putting them all onto the end table. She haphazardly poured out the liquid remaining into one cup, sloshing its contents onto the glass on top of the table. If there is one thing that annoyed me the most, it was clutter and unclean surfaces.

My blood pressure rose as I stood up. "What are you going to do with those?" I asked her, pointing to the growing collection of cups.

Entering the kitchen, I got the garbage can and took it to her in the living room. Collecting the cups, I shoved them in the can—maybe a little too aggressively.

At the sound of cups being shoved into the can, she stopped what she was doing. I caught her rolling her eyes at me. "Some people never change!"

I continued collecting the discarded plates, napkins, and food scattered throughout the condo.

Without looking at her, I snapped back, "You could say that again. I figured you'd at least grow out of your lazy ways."

She gasped and put her hand to her chest. "I am certainly not lazy, but I am also not a jerk like you," she said, poking me in the chest.

I couldn't stop myself. "We are too old for this summer romance crap that we used to do."

She stood with her arms crossed as she tapped her foot on the wooden floor. "Well, it's a good thing that I wouldn't ever fall for the charm of Lucas Miller again."

Tying up the trash bag, I walked to the kitchen to find another one.

She followed me. The sound of her heavy footsteps matched the level of her anger. "Exactly what do you think you are doing right now?"

I opened the cupboard under the sink. "Getting a trash bag." I retrieved one from the box and opened it with a loud whoosh.

Clearly annoyed, she replied, "I don't mean literally, Luke, I mean what *are* you doing right now?"

I am not a mind reader—but if I had to guess, she wanted to know exactly why I was here in this condo picking a fight with her—and not somewhere else. *Trust me, Tess—I'd rather be anywhere else but here in this very moment.*

The thing with Tess is, no matter how far you want to get away from her, she draws you to her like a powerful magnet with the force of a speeding train. The more you fight the draw, the harder the pull. If you aren't careful, not only will you get pulled in, you'll get your heart ripped out of your chest and stomped on. I may have fallen for her antics once, but I would not allow that to happen ever again.

Avoiding her last question, I grabbed the full garbage bag and took it outside to the dumpster, calling over my shoulder as I went, "I'm taking this out. I'll be right back."

Once outside, I walked to the front of the building where the dumpster was and tossed the bag inside. The tree frogs were singing loudly, so I stood there for a moment, not in a rush to go back in. My chest felt tighter than it had earlier, and I could tell I was on the brink of a panic attack. Like my therapist taught me, I took three deep breaths, slow and long. With the additional stress this weekend, I knew I would likely need to call him this week.

The stress in my life was crushing. I was trying my very best to be a wonderful dad, to be a great boss and leader, and to be the best business owner I could be. I really needed this week for some downtime and relaxation to clear my head. If this start was any sign of how my trip was going to be, it certainly would not be the restful week I had envisioned.

The pressure I had on my shoulders had caused mild panic attacks four years ago. I had been doing much better with them— until today. The more I thought about my current situation, the more panicked I felt; my chest getting tighter, my breaths becoming more shallow. I reached out and put my hand on a tree to steady myself. The prickly bark pierced my finger, causing blood to draw.

I remembered the exercises my therapist taught me to do in moments like this—visually notice things around you and say them out loud.

It was a little hard to make out some things in the dark, but I gave it a shot. "Tree, bicycles, bike rack, dumpster, stairs, condos, truck, cherry red convertible that should have been mine, and a stupid blue van that I got instead."

My breathing slowed down, and the panic attack was passing. After a few more deep breaths, a gentle breeze blew across my face as I closed my eyes and listened to the frogs. Here, I was safe, and I would be alright.

I needed a little more time before going back in, so I turned and walked to the back of the condo along the fence that ran to the beach. Knowing there was an entrance to the back doors, I stood directly in front of the back of the condo, a few feet down by the water, staring at the ocean.

It was almost pitch black out here, and though I couldn't see the details of the ocean, I could hear the crash of the waves on the shore. I looked up at the sky to see a million stars for as far as my eyes could see. Counting them in my head, I searched for all the constellations I knew. Because it was my lucky number, I always stopped counting after twelve.

I wiped the small drop of blood from my finger, and put my hands in my pockets. I knew I should go back inside, but I couldn't bring myself to turn around and walk. It was as if my feet were sinking in quicksand. Maybe I'll just sleep out here on the sand tonight. It can't be any worse than the airport sofa.

SIX

SUNDAY, JUNE 5, 2022

Teresa Wright

As Luke walked out the door, I watched him from behind, giving him the space I could tell he needed. One thing I remember about Luke is that he sometimes struggles with anxiety. When things get hectic, he's had panic attacks. In the second year we were here on vacation, I witnessed this firsthand. I had walked in on a conversation between him and his father, as Lucas was trying to convince him he didn't want to play football at college, but wanted to focus solely on finance.

His father wasn't having any of it and told him he was throwing his life away if he followed that path. If I remember correctly, his father's exact words were that it would be "career suicide." I watched Luke power clean in a way that I had never seen him do before. There was so much aggression in his movements, which were usually gentle.

Back then, I watched as he excused himself from the conversation and went outside. Unable to help myself, I peered out the window, much like I was currently doing, and watched as he took deep breaths and tried to calm down.

As I stood in my condo, peering out at a now-grown Luke, I couldn't help but see that same young man—and suddenly, I felt like this was all my fault. I can be stubborn, but perhaps this was an instance where it would have been better for both of us if I had offered to seek resolution instead of pushing his buttons.

I watched his breathing go from rapid to a more steady pace, his hand on the tree next to him, holding him upright in place. Lucas turned around, and I had to duck away from the window to make sure he didn't see me, causing me to lose sight of him for a moment. I waited by the door, thinking maybe he was ready to come back inside—but he never did.

I walked to the back patio to find him. It was so dark out there, but I could make out his silhouette on the beach. Luke stood out there for just a moment longer before turning back to go towards the front of the condo again. I walked over to the entryway and stood, waiting for his knock, which came softly.

I opened the door and smiled softly. "Do you want to sit and try again?" I asked lightly.

He ran his hand through his dark hair while looking down at the ground. "Yeah, sure."

We walked into the living room and sat down across from each other again. Both of us sat in silence, unsure of what to say or do in this moment. I was silent to give him the chance to collect his thoughts before moving ahead in the conversation.

I looked at him clearly for the first time tonight. He wore an expensive suit brand that I recognized, but it was wrinkled and disheveled instead of being pressed neatly. His beard had grown out from what I suspected was usually a neatly trimmed length, but currently looked like he had skipped a day of shaving. His face showed signs of his age with crow's feet and frown lines, but the salt and pepper beard was the biggest tell of all. I hadn't noticed it before, but he looked utterly exhausted.

Lucas spoke first. "So, you said you are here for your business. What kind of business do you have?"

He was playing it safe, so I could, too. "I am an artist, and I am hoping to find a permanent location here for my gallery and studio."

I held back details, not wanting to dump my entire life story on him in this moment.

I looked him in the eyes and smiled. "What about you? You said you are here to help a client, and you have your own firm?"

He quickly replied, "I do."

Like earlier, this is another really awkward conversation, and I am certain that if I can feel it, Lucas can too. Nervous, I stood up and walked towards the patio doors and stared out at the ocean. I reached up to touch the necklace I was wearing, grounding me in this moment.

He cleared his throat, which caused me to turn and face him. Was this the moment Lucas would finally tell me what he wanted to talk to me about?

He threw his hands in the air before fully admitting what he'd been hiding. "Every hotel is completely booked. I don't have anywhere to stay tonight, or for the next two weeks, in all honesty. There is a golf tournament here that starts tomorrow."

Not wanting to react in a way that could further add to his stress, I took a minute to consider this news. I could tell he was under enough stress today.

I replied with what I hoped would be a peace offering, "You can stay here tonight, and I'll help you find something tomorrow."

Relief filled his face, followed by concern as he looked around the condo.

He nervously replied, "Thank you for the offer—but isn't this a one bedroom?"

He definitely looked uncomfortable with this thought. I motioned to the sofa. "The sofa has a pull-out bed in it. You could sleep there if that's okay? I'll stay in the bedroom."

He looked around the room before pulling out cash from his wallet and held it out towards me. "Can I at least pay you for allowing me to stay here tonight? It's the least I can do."

Trying to lighten the mood, I chuckled. "That may cover tonight's rent, but what about the reward for finding your suitcase?"

He tilted his head back and laughed, a deep, hearty laugh that came straight from his stomach. His shoulders shook as his laughter grew louder. This was the Luke I remembered—the carefree and funny one.

He pulled out a few more bills and extended them my way. "Will this cover it, or do I need to head out to the bank to get more?" he said with a mischievous grin.

Unable to hold it in, I giggled. "Your money is no good here, Luke. We are old friends, and friends help each other out. Besides, it's the least I can do after making you run around all night."

He put his wallet back in his pocket, relief visible on his face. "Thank you, Tess—really," he put his hand up to stifle a yawn as he spoke.

I took a step toward the door. "It's getting really late. Why don't I help you bring in your things so we can get you settled for the night?"

I followed him out of the door into the parking lot and was completely surprised as Lucas opened the back of a blue van that looked like it was straight from the nineties. Oh, the memories I had of this van.

I looked at him with my left eyebrow raised slightly and a grin on my face. "Really, Luke? This is your ride? How did you get stuck with this thing?"

In the darkness, I could see him smile. "What? You don't like ole Bessie here? She and I, we go way back," he said as he patted the side of the van.

We both laughed the entire way back inside the condo, our hands full of his luggage.

I dropped the luggage by the table, and locked the door before turning back to him. "I am going to get the bedding from the closet for the sofa bed, and I will help you make it."

I retrieved the extra sheets, blankets, and pillows, and the two of us worked quickly in silence, stretching the fitted sheet over the mattress before layering the blankets. Because he was lost in thought and looked far too serious, I threw a pillow at him, and it struck him in the chest before falling onto the bed. I giggled at the sight of Luke's hair blowing up as the pillow whizzed by. Perhaps I threw it harder than I intended.

I sheepishly smiled. "My bad, that went way worse in real time than it did in my head."

He looked at me, stone cold, devoid of all emotion. "All good, Tess, all good."

The bed was made, and I took this opportunity to stage my exit. "I'm going to use the bathroom real quick to get ready for bed, and then it's all yours. There are towels on the shelves. Help yourself to them if you need to shower. I'll be in the bedroom if you need anything. Have a good night, Luke."

I turned and headed to the bathroom, not giving him a chance to respond after that embarrassing fumble with the pillow. I quickly went through my nightly routine in the bathroom, washing my face, combing my hair, brushing my teeth, and putting on my pajamas.

As I walked from the bathroom to the bedroom, I called out, "It's all yours, Luke."

I softly closed the bedroom door behind me. Once safely inside and out of sight, I sank on the edge of the bed and hung my head in my hands. Why would I think that throwing that pillow was the right thing to do in that moment?

"Read the room, Tess!" I scolded myself internally. That man had clearly been through an extremely hard day, and I just made it harder by trying to be fun—and dare I say—flirty.

I blame it on that blue van. Seeing it in the parking lot reminded me of our first date. He picked me up in a van just like that. We also had our first kiss inside that van. We explored this very island in that van, spending every moment we could together.

All of those feelings flooded me at once, and I wondered what life would have been like if I had gone that last summer instead. Would we have shared a lifetime of love and happiness together? I wondered what kind of life he's had since I last saw him and if he'd had all of his hopes and dreams come true.

Guilt crept in, gnawing at me from deep within. It didn't matter now, because I had made my choice and lived a life that brought me two beautiful boys. They were what made all of it worth it, and I wouldn't change any of that for anything.

Yet, I couldn't help but wonder *what if?* What if Luke and I stayed together and got married? What would our kids have been like? This exploration of feelings turned my guilt into an overwhelming sense of grief.

I shook my head. "No, Tess, we are not reopening this old wound. Stop it." I commanded myself.

I pushed those thoughts back down as far as I could and picked up my book, a cozy mystery, to help distract my thoughts. I pulled back the plush duvet on the bed and climbed in under the covers. As I read, I heard the bathroom door close, followed by the shower turning on. I couldn't help but think about him in the bathroom, literally feet from me. *What are the odds he'd be here right now? Is this my second chance to make things right?*

"Snap out of it, Tess." I scolded myself once more.

I'd already messed up once, and I didn't deserve to get a second chance. To distract myself, I went back to my book and read a few short pages, but could not keep my eyes open. Feeling defeated, I closed my book, placed it on the nightstand, and turned out the light before quickly drifting off to sleep.

SEVEN

Lucas Miller

The smell of coffee brewing hit my nostrils causing me to open my eyes, awakening me from a deep slumber. The sun had already begun to spill in through the patio doors, and I had to squint until my eyes adjusted to the brightness. I glanced into the kitchen to see Tess busily moving about, preparing what I could only assume was going to be a delicious breakfast.

After my shower last night, I went to sleep the moment my head hit the pillow, or maybe even slightly before—I honestly don't have any recollection. Normally, I would have gotten up about two hours earlier and already gone out for my morning run, but I decided that today I would take it easy and try to get caught up on some much needed rest.

I stretched and yawned loudly, which prompted giggles coming from the kitchen.

"Good morning, Tess," I said with a smile.

Her blonde hair glistened in the sunlight through the kitchen window, she tenderly smiled at me. "Good morning, sleepyhead. Breakfast will be ready in about 15 minutes, but coffee is ready now if you'd like me to make you a cup. Still just a splash of cream?"

An old feeling emerged as I tried not to act surprised that she remembered how I liked my coffee. "Yes, that's exactly it, thank you."

As she poured the steaming cup of coffee, I got up to use the restroom and put on my running clothes. Once behind the closed bathroom door, I splashed cold water on my face and looked at myself in the mirror. *Is that what hope feels like?* It's been so long since I have felt hopeful that I couldn't be sure it wasn't just hunger creating the movements my stomach felt.

I needed a chance to clear my mind, and there was only one thing that could do that. After breakfast, I figured I could go for a run on the beach to make up for missing yesterday. I walked back into the living room and quickly disassembled the bed, putting the sofa back together while taking sips of coffee to help me wake up.

I was glad that I decided to give myself an extra week before I had to really get started on this project for William. I haven't had the chance to go on vacation in at least six years. My schedule was free because I had made no plans at all for this week, and decided I would just wing it—something I would not usually do. I preferred structure and schedules that dictated how I would spend each moment available for maximum satisfaction. This was a chance for me to try something a little different.

Happy with how the sofa was now put back together, I carried my coffee cup to the kitchen to offer my assistance to Tess while she finished up breakfast.

I pointed to the block of cheese on the counter. "Would you like me to grate the cheese?" I asked.

Tess looked up from stirring the eggs. "Yes, that would be great. I'm going to need the cheese real soon, thanks," she replied.

I went through every single drawer and cupboard in the kitchen on a hunt for a cheese grater and finally found it in the back of one of the drawers. I grabbed a bowl from the cupboard and quickly got to work shredding the cheese.

Tess stopped me when I had shredded enough. "That will do, thanks for your help. Now, go take a seat, and I'll bring breakfast to you."

I wasn't used to having someone take care of me. "You really don't have to do that."

She shooed me away. "Nonsense, please take a seat. I insist."

I retreated to the table and took my place as she brought the plates over and set them down. We both quickly ate and laughed at how hungry we must have been. I cleared the table and put the dishes in the dishwasher while Tess wiped down the counter and the table.

"Do you have a lot to do today?" Tess asked, with curiosity in her voice.

I thought for a moment. "I am going to go for a run, and then I need to make some calls to find a condo available and to see about getting refunded for this one. How about you?"

Tess looked out the patio doors. "I think I'm going to spend the day outside today. I promised myself that I would take this first week off to relax."

I nodded in agreement. "I hope that once I get these calls made, I'll soon be able to do the same."

With everything cleaned up, I excused myself and went outside to begin my run on the beach. The fluffy sand closest to the condo is really difficult to navigate, but once you get beyond that to where the sand is flatter from the tides coming in, it really makes for a great run. I set my timer on my watch to go off at the point I would want to turn around and come back so that I could hit the mileage I was hoping for today.

As I ran, I allowed myself to clear my mind, taking in only the sights as I listened to music through my earbuds and felt the thud from my foot hitting the sand all the way up my body. I was making great progress when suddenly, my foot found a hole that someone had left on the beach, causing me to take a tumble.

Landing pretty hard on my bad knee, I knew running farther might be difficult without my brace. I stood up and walked, and realized I was okay. I got lucky. Turning around at my alarm, I continued my run back and went into the condo through the fence opening.

Tess was sitting on a lounge chair by the pool with a book in her hand. I didn't want to interrupt her, so I jogged past her and into the condo to get a shower before making some calls. I spent two hours making endless phone calls and really getting nowhere. Frustration returned. I didn't like not being in control of this situation.

Tess stepped back inside. And she looked stunning in her modest black one-piece swimsuit with a flowy beige cover-up. She had on a wide brim sunhat of the same beige color as her cover-up, with a black band. Her hair looked wavier than usual, likely because of the humidity outside. There was that unfamiliar feeling again. My stomach fluttered and my heart beat a tad quicker, reminding me of the power Tess always held over me.

I begged myself to look away before she realized I was staring at her, but it was too late. Our eyes met.

"Did you have any luck?" she asked with a smile.

I cleared my throat before speaking. "No, not really. The best I could do was get a condo booked for two weeks from today. I did, however, get a refund for the double booking."

"Well, you can stay here for as long as you need. It really is no trouble," she replied. "I am going to head back out if you'd like to join me."

She walked over to the refrigerator, grabbing a bottle of water before heading back towards the patio door.

"I am not sure it's a good idea for me to come out and join you right now. I really should keep looking," I said to her as she walked past me.

She sighed. "You're on vacation. It wouldn't kill you to have some fun," she remarked, and out the door she went.

I have to admit—her comment annoyed me a little, and I wasn't entirely sure why—because she was right. I texted William to let him know I was still trying to find a place to stay for the month and asked if he had any connections. Bugging him with my problems was something I really didn't want to do, yet I had no other choice.

With the text sent, I went and changed into my swim trunks. Perhaps Tess was right, some fun could do me good.

I walked outside onto the patio and interrupted her reading. "Are you gonna get in?" I asked.

Not even putting her book down, she replied curtly. "I really just want to read my book. Why don't you go play in the pool?"

Catching her drift, I made a mental note never to interrupt her reading again, but I also decided I wasn't letting her off the hook that easily. I knew what would get her to lighten up and have fun, too. Running, I jumped, pulled my knees to my chest, and landed, drenching her with water

She immediately put her book down and yelled, "That's it! Game on!"

Tess got up out of her lounge chair and did the only logical thing—a perfect cannonball, landing in the pool right next to me with a giant splash.

As she came up out of the water, her wet hair smoothed back across her head and down her back, hanging heavier with the weight of the water in it. *She's even more beautiful than she was back then.*

"I had to just get it over with and go all in. It helps with the shock of the cold water," Tess said.

"So not only are you stealing my moves, now you're stealing my lines too," I teased her.

She completely caught me off guard as she cupped her hands together and splashed water in my face. I had to return the favor, of course, and before I realized it, we were in a full-on water fight. The sound of our laughter echoed all around us as we laughed hard until we were both out of breath.

"Truce, truce," she cried, waving her hands in the air frantically.

Without thinking, I scooped her up and swayed back and forth with her in my arms.

"Do you remember when we used to do this as kids?" I asked her.

She laid her head against my chest. "I remember you always would do a giant cannonball and drench me every single time we met at the pool," she poked at me.

"You were always deep in thought, or nose deep in a book, I had to get your attention somehow," I poked back at her.

She chuckled, "Oh to be young and carefree again…"

I carried her over to the pool's edge, where we floated for a little while side by side, like we used to do, before getting out of the pool to dry off. Once we were out of the pool, we both sat down on the lounge chairs, allowing the hot sun to touch our skin as the drops of water evaporated.

I looked over at her as she put her hat back on her head. "Thanks for convincing me I needed to have fun. I really had a great time."

She grinned at me, clearly pleased with herself. "I needed it just as much, if not more. It really was fun to let loose for a little bit."

The sound of an incoming call on my phone interrupted us. It was William calling me. I excused myself to take the call as I headed back inside the condo.

EIGHT

TUESDAY, JUNE 7, 2022

It was another day of fully embracing the beautiful lifestyle of *vacation mode*. I could get used to spending every waking moment either on the beach or beside the pool. The book I started on Sunday was about three chapters from being finished, and time was no problem. The sun began to set as I kept reading to learn exactly *whodunit.*

Satisfied with an ending I didn't see coming, I closed the book and finally looked up to see lights on inside the condo. It can't be evening already, right?! I picked up my phone to see I had missed a few texts in the group chat from Lynn and Beth.

Lynn Taylor

Are we getting together on the beach this week?

Beth Reed

We are in. What day works best for you all?

After catching up on the missed texts, I quickly replied.

> How about Thursday? My place? Come around noon, we can picnic on the beach.

I went inside and was greeted by the soothing sounds of jazz music playing from the kitchen, aggressive chopping, and a colorful word or two.

Luke was busy chopping an onion, while also wiping at his eyes with the back of his hands. *This man has clearly never been taught how to cut vegetables properly.*

I walked up behind him and wrapped my arms around his waist, settling my hands on top of his to help control his speed and motion of the knife he was using. Once I felt he had the hang of it, I stepped back out of the small kitchen, and let him show me what he had just learned. He was a quick learner, which meant there was hope for whatever it was he was making.

"The trick to consistent cuts is to move at a much slower pace while cutting. The knife tip shouldn't leave the board, but instead, rock on it," I explained.

He seemed amused with his private cooking lesson. "Nobody has ever shown that to me before—thank you. I did not know it could be this easy to cut an onion."

I tried to stifle a giggle, but it escaped me. "What exactly are you doing right now, Luke? Would you like some help?"

He tried to block me from returning to the kitchen by turning his backside to block my entry. "This kitchen is really narrow, Tess. Let me cook you dinner. Consider this my thank you for letting me stay here."

I smiled and put my hands up in surrender. "Okay, but if you change your mind, I'm going to be sitting right there," I said as I pointed to the kitchen table that had the perfect view of what was happening in the kitchen.

I sat down and watched as he struggled to cut up the remaining vegetables. So far, I've seen tomatoes, onions, green peppers, a chili pepper, and garlic. There wasn't, however, anything cooking on the stove as he focused on chopping. I watched as he started pulling out the pots and pans, noting what he was putting in each one. If I had to guess, based on the components, he was making spaghetti.

He had meat frying in one pan, vegetables sautéing in another, and as he was stirring the vegetables, the water started boiling over in the stockpot. I jumped up and came to his rescue. He clearly needed my help. The two of us moved about the kitchen as if we had been doing it for years, weaving in and out of each other, passing the spoons at just the right time, both of us checking, stirring, and tasting as we went.

We reached the point of combining all the sauce ingredients, which drastically reduced the number of pans we had going at one time, so I stepped back to let him take over what was on the stove.

He added a pinch of salt to the sauce and then held up the spoon for me to taste. I put my hand around his and leaned into the spoon, taking a small taste of the red sauce.

I found its taste surprisingly delicious. "Oh my goodness, this is amazing!"

He grinned, pleased with himself. "It's my grandmother's recipe. We don't believe in canned sauce in our family."

I felt warmth spread through my cheeks and was unsure if it was from the steamy pots or the proximity to Luke. He reached up and turned the burner on low to let the sauce simmer longer.

A look of panic washed over his face. "I forgot about the salad and the bread."

I surveyed the disaster in the kitchen. Dishes and food remnants covered every surface. Luke was certainly a messy cook, which surprised me, considering how much he hated messes. I began cleaning up the chopped remnants and cleared a space on the counter to help prep the salads while he put his attention on getting the bread in the oven.

Once the salad was ready, I carried the bowl to the table. I cleaned up the counter once more and put the dishes in the dishwasher. The timer went off on the stove. Luke pulled the bread out and began plating our food.

I grabbed a bottle of pop from the refrigerator and two glasses. Luke and I reached the table together, so he pulled out a chair and motioned for me to take my seat. I sat down and looked at the wonderful meal before me. It was really sweet of him to do all of this for me.

I was grateful for his company and for not having to cook. "Thank you for going through all the trouble of doing this for me. Everything looks and smells amazing."

He smiled down at me. "It's the least I could do for you since you bailed me out this week. Bon appétit!"

While eating dinner, we had idle chit-chat about our day. I was distracted because I thought about how different my life could be if I hadn't ruined my chance with him. He placed his left hand on the table. It was the first time I could catch a good glimpse of it. There was a ring indentation, but no ring was visible. I wonder what happened.

Suddenly, he jerked his hand from the table and put it in his lap. I looked up to see he had caught me looking at his hand. The sudden movement made me wonder if he had secrets he wasn't sharing that revolved around his marriage—kind of like how my dad had a whole second secret family. Hopefully, Luke wasn't the kind of guy my dad was.

To risk being called out, I broke the silence. "Thanks again, this is delicious," I said between bites.

He simply nodded his head in response. I made a mental note to be more careful when stealing glances of him or asking questions, because he was obviously being extremely private about his personal affairs.

This was a whole new side of him I never got to see. He used to always be so forthcoming with me. It was the part of us we both liked, being able to be one hundred percent ourselves in each other's presence. Now, we were both guarding our lives from one another as if the things we had both been through were too personal to share.

After dinner, I helped him clean up, and then joined him in the living room. He was sitting in his usual spot on the sofa, which left the loveseat for me. The television was on, and he was flipping through the guide so fast it was making me dizzy. I pulled out my phone and began scrolling through social media posts while he tried to find something to watch.

It was too early to go to bed, there wasn't anything good on TV, and it was a beautiful night—a perfect evening for a fire.

I interrupted his scrolling. "What do you think about having a fire in the fire pit outside? It's a great evening for that."

Without taking his eyes from the TV, he replied, "No, I think I want to watch this movie. I haven't seen it in years, and it was always one of my favorites."

How did he go from sharing a beautiful moment in the kitchen with me to blocking me out again? I'll admit I got my hopes up. This evening was almost like a date—but I failed to realize he clearly is emotionally unavailable right now.

Annoyed, I got up and walked to my bedroom in search of my next book to read. I chose a romantic comedy, hoping it could add a little spice to my otherwise dull love life. I carried the e-reader outside to the patio and sat in a chair close to the house where the soft light pooled on the concrete.

I tried to read but couldn't concentrate, so I sat the e-reader down in my lap and stared pensively into the darkness. For the first time since I had been here, I realized that my life didn't look like how I had hoped it would. While I had many things to be grateful for, I was also remorseful about a lot.

I stared out at the pool before me. Though it wasn't the exact pool, it still made me smile at the memories that flooded my mind. In the second year that my family came to the island, we coordinated the trip with Luke's family and booked the two condos beside each other. This meant we got to share the pool that was reserved for just the two condos, but we didn't have to share it with anyone else.

Every night after our parents went to sleep, Luke and I would sneak out to the pool and meet under the starry sky. Most of the time, we would lean against the pool wall and float while talking, but some nights we would lazily float in the middle of the pool, looking up at the stars. I was still in my swimsuit, so I stood up, removed my cover-up, and walked to the steps leading down into the shallow end.

As quietly as I could, I walked down the steps into the pool, the cool water making me catch my breath. Once I was a little way in, I went under water quickly to acclimate my whole body. I swam towards the middle of the pool, the spot before it dropped off to the deep end, and rolled over onto my back to look up at the starry sky.

I didn't know what life had in store for me, but I knew that in order for me to be truly happy, I needed to forgive myself for the choices I had made that severely altered my life's course. Tears filled my eyes as I silently poured my heart out to myself and to God, seeking forgiveness for getting things so wrong, and making a promise to do better with the second chance that was before me.

Suddenly, the water all around me became tumultuous, causing me to rock back and forth and go under water. When I resurfaced, I looked around to find the culprit. And much to my surprise—and delight—I saw that Luke had joined me.

He swam over to me. "I watched from the window as you floated, and I couldn't remember the last time I had done that, so I joined you. I hope that is okay."

Reaching up, I wiped the water and tears from my face. "Yes, that is great. Do you just want to float together quietly and just enjoy the beauty of the stars?"

He nodded and rolled over on his back to look up at the sky. I stood in the pool, staring at him for a short moment. The water highlighted his muscular arms and chest. I noticed he clenched his jaw tight as he wrestled with his thoughts. Not wanting to distract him from his moment, I rolled on my back and joined him for the most peaceful moment of my life as we floated in the pool beside each other.

NINE

Lucas Miller

Sometimes you just need a day away to clear your head. I avoided Tess all day yesterday as I drove around the island, although I told her the reason was research for William. There are still some things we really should discuss, but I am not sure I'm ready for those conversations quite yet. I was relieved when I woke up to a text from William asking me to meet him today instead of waiting until next week.

He owns two large commercial buildings and a house that he wants to sell so he can reinvest in something more lucrative now that the island is gaining popularity. He is considering going all-in on an old resort that shuttered after the last hurricane. According to William, it needs some work, but he thinks it could become exactly the cash cow he's looking for right now.

Before I look at the property he wants to purchase, he asked me to meet him at one of his existing properties so we can go over how everything looks on paper.

I pulled into the parking lot behind a row of loblolly pine trees, which left needles scattered everywhere. The building looked modern from the outside, likely boosting its resale value. The pine needles covering everything outside were noticeable, something a new owner might fight, but these trees are native, and it's common here.

I opened the door and walked inside. It was a bright and airy corner building with windows that ran down the front and exposed side. It looked like it was currently being used as some sort of art store.

I spotted William and walked over to him. "Hey man, this place is pretty cool," I said as I reached out to shake his hand.

He matched my gaze around the room. "Yeah, it really is a great place, and it's bigger on the inside than it looks on the outside. Let me show you around."

We walked through the space, which had makeshift areas created by freestanding walls that were arranged in clusters to showcase the art. I couldn't help but think that this could be a great place for me to open my offices, and instead of cubicles, each cluster could be someone's office area. Not traditional by any means, but most businesses nowadays are moving into an open office concept where everyone can collaborate at all times—and this would have that same feel, but offer some privacy.

When we got upstairs, I knew immediately that this space would be perfect for my office. I could have the whole upstairs to myself, overlooking everything down below. This would give me a greater level of privacy, and I wouldn't have to build out anything.

Once the tour was over, I asked William, "What are your plans for selling this space? Any idea of the numbers?"

He opened the folder he had been carrying the whole time. "Ideally, we'd get $1.5 million for this space and $1.25 million for the space next door. I also have a house on the beach in a very nice area, and I'm hoping to get at least $1.75 million from it as well."

I quickly added it all up in my head. "So, you are looking at roughly $5 million all in if you can offload all three. Is that enough to get the other property you want and make the needed repairs?"

He flipped through his papers to confirm. "The estimate for the buyout and cost of repairs came in at $3 million, so I would be two ahead."

I grinned and held my hand up to give him a high-five. "Nice, man, that's what you want—to come out ahead. Did your appraisals match your asking?"

He smacked his hand against mine. "Yes, and actually the house came back higher, but I'd like to lower it with the contingency that they also have to buy one of the commercial spaces with it to get that rate, otherwise, the asking is $2.25 million."

I took this as my opportunity to put in a plug for the space. "Would you have any wiggle room in coming down on the price of this space if I were to be the one purchasing it to open a satellite office here?"

He looked surprised. "Is that something you are seriously considering?"

I optimistically answered, "It has been on my mind the last couple of days, but it's just something I am kicking around right now."

My phone chimed with a text notification. I glanced at it to see that it was from Tess.

Are you joining us? My friends are all here on the beach with me this afternoon, and we'd love for you to come along.

I frowned. She knew I was working right now. I sent a quick response to her.

Can't. I'm working, remember?

Before I could even put my phone back in my pocket, another text appeared.

You are supposed to be on vacation.
Live a little.

Annoyed, I fired off one last text to make my point clear.

Not all of us can waste the day away like kids. Some of us have grown-up things to do.

I shoved my phone back into my pocket and turned my attention back to William. "I'm sorry about that. What's up next?"

William looked at me warily. "Do you want to see the space next door?"

I had time, so I followed him to the space next door. It was not nearly as open and airy—or updated, for that matter. It would certainly need some work to be done, but mostly it would work for offices or a retail store of sorts. I asked him if there had been any showings yet. William told me that while there was some interest, no one had been through yet.

He handed me the envelope he had been carrying all day. "Everything you need to know is inside. Please take the rest of the week to relax a little while you're here before diving into the work."

I chuckled. "Yeah, sure, I'll try. Thanks man, see you soon."

I spent the next hour driving around the island, looking at all the properties William owned before driving to the property he wanted to purchase so I could make my assessment of risk versus reward. The resort property required major work, and I wasn't as optimistic as he was. I jotted down a note to get a second opinion and assessment from someone else not tied into the sale.

The loud grumble of my empty stomach told me it was getting late, and I was hungry. The Driftwood Deli and Grocery was close by, so I ordered my dinner to go and took it back to the condo.

When I got back to the condo, it was oddly quiet inside. I opened the door with dinner in hand, and guilt found its way to me when I realized I hadn't gotten Tess anything to eat.

I smiled at her. "Did you have dinner?" I asked cautiously.

She crossed her arms. "Yeah, I ate."

She was clearly not happy with me, likely because I blew her and her friends off this afternoon for work. I sat down at the table to eat. The silence was deafening. The atmosphere was so electric, you could practically feel it.

She took in a breath as if she was about to speak, but instead of letting her talk, I quickly blurted out, "Why did you abandon us?"

I don't know what brought that out. It was not really what was on my mind, yet here it was out in the open—and I couldn't take it back now.

She was clearly surprised. She shook her head and said, "Ah, there it is. Luke, it's not at all what you think."

What the heck kind of answer was that? It felt almost like a diversion more than a confession.

I swallowed my food down before speaking. "All I know is you never took my calls, and you returned all of my letters. You shut me out and were never to be heard from again."

I waited for her response, but one never came. "I felt like our relationship was just one big joke to you, like you never really even loved me."

She glared at me. "We were just kids. Besides, love isn't forever, Luke."

I shook my head. "Why on earth would you think that?"

"I really don't know if you are ready to hear that without judgment," she quietly answered.

The sadness in her voice reflected on her face. And I knew that in order for us to move forward even as friends, I had to know what happened—but I also didn't want to push her too hard.

I stood up and threw away the remnants of my dinner and went and took my seat on the sofa. She came and sat on the loveseat across from me, like always.

I looked her in the eye. "You have the floor. This is a judgment-free zone."

She took a deep breath in. "This is going to be a long-winded story, so get comfortable."

"It all started the day before we were supposed to leave for vacation in 1997. I had just graduated from high school. Starting college in the fall made me excited, but mostly, I was ecstatic to spend another summer with you. I had spent the whole day packing my suitcases for the trip after trying on every outfit no less than three times, making sure that what I picked would bring a smile to your face," she paused and looked down, her hair falling around her face.

She took a deep breath and continued, "I had taken my last bag downstairs, completely oblivious to what was going on around me. I didn't notice that my bags were next to a stack of boxes. I turned to go into the living room and tripped over a box I didn't realize was there." She paused again to wipe a tear away from her cheek.

I stood up to retrieve the box of tissues from the end table across the room and handed it to her on my way back to my seat.

She looked up at me as she took the box from me, her eyes glistening beneath the tears. "My mom rushed over to check if I was hurt. I asked her what the boxes were doing there, and she told me to take a seat at the table. She needed to talk to me. It was the first time that day that I realized my dad wasn't home. Over the next two hours, Mom shared with me that Dad had moved out the day before—after she discovered he was living a secret second life."

Tess paused for a moment as the heaviness of the memory crushed her all over again. Tears flooded her eyes and fell down her face in rapid succession. Before I could say anything, she steadied herself and continued, "He had another family, another wife, two other children, and even a dog. With him gone, my mom lost everything. She did her best, but we had to sell the house. While she moved into a two bedroom apartment, I left for school early in search of an apartment and job." She stopped and looked at me.

It felt like a bombshell of epic proportions had just been dropped on me. Her parents always seemed to be so in love with one another back then. This wasn't anything I could have seen coming, and it left me unsure how to respond.

I was trying to take it all in. "I'm so sorry, Tess."

Back then, I did not know everything she went through. Accusing her of abandoning me felt absolutely terrible because it wasn't her fault. Her dad had abandoned her. I can see now that in her brokenness, Tess shut everyone out—including me—to protect her heart.

I scooted to the edge of the sofa to be closer to her. I reached out to take her hand. "Tess, I'm truly sorry for the accusation. I had no idea."

Tess looked up at me with a half smile, a sort of sadness behind her eyes. "I'm really sorry for not telling you sooner. I was so afraid that if I continued to open myself up for love, you'd leave me just like my dad left my mom. And I didn't want to give you the chance to break my heart." She put her head in her hands and sobbed.

I walked over to the loveseat to sit next to her, wrapping her in my arms as she cried. We sat there like that for a while—long enough for me to question, *what if this never happened?* If we had stayed together that summer, would we have gotten married?

I tried to push those thoughts away as guilt gnawed at me. My past is something I'd never change. I have two amazing children and a lifetime of memories I will cherish forever, and I am grateful for that.

TEN

Teresa Wright

I leaned into Luke as he held me, releasing years' worth of pent-up emotions I had buried deep inside. He had grown silent, likely unsure of what to say to me. I probably shouldn't have poured it all out like that. But once I got started, I just couldn't stop until he knew the truth. I probably could have just led with something simple like, *"Oh hey, my dad left, and that was why,"* and he would have been okay with that. But no, I had to go and just pour it all out. There was no way I could take it back now.

I had one more thing I had to get off my chest. "My biggest regret in life is never giving us closure. I am really sorry for how I left things."

Instantly it felt as if the weight of a million worlds was removed from me, allowing me the chance to breathe fully once more. He removed his arms from around me and shifted away from me. I turned to face him, unsure of how he was feeling at that moment.

And I realized that, in my earlier anger, I hadn't noticed how nicely he was dressed. He was wearing a pair of khaki pants and a long sleeve button down shirt that was a medium blue hue, reminding me of the ocean. He had unbuttoned the top four buttons, which exposed parts of his tanned chest. Blue was a good color on him. It complemented his brown hair and eyes, while also accenting his muscular arms with the snug fabric clinging to them.

He sighed as a serious look filled his face. "It's really okay, Tess. Your leaving me is what led me to Lisa."

He looked like a deer in headlights after saying her name. *Who is Lisa? Is that his ex?* Suddenly, I needed to know more about her to help put my mind at ease. But was it because I was genuinely interested—or the slightest bit jealous that he could have loved anyone other than me?

I asked softly, "Do you want to talk about it?"

He ran his hand through his hair. "There's not much to talk about."

He stood up and walked into the kitchen to wipe down the table where he had eaten his dinner. Luke has the tendency to shut down and clean when things get uncomfortable. I know this as a sign to back off and not push him. Admittedly, I was extremely annoyed that he shut me out so quickly—and right after I had just poured my heart out.

I needed fresh air, and I needed it now. On my way out, I grabbed the lighter and fire starter to go to the beach. I walked past the pool and out onto the sand to the fire pit. The sun had been down long enough that the sand was cold on my bare feet. Reaching into the fire pit, I arranged the logs like Rob had shown the boys on the farm. Underneath the logs, I placed the fire starter and tried to spark a flame with the lighter. I kept clicking the trigger, but nothing came out.

I was getting frustrated when I heard the patio door close and the sound of Luke coming towards me. He reached out his hand for the lighter, which I happily handed over. Luke got it on the first try. With the fire going, I went and grabbed two of the beach chairs from the pool shed for us to sit in and put them up next to the fire.

We sat by the fire in silence for a short time. The crashing waves and crackling fire were the only sounds we heard.

He broke the silence. "Lisa is my wife…"

I broke in, "Oh, I'd love to meet her. Is she coming down?"

He replied softly, "No, she passed away five years ago."

I immediately felt terrible for putting my foot in my mouth. "I am terribly sorry, Luke—I just assumed."

He shook his head. "Don't worry about it. It happens all the time."

He grew silent again. I watched as he clenched his jaw and fiddled with his hands while staring at the fire. There was a warm glow cast on his face from the light of the fire, which only enhanced his features more. The level of sadness evident on his face told the story he wasn't ready to share, and I understood then the magnitude this loss had on him.

I didn't want to pry, so I shared more about my situation with him. "I met Rob at the beginning of my sophomore year in college. We dated casually up through the start of our junior year in college, when I found out that I was pregnant in November and would have a baby the following summer." I paused to see if he'd react, but got nothing.

I continued, "That pretty much sped things up for us. He proposed, I dropped out of college, we moved in together, and built a life that eventually led us to purchase a farmhouse and have a second child. We were together for 21 years, but we never got married."

I was so nervous about how Luke would take the last part that I couldn't even look at him. I was afraid of being judged not only for my choice not to marry Rob, but also for getting pregnant during college and never finishing school.

My life was a far cry from the aspirations I once shared with him in secret late one night in the pool. I have always put the needs of my children above my own, ensuring they had everything they needed when they needed it. Now that they are adults, I was leaning more into the things that I wanted to do.

He cleared his throat before speaking. "Did you ever go back and finish school?"

I looked over at him. "I finished online school three years ago and got my degree."

He looked relieved. "What do you do for your profession?"

I don't know why this question always embarrasses me. I'm proud of what I do; I just have a hard time explaining it in a way that others understand the validity of my choices.

I raised my chin a bit and confidently responded, "I am an artist."

A look of confusion filled his face. "What happened to becoming a lawyer?"

Disappointed in his response, I answered, "Having two kids forced me out of that profession. I stayed home to take care of them and their needs until they were old enough to be out on their own."

He looked at me unchanged in emotion, "And Rob was okay with letting you throw away your dreams?"

No one had ever asked me that before. "Rob never knew that was my dream. Because of the situation with Mom and Dad, money was tight, and law school was no longer an option for me.

I attended a local college and was working towards my Bachelor of Arts in Business."

He asked me cautiously, "Why did you never marry him?"

That was the one question I had hoped he wouldn't ask. "Because, Luke, love never lasts. People move on, they find someone else, they stop loving like they used to," I answered honestly.

He didn't reply, which left me alone to wrestle with my thoughts. Did I believe what I was telling him? I always looked up to my parents, and their relationship was, by my definition, what true love looked like. Until suddenly it wasn't. My dad completely crushed the definition of true love, and I could no longer see what was real and what was fake when it came to matters of the heart. The only thing I was certain of was that I would never put myself in a position like my mom had gotten into.

As I was deep in thought, my chair shifted from under me and gave way as I came crashing down on the sand below me. Luke jumped up to help me up. I slowly stood up; my body ached from the fall. As he held on to me, I brushed the sand off my clothes. Looking up at him, our gaze held longer than it should have.

The warmth of his touch and the closeness of his body to mine stirred up a well of feelings inside of me I wasn't fully prepared to feel. His breath was warm on my face and smelled of peppermint. I leaned against him, resting my head on his shoulder. My face was turned towards his, our lips nearly inches apart as he looked down at me. I had my right hand on his chest, his hand was over mine, and I could feel his heart rapidly beating.

My heart pounded in the same rhythm as his, a sweet melody of a forgotten love. I closed my eyes and took a deep breath in. His signature scent of sandalwood and cedar mixed with citrus filled my nostrils. He pulled away suddenly, which made me feel as if I had done something wrong.

Panicked, I started giggling uncontrollably. "Leave it to me to ruin a serious moment," I said before turning and running inside the condo, leaving him on the beach alone.

Going back into my bedroom, I sat on the bed's edge, reliving the moment. I couldn't get the smell of his cologne out of my mind, likely because it was now on my shirt and was still very much present in the room with me. It's crazy what a great smelling man could do to a woman.

I replayed every conversation we shared this evening, looking for any indication that Luke was feeling the same way about me as I was about him. Being back on the island with him has reopened a desire never to leave his side. The contradiction between what my head was telling me and what my gut was saying was enough to confuse my heart.

If I were to believe the very words I say all the time—love never lasts—then why does it feel as though love with Luke never left? Perhaps it was possible that I had been wrong all along. However, I would certainly need more evidence to debunk that theory. Besides, what are the odds that he still loves me?

I have been receiving mixed signals from his words and his actions from the moment we reconnected, and the inconsistencies they both have. If tonight left me with anything, it was the greatest question of all—*is he ready to move on from his loss?*

ELEVEN

FRIDAY, JUNE 10, 2022

Lucas Miller

Waking up to the smell of bacon, eggs, and coffee will never get old. I had completely forgotten what it was like to live in the same house with a woman who enjoyed cooking and was good at it. I haven't eaten this well in so long, my waistline was already showing signs of trouble ahead if I didn't get back into my workout routine.

Last night, we had a serious conversation where I told her about Lisa, and she shared with me about her ex—which had me still wondering why she never married him. I'm not buying the whole "love never lasts" line.

The Tess I knew was a hopeless romantic who loved love so much that she forced me to watch romantic comedies every year on vacation. We had even had a date at the movie theater here on the island to watch a new release that she couldn't wait to see. *Nah, the Tess I know puts the swoon in swoon-worthy.*

I'm sure there is more to that story, and I will get it out of her. But I have to be strategic about it. Timing is everything, and one thing I know about our situation—we have all the time we'll need.

"Breakfast is ready," Tess called out as she placed the plates on the table.

I walked over and sat down next to her. "This looks delicious. Thank you for making it."

She smiled at me, took a bite of a pancake and mumbled, "We need to get some things before tonight's big party."

I reached up and wiped away the syrup dripping from the corner of her mouth with a napkin. Her cheeks flushed, but she held my gaze as she swallowed the bite she had taken.

"Thanks for that," she said casually before taking a second bite, this time more carefully.

"Tell me more about this party. What is it? Who's coming? And do we need more than food and drinks?" I asked her.

She chewed faster, and after swallowing, responded, "It's a farewell party for my friends—it will be casual. Today is their last day here on the island. I figured we could have a fire in the fire pit, food and drinks indoors, and plenty of seating outside for everyone."

I thought for a moment before replying, "Do you think it would be okay if I invited William to join us? He is my client, but he is also a good friend of mine."

She smiled. "Sure, that sounds great. The more, the merrier."

Over the next half hour, we worked out a list of items needing to be picked up at the store before the party. Based on our list, we could get everything at Driftwood Deli and Grocery, so we only needed to stop once.

I picked up the list. "I'll go to the store to get everything. You can stay here and relax."

She frowned at me as she stood. "No, Luke, I'll come with you."

I smiled and tried to reason with her. "Really, Tess, I can get this. It would be my pleasure."

She shook her head at me in disagreement. "Oh, I don't know. I really would like to come with you."

"You are quite the perfectionist. Don't you trust me?" I teased her.

Pink slowly crept across her cheeks. She put her face in her hands and shook her head back and forth as if to say no. I reached out and took her hands in mine, gently guiding them down from her face and onto the table. I kept my focus on her and watched as she went from looking down at the table to looking up at me.

Her eyes met mine, and I smiled at her. She returned the smile, and we sat in silence for a moment, holding hands across the table, not looking away from each other.

"You can join me. It could even be fun," I said to her.

She grinned, clearly excited. "Okay, go get ready, because I'm already ready!"

I got up and took a shower, followed by my daily morning routine that apparently was taking entirely too long for her liking. She had come back to check on me twice already, based on the sound of the footsteps I heard outside the bathroom door. I moved as quickly through my morning routine as I could, being careful not to miss a single step because it would throw off my entire day.

Few men care about their appearance nearly as much as I do, but good hygiene is something that I take seriously. And skincare was essential to me. One thing that I learned in the wake of Lisa's death is that taking care of your skin is crucial for many reasons. Most people likely don't check every single mole or blemish daily like I do, but then again, most people also likely didn't lose their spouse from skin cancer.

The last thing I put on my face, neck, and arms was sunscreen. Stepping back, I looked at myself in the mirror. I had done a little more than usual because I wanted to look good for Tess.

"Man, what are you doing? Are you really ready for a potential relationship right now?" I asked my reflection in the mirror.

I shook my head at myself at the preposterous notion that I would think I was ready for this. But life is short, so I had to snap out of it and at the very least give it a shot. Besides, what are the odds that it would fail epically? I might actually be surprised—it may be the best thing for me.

I heard footsteps coming towards the door and a soft knock. "Luke, are you ready yet?"

I sprayed on my cologne before opening the door to see Tess standing there, waiting. Tess stood staring at me, and her eyes intently scanned my body from head to toe, confirming my choice in clothing was on point and that I had spent the extra time getting ready wisely.

I smiled at her. "All set, let's get going."

She remained frozen in place, so I gently guided her down the hall towards the door.

"Do you want me to drive the van, or do you want to drive?" I asked Tess, hoping she would have a better vehicle than in my current situation.

She held up her keys. "Oh yeah, no, I'm driving. We are not taking that van."

I followed her out to the parking lot, quickly scanning to see if I could guess what vehicle was hers. It was likely the black sedan that looked like something she would drive. I was surprised when she turned left, which was the opposite way from the sedan. I guessed wrong.

Nothing could have prepared me for the sound of the unlocking of a cherry red convertible. *She is the one who got my car? How is this even possible?!* I don't know whether I'm relieved, angry, or ecstatic right now.

I looked at her curiously. "You are driving the convertible?"

Tess smiled as she put on her sunglasses. "Of course, why on earth would I drive anything else? I'm on an island, my SUV is in the shop after my accident on the drive here, and I plan to enjoy every single moment of sunshine that I can."

"Wait, what? You got into an accident on the drive here?" I asked, surprised that this was the first time she's mentioned it.

"Yes, I was about an hour from the island after driving through the night to get here from Ohio. A young woman was texting while driving and hit my car on the front driver's side with such force that it completely broke it. I had to have it towed to Savannah, and I picked up this rental there."

She got behind the wheel and started up the car, immediately putting the top down. From her bag, she took a baseball cap and put it on, her hair coming out the back. I don't think I've ever seen anything more captivating. She definitely had my attention.

I watched as she buckled the belt and followed suit. Tess backed out of the parking spot and headed towards the main road. It was a short drive to the store, which made me sad. I wanted to ride around in this car on the island. It was *the car* I had requested but didn't get.

I decided I had to ask the question on my mind. "How did you get so lucky to get this car?"

She grinned at me. "That's just it. It was pure luck. The original person who requested it was a no-show. When I arrived at the counter, she asked if I would be interested in the convertible, and I said absolutely!"

I shook my head in disbelief. "Unbelievable! I think you've got my car!"

She looked at me with her left eyebrow raised. "Were you a no-show?" she grinned when she asked.

I laughed so hard my stomach shook. "In my defense, it wasn't my fault at all. But I should have called them to tell them I'd be late. They said they had one coming back in a week, so I'm on a callback list. How long do you have this one for?"

She smiled bigger before breaking out into a laugh. "Just for this week! I couldn't pass up the chance to get it because it's perfect. My SUV should be finished at the end of the week. I'm just glad I didn't get stuck with the van!"

We both laughed at the luck we had in the whole situation. One may say that this was all preordained as a way to bring us back together. I suppose it depends on how you feel about divine intervention.

We walked into the store together. She grabbed a cart, and I followed her down each aisle. She meticulously checked her list, ensuring we grabbed every item. I never knew grocery shopping was such a serious event.

We came down what I referred to as the forbidden aisle. Row upon row of delicious sweet treats lined every shelf. She surprised me when she grabbed a box of cookies and put it in the cart.

Teasing her, I picked them up and waved them in the air. "Hey, these are most definitely not on your list. I think they should go back," I threatened to put them back on the shelf.

She grabbed them from me and tossed them back into the cart. "Don't you dare. These are for me. I'm all out."

We turned down the next aisle. This one is more my speed, and it reminded me I never picked up any protein powder. I reached over and grabbed a canister of powder and set it in the cart.

She picked up the canister and held it out in front of me. "Hey, this for sure isn't on my list. It's gotta go back," she teased me right back.

I held up my hands in truce. "How about we both make an exception for each other? You with your delicious cookies, and me with my nutritional powder."

She laughed as she said, "Deal. Consider me looking the other way."

We went down the final aisle, where all the drinks were. I reached out to grab a bottle of pop at the same time she reached for it. Her hands touched mine, which sent a million volts of electricity throughout my body. There was just something about the way she touches me that makes me feel alive again.

"Oops, sorry, you get that one; I'll grab the next one," she said as she let go of my hands to reach out for a different bottle.

Never in a million years would I have guessed that a trip to the grocery store could be so revealing of a person's hidden feelings. *Is it possible I still have feelings for Tess after all these years?* It has been a lifetime without her, yet it feels like it was just yesterday that we were together.

Five years doesn't feel like long enough to grieve the loss of Lisa's life, but five years feels like a long time of living alone in grief. I missed being touched by a woman. These thoughts brought up another new feeling—guilt. I felt guilty for thinking of another woman in this way, almost like I was betraying Lisa by considering moving on without her.

I tell myself that nothing is happening—I am simply noticing there are feelings resurfacing surrounding Tess. This is normal and nothing to feel guilty about at all. But I need to decide if now is the time I can open myself back up without reservations to give love a second chance.

TWELVE

FRIDAY, JUNE 10, 2022

Teresa Wright

Music floated on the breeze coming off the ocean. My friends were all dancing and singing along to one of their favorite songs from a new up-and-coming artist, Blade Williams. I stepped back to take in the scene before me, as if to etch it forever in my memory. The bonfire was a touch bigger than I think Luke had expected, but the crackle and pop along with the giant blaze really added to the poignant moment.

Lynn and Beth spotted me off by myself and joined me. "So, Tess, how has it been living with Lucas this week?" Lynn asked curiously.

Warmth filled my cheeks as I looked over at him dancing and smiled. "I have really enjoyed my time with him. We've had some really awkward moments, but we have also had some really amazing ones."

Lynn gave me a sharp look as she gave me a word of caution. "Be careful, Tess. From what you've shared with me, his heart is fragile, and so is yours. Take this one slow and be thoughtful in your approach."

The girls nodded in unison. "That's why I think I'm holding back. I'm unsure if he's ready for more than friendship, and I won't push him."

Beth looked at me with a questioning look. "Does this mean you want more than a friendship with him?"

A sigh escaped me as I offered what was on my heart. "It's what I've always wanted. You both know that." I looked away as sadness came over me.

Beth put her arms around me and squeezed. "We know, Tess. We just needed you to say it out loud."

"What are we saying out loud?" Louise came up behind us.

I looked over at her and smiled. "Oh, you know, regular girl stuff, like how amazing Blade Williams' new song is, and that I still have strong feelings for Luke."

Louise's eyes lit up and a huge smile spread across her face. "I *knew* it! It's about time you admitted it. When we were here yesterday and you were disappointed that he didn't come join us, I had my suspicions, but you kept saying no."

I shook my head. "Oh, that's because I was annoyed he couldn't come join us after telling me he'd try. But we had a great conversation last night and an amazing morning today. So maybe there is some hope." I almost believed the last part.

Beth lovingly reminded me, "There's nothing wrong with having hope that love can be found, even after it has been lost for so long."

I was such a lucky woman with the very best friends. They always knew the right thing to say. When it comes to Luke, however, he still has a hold on me that makes my heart skip a beat, and I get all tongue-tied. I glanced over to see him talking with Beth's husband, David. Standing up, I excused myself to go mingle with Luke's friend William and his guest Jason.

I walked up to the two gentlemen to greet them. "I hope you are both enjoying yourselves," I said casually.

William responded, "The best time, it has been good to meet everyone. You and Luke throw a really great party together."

Jason chimed in. "I must ask, who is that woman over there?" he asked, pointing to Louise, who was sitting by herself near the fire.

After following his direction, I smiled. "Oh, that is my cousin, Louise. She's amazing. Would you like an introduction?"

He thought for a moment before responding, "No, I think I'll go over and do that now, but thank you for offering."

William chuckled. "He wastes no time. He is a great guy. I think he is just really lonely now that he's moved here."

"That is actually one of the worries I have about moving here, especially since I don't know anyone on the island," I said.

William held out his hand for a handshake. "Hi, I'm William. Now you *do* know someone on the island," he said with a chuckle.

I couldn't stop myself from giggling. He had a great sense of humor, so I could see why he and Luke were good friends.

I shook his hand. "Well, it's nice to meet you officially, William. How long have you known Luke?" I asked.

He used his fingers to count. "About 25 years or so? We met in college during sophomore year back in 1998. He's the numbers guy and would have known that answer without having to use his fingers to do the math," he laughed at himself.

I laughed with him. "Don't worry, I get that too. I am not a numbers person. You've known him almost as long as I have. We met in 1995, but lost touch in 1997."

William shifted the conversation. "So, Teresa, tell me a little about yourself. What is it that you do?"

I felt relaxed with him and couldn't help but think he would make a great companion for Lynn. "Please call me Tess; it's what all my friends call me. The short version would be that I am a single mom of two adult boys, I am an artist, and I enjoy teaching others how to paint."

He looked interested. "Do you have your work on display anywhere?"

Not wanting to divulge too much information, I simply smiled at him as I responded. "Oh, it's here and there, I'm sure. What about you? Tell me more about yourself and what you do." I changed the subject back to him.

We stood and chatted for a while longer, getting to know each other. I really liked William. He is a nice guy, and I hoped we could become friends here, too. As he was talking, I looked over to see Luke talking to Lynn and Beth. The sight of him laughing with my friends made me catch my breath. He is getting along with them so well.

I watched as he tossed his head back and laughed, his eyes lighting up as pure joy filled his face. I'm seeing the old Luke resurface, and I couldn't be happier.

I excused myself from William and picked up some empty cups and plates that were scattered throughout the beach to take them inside. I had just finished putting them in the garbage can and turned to go back outside. And I found myself bumping right into Luke.

Flustered, I quickly said, "Oh my goodness, I'm so sorry, Luke, I didn't hear you come in behind me."

He smiled at me and reached around me to toss the garbage he was holding. "I saw you picking up and wanted to help out."

His thoughtfulness was touching. "Thank you for helping me. I thought maybe I'd sneak away real quick to clean up a bit and refill the food bowls," I said as I walked into the kitchen.

Luke didn't hesitate to join me, as together we added more chips to the bowls, put out more cheese and meats, and even filled the dessert plate and candy dish that appeared to have been hit the hardest.

Tossing away empty wrappers as I went, I cleaned up, which prompted Luke's response. "I think I may be rubbing off on you a bit, Tess. You never cleaned up as you went, if I recall."

I poked him in the ribs. "You are rubbing off on me. You had to ruin the good thing I had going," I teased him.

We both laughed and headed back outside with the others. A slow song came on, and everyone coupled up to slow dance by the fire. Even William and Lynn were dancing together, which made me happy for her.

Luke held out his hand as he asked, "Would you like to dance?"

I placed my hand in his and let him guide me out onto the sand. He didn't let go of my hand as he held it close to his chest and rested his other hand on my waist. I placed my free hand on his shoulder as I stepped in closer, our faces merely inches apart.

We danced in silence, gazing into each other's eyes, feeling the music as we swayed back and forth and spun around. It reminded me of the first time we danced like this on the beach. It was the second year we both came here for vacation, and my parents hosted a party for his family to join us. I can still remember how happy he looked that night as we danced the night away.

Luke was the first to speak. "This has been a really great party. Your friends are wonderful. I've enjoyed getting to know them better."

I smiled up at him. "William and Jason are great, too. I can see why you are friends, and I'm glad you invited them."

He smiled down at me, and for a moment, I thought he was going to kiss me. Perhaps it was wishful thinking, and I was getting my hopes up for nothing. But still, I couldn't help but hope he would kiss me.

Unfortunately, the moment passed as Jason came over and put his hand on Luke's shoulder and said he was going to head out. Luke pulled away from me and walked Jason back to the condo to see him out. I couldn't help feeling disappointed as our dance ended and I watched him disappear into the condo.

I took a seat next to Lynn, who was deeply engaged in conversation with William. I could tell that she was a little shy, but interested in him. There was an awkward pause, and I took that as my cue to interrupt.

"So, Lynn, how have you enjoyed your time on the island?" I asked her.

She turned to me as she replied, "I have really enjoyed it. It's going to be really difficult for me to go back home. I can see why you want to move here."

I chuckled as I responded, "You could always move here with me, then I would know more than just William on the island."

William interrupted our conversation to ask Lynn to dance again, and I watched as the two of them swayed back and forth. I was so lost in thought I didn't notice Luke had come and sat down beside me.

Luke leaned over and whispered, "What are we watching?"

His warm breath brushed my ear, creating a wave of goosebumps to break out all over my body. "Nothing, really, just staring out into the void, lost deep in thought."

"What's on your mind, Tess?" he asked with concern.

I felt sad at that moment. "I am going to miss having them around all the time. This is the last time we will all be together like this for quite some time."

He leaned in closer. "Do you regret deciding to move here? Are you reconsidering?"

I thought for a moment before answering confidently, "No. This is what I have wanted for so long. I owe it to myself to see this through."

He looked at me questioningly. "What exactly is it you have to see through?"

I wasn't sure how to explain this in a way that would make sense to anyone else. "All my life, I've done things that others either wanted, needed, or expected. I am finally at a place in life where I can do the things I have always wanted to do. Living here has been a dream of mine for as long as I can remember. That dream has never faltered. I love it here, and it's the perfect place to find inspiration for my next collection."

There was a sparkle in his eyes as a smile crept across his face. "I am glad you are finally putting yourself first and doing what makes you happy. Is art what you want to be doing for the rest of your life?"

"Yes, absolutely. I can't imagine not having art as a part of my life. I feel so free when I'm in the zone, like I am one with what it is I am painting; I can express my feelings through my art," I replied passionately.

He looked me in the eye as he grew serious. "When will you let me see your paintings?"

I froze. I don't share my paintings with anyone I know. Mostly because I am a very private person, but I have never had anyone ask me to see them before either. I dodged the question by way of a diversion.

I stood up and held out my hand to him. "Walk with me to the water's edge?"

Without speaking, he stood up and put his hand in mine. We walked away from the music and fire in silence, welcoming the change in volume as it grew quieter. We reached the water's edge, and I stood with my head tilted to the sky, eyes closed as the cool water lapped at my feet.

Luke stepped in place behind me and wrapped his arms around me from behind, pulling me into an embrace like he had never done before. I never wanted this moment to end. Life has changed us. And I know picking up where we left off isn't possible—but perhaps we could have a fresh start—beginning tonight.

THIRTEEN

SUNDAY, JUNE 12, 2022

Lucas Miller

The day I have been waiting for has finally arrived! Her convertible has to be returned by 10:00 am for me to swap with my van. I planned a whole day for Tess and me in Savannah that I hope she will enjoy. *It all starts now.*

Tess and I walked hand in hand to the van—our last walk of shame as empty nesters with a family vehicle. We hugged before getting behind the wheels of our respective vehicles. My drive to Savannah took 45 minutes, but with her following behind me, it felt much longer.

I pulled into the lot and parked next to a black SUV, wondering if it was hers before we headed inside to do the swap. They had us in and out in no time. While Tess wrapped up her conversation with the dealership representative, I went back outside to admire the convertible I wanted to drive since I first sat in it next to Tess.

We left her SUV at the airport parking lot for the day, as I drove us around town in the convertible with the top down, ready to explore. The historical charm was evident in the style of the buildings and iron fences that lined the streets. I turned toward Savannah Harbor Marina and found an empty parking spot in the shade.

"Are you up for a walk along the docks?" I asked Tess.

She smiled at me and replied, "Yes, that sounds fun."

Her smile made my heart skip a beat, and an unfamiliar feeling filled my abdomen. Dare I say—she gave me butterflies again? It feels strange to even think about—it has been quite some time since they've taken up residence in the pit of my stomach.

I got out of the car and crossed over to her side to open her door and help her out. We walked hand in hand towards the dock in comfortable silence. We stopped along the pier to watch yachts coming in and taking their places along the docks.

I looked over at Tess and saw that the wind had blown her hair into her face. I reached up to tuck a stray strand of hair behind her ear. She turned to look at me and smiled.

"I have been kicking around the idea of buying a yacht for quite some time, but I just haven't done it yet," I confessed.

She looked up at me, questioning. "Why haven't you?"

I nervously ran my hand through my hair. "Honestly, I don't know. The money is available, and I know roughly the size I want. I guess what it comes down to is not having anyone to share it with."

She squeezed my hand as if to reassure me. "You have your children, and their families will come with time. If you plan to have it here, William would likely join you, and I would, too."

I squeezed her hand back. "True, I hadn't considered that as a possibility. I could have friends on board and invite the kids here too. It would be a lot of fun."

She looked around the marina, and a big grin stretched across her face. "Let's be spontaneous and look at the yachts for sale."

I followed her gaze to see that she had spotted the very place I wanted to take her today. Our synchronicity was beautifully eerie; we were thinking the same thing at the same time.

I checked my watch to see that it was almost time. "Actually, we have an appointment with them in about five minutes."

Her face lit up as she threw her head back and laughed. "Well, I suppose this counts as you being spontaneous, even if you have a schedule."

"In my defense, I decided yesterday after we talked about swapping the rental, so I had little time for preparation," I replied, my hands up in surrender.

Both of us eager to see what awaited, we hurriedly walked over to Sea Spray Yacht Club. Once we reached the front doors, a man dressed in designer clothing without a single wrinkle immediately met us.

He extended his hand to me as he introduced himself. "Hi, I'm Toby Wells. You must be Lucas Miller."

I shook his extended hand with a firm grip. "Hi Toby, I am indeed Lucas Miller, and this is Teresa Wright."

He extended his hand to Tess. "Pleased to meet you, ma'am."

She looked at me with her left eyebrow raised before turning back to Toby. "Please call me Tess," she replied as she returned the handshake.

Toby turned his attention back to me. "Are you ready for your tours?"

I couldn't stop grinning. "Please lead the way!"

Tess and I followed Toby down the dock, where six similar yachts sat in the water beside each other. The only thing between them was a small dock to get on board.

Toby stopped in front of the first one we came to. "This is where I'll be during your walkthrough. You can spend as much time as you need on each vessel. Come back to me at the end, and I'll happily answer questions you have before moving on to the next one. There are six for you to board that fit within the criteria you supplied me with yesterday."

We thanked Toby before stepping up into the first yacht. I had already seen all six of these online before coming here, and of the six, this was my least favorite. The layout just wouldn't work for me. It felt too closed off in most areas. However, I wanted to at least see it in person in case the online photos were misleading.

Now that I was standing on the main deck, I knew I could rule this one out—but I wanted to see what Tess had to say.

I watched as she effortlessly walked around and looked at everything closely, not saying anything. We went down to the lower deck to see the living quarters, and I watched as her face showed disdain.

Curious to know what was on her mind, I asked, "What is it?"

She turned to look at me as she explained. "This feels so closed off and boxed in. Not just down here on the lower deck, but even on the main deck."

Her knowledge of correct boating terminology impressed me. "I agree. I don't think this one is it."

We didn't even finish the tour to the flybridge and made our way off the yacht to meet back up with Toby.

He greeted us. "What did you think of this one?"

I replied, "It's not the one for me. Which one is next?"

He led us down to the next yacht and allowed us to board it. It was a little more promising, but still not it—and, like the first tour, this one ended quickly.

The third yacht was one of the top three as a potential, and one I was eager to see. We boarded and walked through the main deck much more deliberately. It felt like a more natural flow of things, and I couldn't help myself. I sat at the helm station. I put my hands on the wheel and tried to picture myself out on the water. But for some reason, I couldn't.

Guilt gnawed at my chest. How much of my life had I let go by since Lisa died? I have lived the last five years on pure instinct and survival, not living life to its fullest. She would be so disappointed in me.

Tess walked up behind me and placed her hand on my shoulder. "I could see you in this chair, taking us out on the water. This main deck is definitely the best one we've seen yet. Its open flow will be great to have the kids sit here behind you in the shade from the flybridge."

I turned and looked behind me and tried to picture my kids sitting behind me—and again—I couldn't visualize it. Could it possibly be that this wasn't the one for me?

We toured the lower deck, which had some things we both didn't like about it, but this was the first yacht where we toured the flybridge.

I followed Tess up the stairs and heard her gasp before I could see what had captured her interest. Once I stepped out onto the flybridge, I could see the water going out into the ocean. It was breathtaking.

She walked up to the helm and took a seat. "Wow, what a view from up here! It's incredible!"

I sat down beside her and reached for her hand. "It certainly is."

We sat there for a brief moment before finally retreating to the main deck and down to meet with Toby.

He greeted us as we slowly made our way to him. "Ah, we are getting somewhere, no?"

Still unsure, I half smiled at him. "It was one of my top three, and it will remain there for now, but there are still others to look at."

He led the way to the fourth boat, which, like the first two, was immediately ruled out, and we moved on to the fifth boat, which was number two on my list.

The concern I had about this boat was that it was at the high end of my budget. If I were to go with it, that didn't leave me a lot of wiggle room for purchasing a house. The vessel was exquisite. It matched my taste in style perfectly—but it was also a foot smaller—which meant the rooms were also smaller.

Tess and I agreed that the extra foot makes a big difference in the sleeping quarters, and so we disembarked and made our way to the final yacht. This was the one I was most excited about.

As we walked up, Tess looked back at me with a sparkle in her eye. "Already, Luke, this one looks the most like you."

"Hopefully we saved the best for last," I replied.

We boarded, and instantly it felt like home. I made my way to the helm station and sat down. I could see myself out on the open water in this vessel. Tess joined me and put her hand on my shoulder.

"Can you see your kids sitting behind you on this one?" she asked optimistically.

I turned to look at the seats behind me, and I could see where our kids could sit together as one unit, a blended family brought together by two people who have always been drawn to each other.

I placed my hand over hers. "I can see our kids sitting behind me on this one."

Tears filled her eyes, and I feared I might have been overly ambitious in my confession. I stood up and placed my hands at the nape of her neck and tilted her head towards mine. I wiped away a tear with my thumb as it fell down her face.

"What's on your mind?" I asked gently.

Another tear fell down. "I can see it too," she said while looking deeply into my eyes.

I couldn't help myself. Suddenly, it was all so clear that I wanted her in my life. I tilted her chin up and leaned in as our lips met. She parted her lips and returned my kiss with passion and longing that filled my body with warmth from head to toe as my heart beat loudly.

We pulled away breathless, and as I looked into her eyes, I knew I wasn't ready to end this moment. She grabbed me and pulled me back to her, confident, yet gentle and loving. It had been so long since I had last held a woman in my arms, let alone kissed one. This kiss was effortless. Tess felt like home to me.

I followed her lead this time, only stopping when she was ready to stop. We both took a step back and looked at each other. Her face was flushed. She put her hand on her stomach as she looked at me knowingly.

I wasn't sure how she was handling this moment. "Are you okay?"

She giggled as she held onto a nearby railing to steady herself. "I'm going to need just a minute. But yes, I'm good."

I don't know much about women, but one thing I know about Tess is that usually when she giggles like that, it's a good thing.

I held my hand out for hers. "I think our tour is done. This is the one for sure."

We quickly disembarked and met back up with Toby, where I told him I would get back to him in a couple of days with my decision. I wanted to make him sweat it out a bit to see if he would be up for price negotiations later.

On our way out, we stopped in for lunch at Antonio's Pizza and Pasta, where we talked more about Lisa and Rob and what they both were like. Afterwards, we went to Double Scoop, the old fashioned ice cream shop next door, for dessert.

She asked about my kids, and I told her how hard it has been on them when they lost their mom. I asked her about her kids and watched as her face lit up every time she talked about how proud they made her. She held my hand across the table, and our knees touched underneath, sending shivers down my spine every time she shifted.

When we finished our dessert, we went back to the airport to separate for the drive back. The convertible felt empty without her next to me in it, and I caught myself looking in the rearview mirror to make sure she was still safely behind me.

Lost in thought, I tried not to compare how I was feeling with Tess to how I felt with Lisa. I loved Lisa, but I had to be honest with myself that I have always loved Tess as well. A part of me worried she'd leave, and I doubted her ability to love me in a way I needed.

Losing someone I love again felt impossible to recover from. But living the rest of my life alone would feel isolating. Imagining the rest of my life with Tess by my side gave me hope. Giving love a second chance sounded terrifying, but it also felt exhilarating.

FOURTEEN

Teresa Wright

After a season of creativity block, I woke up this morning with an idea for a new collection. It was the perfect morning to spend the day painting the largest canvas I had brought with me. After spending a couple of hours on the beach painting, the canvas was complete. It was perfect for the show-stopping piece, and it captured the spirit of the entire collection. Not wanting it to be seen, I hid the painting in the closet on my vintage easel, gifted to me from my Nonna Rosa.

With the painting safely tucked away, I grabbed my laptop and began a search for potential houses to buy. The prices were much higher than I had expected, which worried me. I wouldn't be able to afford both a house and the gallery space comfortably. It would be a stretch financially until my gallery took off.

Discouraged, I switched gears and started searching for long-term rentals near me. Maybe it wouldn't be a bad idea to rent a space for a year to live while building the gallery up and growing my savings. I wrote a list of potentials to have on hand when I would find a local realtor to work with.

Satisfied with my list, I closed the laptop just as my phone rang. It was Ted, my agent back home. "Hi Ted, what news do you have for me today?"

"We are ready to move forward with the closing. I have paperwork being overnighted to you today. Once you receive it, please sign and send them back in the provided overnight envelope," he said.

I danced in place, excited to move forward. "Woo hoo! This is great news, Ted! Thank you! I will be so glad to get this behind me."

We chatted a little longer about the details of the sale, and he gave me an estimated end date—just a few days away pending receipt of the signed papers. Once the sale was final, I could get more serious about putting an offer on the gallery space.

I spent some time working on a business plan, giving myself permission to dream about the impossible. I love teaching others how to paint and am well-versed in several mediums. The loft at the gallery would make an excellent classroom that could hold about twenty students with easels at once comfortably and up to forty students if needed.

I would build out a stage at the front of the gallery for live subjects or for an elevated platform for me to teach from. My paintings would be on display and for sale downstairs, and there was one area that I felt would make a great spot for other local artists to showcase pieces on a commission basis. This could help newer artists build a clientele while freeing up my financial risk.

I would also want to get heavily involved in the local community and made a note to join local groups to connect with other business owners. Becoming fully immersed in Sanderling

Pointe was my biggest goal right now—along with spending more time with Luke.

As if on cue, my phone dinged with a text from Luke.

> Working late, go ahead and eat without me. I'm grabbing a quick bite now before coming home.

It was the first time he called this condo home, which melted my heart. Building a home with him is something I could get used to. I never meant for anything like this to happen on my trip here—but I'm certainly not mad about it.

I grabbed a quick dinner of leftovers before relaxing on the sofa to read my book. I realized my schedule had been busy, and I didn't have as much time to read recently as I did when I first arrived. The air in the condo was quite chilly, so I grabbed the blue sherpa throw on the sofa and wrapped it around me.

The blanket was warm and comforting—and it smelled like Luke—which kept distracting me as I tried to read my book. I couldn't help but stop reading long enough to breathe in the scent of his cologne. I kept losing my place and repeating the same sentence.

Luke had a hold on me from the moment we met. It was always present. He is like a powerful magnet that attracts me to him in a way that cannot be separated no matter how hard you try.

It was getting late, and the more I thought about him, the more I missed him. I was wondering when he'd return.

Again, as if on cue, I heard the code being punched into the lock, and my heart skipped a beat. I couldn't wait to see him again, so I tossed off the blanket, jumped up from the couch, and ran to the door to greet him.

He came in the door and looked a little stressed from his long day as he loosened his tie. "I think the perfect way to end the day is with a late night swim. Would you like to join me?"

He leaned down and pecked my cheek. "That sounds wonderfully refreshing, actually."

We changed into our suits and headed out to the pool together. I tossed my cover-up and our towels on the chair as we went by. I walked over to the edge to dip my toes in, and it was cooler than I was expecting, considering how warm the day was.

He held out his hand to me and took one step closer to the pool's edge. "You know, the only way to adjust to the temperature of the water is to jump right in."

I placed my hand in his, and together, we jumped in feet first. Once I came up from the water, I swam over to him and put my arms around him like I used to do when we were younger. I quickly regretted throwing myself on him like that, so I pulled away and apologized.

He reached out and pulled me back to him. "Tess, I love being with you. You don't need to apologize for anything—you did nothing wrong."

There has been a nagging question at the back of my mind all day after the kiss we had yesterday. I just couldn't stop thinking about his lips on mine and the way he filled my heart with longing in a way that no one else could.

As he held me, I quietly asked, "Are you ready to open yourself up to love again?"

It felt like he'd taken an incredibly long time to answer despite his response being fairly quick. "With the right person—yes, I am ready," he answered.

We were both quiet for a short time before he spoke next. "I was thinking yesterday about how the last five years have gone by both painstakingly slowly—yet so quickly. I have come to realize that time is precious, and it's time for me to start living life again."

I looked up at him as water dripped from his hair, leaving ripples in the water below. "There is still plenty of life to live ahead of you with someone by your side."

He smiled down at me as he swayed back and forth, the water splashing up over my body as I moved with him. "How about you? Are you ready to open yourself up to love again?"

In my heart, I know that I have never stopped loving Luke. Not wanting to scare him away, I smiled and simply responded, "With the right person—yes, I am ready."

Shivering in the night's cool air, he asked if I wanted to sit by the fire pit on the beach. I could never turn down an evening on the beach by the fire, and we made our way out of the pool. He built the fire, and I dried off and grabbed a blanket from the closet inside. I took the blanket out to the beach and spread it out as close as I could get to the warmth coming from the growing blaze.

With my towel around my body, I still couldn't seem to get warm as a gentle breeze blew off the ocean. He reached his arms around me to help me get warm. Cold water from his hair dripped onto my shoulders, only making me colder.

I shivered in the cool night air as I turned to look at him. "You are still wet!"

He turned and ran to grab his towel, drying off and pulling his shirt on. On his way back to me, he grabbed my cover-up. "Here, this should help you."

I dropped my wet towel and put on the dry cover-up while inching a little closer to the fire. Luke came and stood next to me, unsure of what to do next. I stepped closer and wrapped my arm around his waist. He pulled me closer to him, the heat from his body radiating towards mine while the fire warmed us both.

He reached out and cupped my chin, tilting my face towards his while leaning in to kiss me. His kiss sent a surge of electricity straight through me. Perhaps this is an indication that he could be the right person to open myself up to love again.

We parted just enough for me to lay my head on his chest, where standing together for a little longer before finally sitting down on the blanket together.

He tossed a stray branch into the crackling fire. "Did you have a good day today?"

I realized in my excitement of seeing him, I had never asked him how his day had been. "I did, how about you?"

He let out a sigh. "I quickly realized that I might need to consider opening a satellite office here permanently. There's so much work to be done."

I hoped this meant he was considering moving here, too. "That would be great for your business. Would you run it, or would you hire someone else to run it for you?"

He ran his hand through his hair and looked away from me for a moment. "I am not sure about that yet."

I was a little sad that he wasn't at the point of committing to moving here. I started to recognize a pattern in Luke that I wasn't sure he was aware of. He couldn't commit to a yacht because the idea of moving here felt like too much. He can't commit to moving here and running the satellite business because he just doesn't know if that is what he would want to do yet.

Part of me had hoped he'd realize that by saying yes to both, he was also saying yes to us. Whatever *us* was. Since it wasn't defined, I wondered if our relationship would be long-lasting or short-lived.

Sensing my overthinking, he interrupted my thoughts. "I think it depends on what you had in mind."

I was surprised at his statement. "Why is it dependent on what I have in mind? It is your business, you have to decide what is best for it."

Luke threw his head back and laughed a deep, hearty laugh. "I'm not talking about the business, Tess. I'm talking about us."

What did I miss? Because I don't recall him ever making us official in any capacity. "So there is an *us*?!"

His warm smile showed me he was genuine in what he was saying. "There will always be an *us*, Tess. The question is, what do you want *us* to be?"

I thought for a moment before answering him. "I want us to be us. Two ships passing in the darkness of the night, each on their search for a shining light to guide them home. Two people who connect together to arrive safely on shore."

He looked surprised by my response. "Wow, Tess, that was beautifully said. I believe that as long as I'm connected to you, I'll always be safe at home."

I felt our conversation couldn't have gone any better. I received clarity on what it was we were doing as a couple, which filled me with hope. I can't help but feel that just maybe, Lucas has never stopped loving me after all these years, too.

FIFTEEN

Lucas Miller

Not wanting to waste much time, William called me in for a meeting at the second retail space next to the gallery. I brought a stack of paperwork for him to sign to get the ball rolling on some additional investments. I recommended them to him because I felt they would bring greater returns long term and had little to no risk associated with them. This would help bring his financial portfolio up to the next level that I knew he was aiming for.

I walked into the building, seeing the space with a fresh perspective. I wasn't sure if that was because everything looked so much better now that I was with Tess—or if I had simply been so preoccupied the day I toured it initially that I didn't notice how great it would be for offices.

William seemed to be in a hurry, so we jumped right in and signed all the documents. Just as I closed my folder, the door opened and in walked six men I had never seen before. They must be touring the location, which would explain why William was in a hurry. One man walked over to us quicker than the rest and reached out his hand to shake William's hand.

After shaking his hand, William turned to me to make the introduction. "Todd, I'd like to introduce you to Luke. Luke, this is a colleague of mine, Todd."

I reached out my hand toward Todd. "Nice to meet you, Todd."

The five other men caught up with us, and William quickly introduced us. "Guys, this is my financial advisor, Luke. Luke, meet Shawn, Mike, Matt, Alexander, and Josh."

During introductions, I shook each man's hand and tried to remember one physical thing about each to avoid later confusion. Todd was the tallest and had blonde hair, so in my head I referred to him as Tall Todd. Shawn was the shortest, so Short Shawn it is. Mike was the most muscular of them all, so he got Mighty Mike. Matt is the thinnest of them all, so Flat Matt. Alexander was the most jovial of them all, so I called him Alexander the Great. Josh was the best dressed, so I went with Posh Josh.

Now, I was fairly confident I could remember who was who by giving them all a nickname that helped me remember. They were all chatting together when William cleared his throat to get everyone's attention.

"I invited you all here because you each expressed an interest in investing in this great island of ours to help build it back up. Luke is the best financial advisor there is, and I think you could really benefit from his help. Within a week, he helped me change my investments to more lucrative options, and I'm pleased to report I'm up five million already," William said with a huge grin—though he may have oversold me a bit.

One by one, the men came to talk to me about their current investments and where they hoped to be. I am usually a good judge of character, and I could tell in speaking with them all that

I would likely work best with most of them. But there were two who would require more work on my part to convince—Posh Josh and Mighty Mike.

As suspected by the end of our time together, I was writing contact information for Tall Todd, Flat Matt, Short Shawn, and Alexander the Great so I could send them each a contract to begin their portfolio takeover. Both Posh Josh and Mighty Mike shook my hand before leaving, and took my business card while assuring me they'll be in contact should they require my services.

Once they had left, I turned to William. "That felt promising. If I can get the four of them to sign, I will need to open up shop here in order to better service everyone here."

William fist-pumped the air in excitement. "Yes! That's what I'm talking about!"

I laughed at his eagerness. "I appreciate the punt. My odds are greater with you stacking the deck."

William shook his head in disagreement. "That was all you, my friend. Hey, do you want to see the house I have? I haven't put it on the market yet, but I was planning to soon."

I scheduled a time to meet William at the house and headed out. I reached my car and decided I wanted to celebrate my wins—so I drove straight to Laughing Gull Marina. I walked up to the boat rental desk and rented a boat for the rest of the day. Boat keys in hand, I went back to my car and drove to the condo to pick up Tess.

I jogged into the condo and found her sitting poolside, reading her book. "Hey Tess, I rented a boat to go for a quick ride over to Savannah to look at the yachts again. Would you like to come with me?"

She immediately jumped up. "Yes! That sounds like a lot of fun. Let me change and grab a few things."

She moved quicker than usual, and in no time, we were driving back down to the marina to get into our rental boat.

Once on board, Tess moved in closer to me. "So, what made you decide to do this?"

I leaned over and kissed her, her lips soft and silky against mine. "I wanted to celebrate landing four new clients here on the island."

She looked at me with her left eyebrow raised, questioning what she had just heard. "If you keep it up, you'll have to set up an office here and move to the island for good."

I thought about what she said for a moment. "Actually, that thought keeps crossing my mind. It looks more like a possibility now than it did when I first arrived here."

She put her hand on my shoulder to steady herself as I sharply steered the boat into the dock at Savannah Harbor Marina. I tied the boat to the dock and escorted Tess off. We walked hand in hand to Sea Spray Yacht Club, where we were greeted by a smiling Toby.

He extended his hand toward me. "Good to see you again, Lucas. Are you ready to look at your top three again?"

I shook his hand in return. "Yes, I have something I wanted to check on each of them to help me decide."

We followed Toby back down to the docks, where the three yachts sat, side by side. I wanted to make sure I picked one that would fit my kids and their families, as well as Tess's kids and their families. It was important to me that it fit us all at once comfortably.

We walked through each boat, concluding that the one we both originally said we liked was the one big enough for everyone to sleep comfortably. I made my decision, and we walked back to the office with Toby to sign the paperwork. The staff helped me set up a dock at Laughing Gull Marina on Sanderling Pointe Island and promised to clean up the yacht and deliver it by the end of the day.

After grabbing a quick dinner nearby, Tess and I boarded the rental boat and began our ride back to the island. Suddenly, I missed my kids, wishing they were with me as I pictured all the kids on the yacht.

Tess jolted me. "Penny for your thoughts?"

Trying to hide my sadness, I smiled up at her. "I was just thinking about the kids. What do you think about getting all the kids together for the first time and spending the weekend on the yacht?"

Her smile changed as a look of panic filled her face. "I know we've known each other a long time, but to them, we've only been back in each other's lives for a couple of weeks. Will they think it's too soon?"

I love how concerned she is about her kids, but I also wanted to make sure she remembered to put herself first. "I'll leave the choice up to you to decide. It's okay to put your life first, but it's also okay to consider the kids' feelings as well. You are in the middle, kind of like me—and I understand that."

The hour boat ride back to Laughing Gull Marina went quicker than I thought it would. Being on the open water with the wind in our hair felt really great. Tess looked like she belonged on a boat as she glided effortlessly across the bow, upright.

We made it back to Laughing Gull Marina at sunset and watched the sun disappear into the horizon before disembarking from the boat and turning in the keys. We drove back to the condo in silence, each of us deep in thought about the possibility of bringing our families together.

When we got back to the condo, we sat on the sofa next to each other to watch TV. I had my arms around Tess, and she was leaning back against my chest. Her hair smelled of raspberries and vanilla, and her skin was silky smooth to the touch. She felt so good in my arms. I never wanted to let go for fear I might lose her again.

Suddenly she jumped up from the sofa. "Okay, let's invite them. I'll call mine and you call yours. Once confirmed, I will set up the plane tickets for all four to come in on Saturday morning and back out on Sunday evening so they won't miss any work or schooling."

I stood up and kissed her on her forehead before walking outside to call my kids, leaving her inside to do the same. I wasn't sure how they would react to the invitation, but both were thrilled and excited to meet Tess. After hanging up with Jacob, I couldn't help but notice the uncertainty in his voice. He took it the hardest when his mom died, and my moving on could be difficult for him. I knew I'd need to keep an eye on him during our time spent together.

I spent a short time looking out into the darkness. "Lisa, if you can hear me, please know that I'll always love you—while also loving Tess. There's room in my heart for you both. Your memory will never be forgotten."

I took a deep breath and headed back inside just as Tess hung up the phone. "They are in! Both of them said they would come," she exclaimed.

"Both Emily and Jacob can make it in too. It actually went much better than I thought it would." I exhaled.

She crossed the room and looked up at me. "But what about you? Are you okay with how quickly things are progressing?"

I reached out and pulled her close. She laid her head on my chest, and we stood there together in the kitchen for several minutes before I could find the words to say. "We are progressing at just the right speed."

I couldn't help but feel that this was a clear indication that our families would do well together, especially since all four kids agreed to come without a single objection. My kids were always objecting to things, so the fact they didn't object told me that this is a different situation.

I just hoped that they truly were ready for me to move on in life. I'll just have to make sure that they understand that in no way, shape or form am I trying to replace their mother with Tess.

Their mother is irreplaceable. She will always be the same in my mind. But Tess is a wonderful addition to the family, and I know they will grow to love her, just like I do.

SIXTEEN

Signing the paperwork for the sale of the farmhouse brought more emotions than I thought it would—and resulted in a delay of signing. The forms sat on the table in front of me, begging me to sign them. But instead, I was purchasing flights for all four kids to come in this weekend for some fun together.

Blending the two families may prove to be interesting, and I wasn't sure how Luke's kids would take the news that their father had decided to try love again after losing their mom. It's such a delicate situation that we are all in together, and I want to make sure that I'm being respectful of their feelings throughout the whole relationship.

Losing a parent at any age is hard—but when you are young, it's even harder. You feel robbed of time and joy as you navigate grief and all the emotions it brings. It was a feeling I understood well. Even though my father hadn't passed away, he chose his other family over me. In fact, I never saw him again after he left.

I had to grieve that loss in a way my eighteen-year-old brain could comprehend. It was easier to tell my friends that my dad was dead than to explain to them the complexity of the situation. And to me—in a way—he was dead. He was gone, and I would never see or hear from him again.

Snapping back to reality, I heard the computer notification ding. The email confirmations for the tickets finally arrived in my inbox, and I forwarded them off to my boys and Luke so he could forward them to his kids. I thought it might be awkward coming from me. As soon as I hit send, my phone rang. Glancing at the screen, I saw it was Ted—and braced myself.

"Hello Ted, how are you today?" I asked.

"Good, good, I just wanted to make sure you received the paperwork yesterday and see if you looked it over," he replied.

I had a feeling I'd be getting this phone call. "After reviewing them last night, I have them right here, ready to be signed. I'll sign them shortly, and then I can run them out to be shipped."

"Great! Once I get them here, they asked me to call right away—so if you can get it out today, that means tomorrow we can close," he said, a little too enthusiastically.

Finishing this fast surprised me slightly and filled me with panic. "Wow, that quickly? I thought for sure it would take another week or so," I asked.

"Everything is all set. We just need to sign the documents and hand over the keys. That is the final part of the sale," he said.

"Well, okay then, I'll get that signed and out this morning. You should have it tomorrow," I replied.

We said our goodbyes and hung up the phone, leaving me in a slight state of panic. It makes me happy that this part of my life is ending. But I've had so much fun with Luke, I neglected finding housing and looking into the gallery. I don't even know if the gallery is still available, and the last time I looked online for a house, the prices were out of my budget range.

Quickly, I typed *homes for rent near me*, and began looking through the options. It quickly became clear that I was hitting dead ends because most listings were outdated or had broken links.

Frustrated, I slammed the laptop shut and grabbed the stack of paperwork waiting for my signature. I went through every single page and signed next to the flags that Ted had put in place.

The stack was so thick it took longer than I realized it would, but once I reached that last sheet, I was grateful to give my hand a break. I put the paperwork in the overnight envelope, grabbed my purse and keys, and made my way to the car to drop it off.

When I pulled into the parking lot, I noticed a sign on the building next door for a local realtor—and I knew I needed help finding a place to live. After dropping off my package, I walked through the front door of the agent's office. The front desk associate looked up at the sound of the bell ringing. After a quick discussion, I learned both agents were out with clients. I left my contact information for one of them to get back to me when they returned.

I went back to my car and decided that a drive around the island would be good to clear my head. It was no coincidence that I pulled into the gallery's parking lot. I didn't intend to go here, yet here I was. The sign on the door read *Open*, and I saw that as the perfect invitation to talk to Eloise.

I walked through the front door, and Eloise quickly greeted me. "Hello—Teresa, correct?"

The fact that she remembered me made me feel good about being here, almost as if I belonged. "You have an excellent memory, Eloise! You are correct."

She made an excited gesture with her hands. "I still have it after all these years. What brings you here today, Teresa?"

I looked around the gallery as I answered her. "I just love art, and today has been one of those days where I just needed a little pick me up"

She smiled at me softly. "Would you care to sit down and chat?"

I followed Eloise over to a small table with two chairs overlooking the gallery. Eloise offered me a bottle of water, which I politely declined. We settled in quickly and had some idle chatting before Eloise asked me a hard question.

"What makes you love art so much, Teresa?" Eloise asked with poise and elegance.

Nervous, I smiled awkwardly. "I have loved art for as long as I can remember. In my teens, I knew I wanted to be an artist someday, but life, and children, got in the way of that for a while."

She reached over and patted my left hand as she looked me in the eye. "You are a great mother for putting your ambitions aside for their needs."

I placed my right hand on top of hers, not breaking our gaze. "Thank you for graciously saying so. I am an artist now, but I feel like something is still missing."

We let go of each other's hands as Eloise kindly asked, "What feels like it is missing?"

I thought for a moment before quietly confessing, "Me. I gained popularity as an artist, but I have used a pseudonym because I was afraid no one would like my art. And honestly, it offered me the chance to hide behind the name. To be someone else without fear of rejection or humiliation."

Eloise didn't seem at all fazed by my confession. "Have you ever told anyone else that you do this?"

I shook my head and looked away from her. "Actually, no. No one has ever even seen my art—well, not from me personally—but I suppose they could have seen it on display somewhere and not known it was mine."

I wondered if Eloise thought I was crazy—because I felt as if I sounded like a woman who had completely lost it. Back then, I thought that if I had a pseudonym, it would give me the chance to create freely in a way that allowed me to share what was on my heart through my paintings—with no one realizing the story behind the paintings. Fearing exposure, I worried that if they knew the paintings were mine, they would see my broken heart, wounded by lost love and an unfulfilled existence.

Eloise cleared her throat to get my attention and then smiled softly when I looked back at her. "May I ask what your pseudonym is?"

I felt heat flood my cheeks, and I looked down at the table. "I have told this to no one before." To ensure we were alone, I nervously looked around the gallery. "It's T. Bianchi," I said quickly and quietly. "I picked this name to honor my mother because it's my Nonna's maiden name. It's the perfect blend of the three of us in a name."

Eloise stood up and motioned for me to follow. "I would like to show you something, Teresa."

I followed her through the gallery, taking time to look at the paintings along the way. She led me to the window display on the other side of the gallery. Behind it was a wall that was built up to hang pictures that those walking by could see from the windows. But what they couldn't see from outside, we could see as a staged setting on the inside, with one single painting above a chaise.

I was speechless to see one of my paintings hanging there alone. "You have one of my paintings!"

Eloise smiled so big her eyes crinkled up at the corners. "Walk to the other side of the wall, dear."

I gasped when the side visible to the outside world came into my view. "It's the whole collection!"

Eloise spoke a little louder so I could hear over the wall. "It came in last month, and with closing, I wasn't sure if I would have time to set it out. I decided that it needed to be the prominent display for the farewell party. The whole collection is full of emotion and really speaks to me."

I walked back towards Eloise, still incredulous that my paintings were on display. "Well, I am absolutely honored that you have these. Thank you."

Eloise clasped her hands in excitement. "Would you consider speaking at the gallery's farewell party?"

Shaking my head, I said, "Oh, no, no, I couldn't do that. I'm so sorry. For the time being, I want to remain anonymous and not announce myself."

Eloise looked surprised by this. "Do you think you'll ever share with others that it's you?"

Thinking about it made me smile. "Actually, yes. I would like to open a studio that also has a gallery of all my collections and a place to teach painting classes. If I could pull this off, I have always imagined the big reveal being the grand opening of the studio. I must admit, if I could get this space, it could be a lovely way to transition from your gallery to mine—so I'll consider your generous offer to speak."

Eloise seemed pleased with this answer. "If there is anything I can do to help you get this space for your studio, please let me know. Keeping it within the arts community would make me happy. Your plans sound like a great opportunity for the locals."

After thanking Eloise, I walked out and turned to see the display. I stood looking at my last collection through the window, a glimpse into what this space could be for me. With the way Eloise had it on display, it really made the artwork shine in this setting. It was as if you could picture it hanging up in your space. She staged the art in a way I loved—making it feel like a home, not just artwork. I would want to continue the same feeling in my studio.

After standing for a moment, I turned and walked to my car. But once I was behind the wheel, I couldn't convince myself to start the car. *Is it finally time for me to step out of the shadows and be more present with my artwork?*

It's only been a couple of days, but I feel like Luke's *"life is short"* moment of buying a yacht made me realize just how short life is. I wasn't ready to make my decision yet about whether I would speak at the farewell party, but I was giving it some serious consideration.

SEVENTEEN

SATURDAY, JUNE 18, 2022

Lucas Miller

Saturdays are for living is a motto I've always shared with my kids. It seems fitting that today is a Saturday and we are going to be doing a whole lot of living today.

Jacob, Emily, and her husband, Brandon Snyder, were the first to arrive and board the yacht. I introduced them to Tess fairly quickly, followed by a tour of the yacht to show them each their quarters so they could drop off their bags and get settled in before Tess's kids arrived. They weren't far behind, so after telling my kids to make it quick, Tess and I headed back up to the main deck to await their arrival.

I could tell Tess was nervous, and to remind her I'm right here with her, I reached out and squeezed her hand. She looked at me and smiled, which made time slow down as we shared this special moment together. Emily and Brandon came up from the lower deck just as Aiden and Logan boarded the ship with Jacob rushing back upstairs.

Tess quickly helped Aiden and Logan with their bags before bringing them over to the three of us. "Aiden, Logan, this is Luke and his kids, Jacob and Emily, and her husband, Brandon," she said as she quickly made introductions.

We went around, each taking turns acknowledging them in our own ways with nods, high fives, and me being the awkward dad who still believes in a good solid handshake. "Boys, would you like to take your bags down to your living quarters before we head out?"

Tess took charge, making sure the boys knew how to get down to their living quarters while I started prepping the boat for departure with Jacob and Brandon's help. The boys surprised me with how quickly they learned how to undock the boat.

Tess and her boys joined us on the main deck, where I sat at the helm station with them all seated together behind me. It was just as I had imagined the first day I toured this vessel, and Tess was right—it was the boat that was most like me.

Steering the ship and taking part in conversation was difficult for me as we headed back to Sanderling Pointe after picking up the kids at Savannah Harbor Marina. Having everyone on board must have made me a bit more anxious than I thought it would. I have navigated these waters many times in this boat already, but suddenly having precious cargo on board changed my approach.

Once we were out on the open water, I was able to relax a bit more and enjoyed captaining the ship. Not wanting to rush back to Sanderling Pointe, I broke the trip up by stopping halfway and anchoring the boat so we could spend time together on the flybridge.

Jacob was showing a real interest in learning how to captain the ship, so when it was time for us to get moving again, I taught him how to bring the anchor home and put the ship in gear. Once we got going, I let him hold the wheel because there wasn't much traffic and I could keep an eye on him.

As Jacob controlled the vessel, I couldn't help but remember not that long ago when he was a little boy. Jacob had recently turned 18 and graduated from high school. But instead of seeing a little boy before me, I could see that he was growing into a fine young man. His mother would be so proud of him.

After a while, I took back over the controls so Jacob could join the others. Tess was tending to everyone and taking turns talking to each of them between their video and photo sessions. Everyone seemed to enjoy themselves on the yacht and was making the most of their time.

We arrived at Sanderling Pointe, and I quickly backed into my spot on the dock. Giving instructions, I shouted to Jacob and Brandon to secure the lines on the dock.

With everything secured, I shut off the boat and gathered the troops. "Alright gang, the game plan is we will head to the beach for a day of sun. Then, we will stop for some lunch and get back on the boat to head back out onto the water to the place where we will drop anchor for the night."

Tess stepped in to add to my sentiments. "If you'd like to get changed and pack your beach bag, now is a great time to do that so we can head out."

The kids all scattered, leaving Tess and me alone on the main deck. I crossed over to where she stood and put my arms around her to pull her closer to me. "This is going to be a great day," I said while nuzzling her hair, breathing in her scent.

She rubbed my arms, which gave me goosebumps. "A great day indeed," she said, turning to face me.

Not being able to resist her any longer, I put my hands on her face and turned her lips to mine, drinking in the taste of blackberry sparkling water that lingered on her lips. The sound of Brandon clearing his throat behind me caused us to cut the kiss short and pull away from each other awkwardly. We hadn't yet told the kids about the seriousness of our relationship, but we also didn't want them to find out this way.

Tess pulled away from me and picked up her bag. "Let's go, boys! She yelled down the stairs to speed up her kids."

I walked over to Brandon. "Do you need any help with your bags?"

He held up one bag. "I think I can manage this one, but let's wait and see what Emily brings. You may need a forklift for it!"

We both chuckled at the thought as Emily came upstairs. "What's so funny, you two?"

Brandon reached out for her bag while giving me a knowing glance. "Oh, nothing, honey, just us being us," he said as he pretended her bag weighed a ton.

With everyone now up on the main deck, we all disembarked and made our way to the vehicles. My family rode with me in front, while Tess's boys rode with her behind me on the way to the beach.

When we arrived, it was a bit of a struggle to find two parking spots close to each other, so I purposefully drove past a closer spot so Tess could have it and took one that was further away.

"That was very considerate of you, Dad," Emily said.

I looked at her in the rearview mirror. "Just trying to be helpful. Most of the items are in her trunk," I winked at her.

Jacob spoke up. "Dad, are you two dating?"

I wasn't quite ready for this conversation, but Jacob was always known to be direct. He called things as he saw them and did so unapologetically.

"Yeah, bud, is that okay?" I asked cautiously.

Emily spoke up first. "I think it's amazing. She is lovely, and so are her boys."

Brandon chimed in as well. "I really like them, too. They are all really nice."

I pulled into a parking spot and put the car in park. I turned around to look at Jacob. "How about you, bud?"

He ran his hand through his dark hair, a habit he picked up from me, no doubt. "I like her just fine," he said—while not at all looking fine.

I turned to Emily and Brandon. "How about you two head on up and see if you can help Tess get everything down to the beach? Jacob and I will be right behind you."

Once Emily and Brandon had gotten out of earshot, I turned back to Jacob. "Do you want to talk about it?"

He looked at me. "I just miss *her*, Dad. Like, all the time. And it's okay that you are ready to move on. It's been five years, and you deserve to be happy. I just really miss Mom."

I sighed and put my hand on Jacob's shoulder. "I do too, bud, more than you may ever know. There isn't a day that goes by that I don't think about her. She made me promise her I would go on living when the time was right, and I feel ready. But in no way does that mean that Tess will ever replace your mom."

He looked relieved. "Thanks, Dad. I know Mom would have loved the yacht. It's great, and I'm glad you have someone to share it with here."

The two of us headed up to meet the others on the beach. We spent the rest of the morning tossing footballs and swimming in the ocean. Tess even convinced everyone to build a sandcastle with abandoned toys we found on the beach. It was the best day on the beach I've had in a very long time, and it felt like things were moving in a direction we could all benefit from.

My stomach growled loudly. "Who's hungry? Let's head out and get something to eat," I suggested to the group.

Not surprisingly, everyone agreed and hastily picked up everything that we had scattered throughout the sand during the short time we were there. We had a quick lunch at the Souper Grouper and then headed back to the boat.

We made great time getting off the dock and back out into open water, where I let Jacob steer again before taking over and getting us in position for the night. I taught Jacob how to drop the anchor and secure the vessel to ensure we wouldn't drift away during our sleep at night.

The kids snorkeled while Tess and I sat on the main deck and watched the five of them explore the area and play with the water toys we had. I put my arm around her shoulders and pulled her a little closer to me.

"How are the boys doing with all of this today?" I asked curiously.

She turned and faced me. "I think okay. They haven't really talked much about it, and I haven't brought it up yet. I think we will need to have a discussion soon with them, though, because I'm having a hard time keeping distance from you."

It pained me to hear that she was holding back from us a bit, but I understood. "You have to do what you are most comfortable with. If you need me to be there during the conversation, I will gladly help."

She stood up to walk to the bow to check on the kids, who had swum out of sight. "Thank you, Luke. I really appreciate that offer. I'll talk to them before dinner."

Eventually, the kids grew tired of being in the water and boarded the ship once more. We all went up to the flybridge to get some sun so we could dry off. Emily and Brandon were the first to go back down to shower and change for the night. Jacob asked me if I could show him how to tie knots on the main deck, so that left Tess and her boys alone upstairs to have the conversation they hadn't had yet.

Satisfied with his knots, Jacob hustled downstairs to shower and change before dinner, followed by Aiden and Logan, leaving me alone with Tess on the main deck once more. "So, how did it go?" I asked optimistically.

She let out a sigh of relief. "It went really well. They had some questions, but mostly, they were okay with me dating again—and both of them really like you."

It was my turn to let out the breath I had been holding. "Whew, what a relief. This is a good step forward." I leaned and kissed her on her forehead.

She turned to head for the galley. "I am going to get started on dinner, should be ready in about 30 minutes or so. Can you keep them entertained?"

I nodded eagerly. "Of course I can! Entertainment is my speciality."

She chuckled as she walked away. "Just don't hurt yourself. You're not as young as you once were."

Dinner that night was a lot of fun. We all went around the table and shared with each other their favorite things about the day. After dinner, I helped Tess clean, while the kids all went off to do their own thing for the night. I checked all the stations once more to ensure the anchor was still secure before heading down to the lower deck with Tess to our shared sleeping quarters.

Once we were in our room, I motioned to the bed. "Tess, I will sleep upstairs on the couch. You take the bed."

She laughed nervously. "Don't be ridiculous. This is your boat, so I should sleep on the couch upstairs."

Not having it, I was firm in my response. "Nonsense, you get the bed. I'll be perfectly fine on the couch."

She stood with her hands on her hips, staring me down. "Would it be weird if we just shared the bed?" She asked.

I watched her as she climbed into the bed. "If it's too much to share a bed, I could always go up and sleep on the couch. Though it may get chilly tonight and I'll have to find something to keep me warm. You could join me up there."

She picked up a pillow and tossed it at me. "What are we, twelve? We are old enough to be respectful and responsible. I appreciate your willingness to sleep on the couch and let me have the bed to myself. We can share the bed tonight." She patted the bed next to her.

I sat on the bed as close to the furthest edge as possible. "There. Are you satisfied now?"

She got a serious look on her face as she watched me. "There is something I've been meaning to tell you. Even though I loved Rob, the reason I couldn't marry him was that I was worried it would end just as quickly as it had begun. Time kept passing, and while I loved him, the love I felt wasn't as strong as the love that I felt for you when we were younger."

Suddenly, I didn't know what to say or how to respond. This was moving faster than I was comfortable with, and I needed a moment to wrap my head around what she had just told me. I could sense that my lack of response was making her nervous.

After running my hand through my hair, I quietly replied, "We were just kids, Tess. We were just learning what love was back then. Did you really love me that much?"

She spoke so softly, I almost didn't hear her. "Yes, I did. I was just too afraid to show it."

Unsure of what to say or do next, I stood and prepared my spot on the bed to go to sleep. "Thank you for opening up and being honest with me. I'm exhausted. It's been a long day. Let's get some sleep," I said as I turned off the light and settled in on top of the covers.

We lay there in silence, and I listened to her breathing deepen as she fell asleep, leaving me alone with my thoughts. Hearing that she loved me that much for all those years proved one thing—*Tess could open herself up to a lasting, loving relationship.*

And I had to admit that I never stopped loving her. After losing Tess, I learned how to cope without her and found love in other places, with other people. I don't regret the way my life has turned out up to this point, but I am looking forward to a new life with Tess by my side.

EIGHTEEN

SUNDAY, JUNE 19, 2022

Teresa Wright

Waking up mere feet from Luke made me feel safe. Not wanting to disturb him, I slid quietly out from under the sheets and quickly went into the restroom to get dressed.

Once I was ready, I went up to the galley to make everyone breakfast. I was looking forward to a nice family breakfast with all our kids. It would be a good look into the future of what this family could be if our relationship continued to blossom.

I moved quickly through the galley, making fresh baked cinnamon rolls, bacon, eggs, hash browns, and sausage. With the warm foods cooking, I cut up some fruit and greens to help create a balanced plate. Luke was the first to arrive just as the coffee pot finished filling. I grabbed him a cup and served him while icing the cinnamon rolls.

He walked over to retrieve the cup from me and gave me a quick peck on the cheek. "Good morning, beautiful. This all smells amazing. You must have gotten up early. I didn't even hear you leave."

Not slowing down my cooking, I replied without looking up. "I didn't want to wake you. Knowing everyone would be hungry this morning, I tried to be as quiet as I could. With having a smaller stove than I am used to, I figured I'd get a head start on cooking."

One by one, the kids made their way upstairs and took a seat at the table I had set for them. Logan was the last one to arrive and seemed to have quite the attitude this morning. He is my youngest and sometimes gets this way if I haven't been spending enough time with just him. Yesterday was such a whirlwind, and I know we shared some moments together—but I should have attempted to do more.

I picked up the cinnamon rolls to serve Logan. "Hey Logan, would you like a cinnamon roll?"

He snatched the plate from my hand with a quick jerking motion. "I can serve myself, Mom. I'm an adult, you know."

I laughed nervously. "Yes, of course you are. I know that. My apologies."

Others chattered, which helped get past the awkwardness of Logan's gloomy attitude at breakfast. I was grateful for the chance to listen to what the others had to say and get to know them a bit more too. We were all laughing and having a great time when I realized not everyone was smiling. Logan looked like he was on the verge of tears, and I couldn't quite shake the feeling that something was wrong.

I leaned towards him and quietly whispered, "Everything okay, Logan?"

He looked me dead in the eye, face unchanged. "Why didn't you ever marry Dad?"

His question shocked me. He had never asked it before, and I felt very much on the spot. "That is between your father and me."

Red flooded Logan's face as he retorted, "Then why did you tell him it was because you still loved him?" he demanded, while pointing at Luke.

Luke interrupted the conversation. "After breakfast, we are going to head back to Savannah to spend the day together there before you check in at the airport for your flights this evening."

Everyone seemed confused by the sudden change in dialog. Logan grabbed his plate and stormed up the stairs to the flybridge. The best approach, I knew, was to give him space, allowing him to sort out his feelings, and then discuss the topic with grace. I told the kids to all head back down to get ready for the day, and I would clean up breakfast. I really could use some time alone to think.

Once everyone but Luke went to get ready, I started clearing the table. As I was scraping dishes, I also wiped tears from my eyes with the backs of my hands. This was not the lovely breakfast I had envisioned we would have this morning.

Luke walked up behind me and put his hands on both of my arms and began rubbing them to soothe me. As tears fell freely, I leaned back against him. "I don't know why I'm so upset by this. I just really wanted a nice breakfast with everyone this morning."

Luke sighed. "It was a nice breakfast. Everything was delicious. Thank you for preparing it for us all. Try not to let his outburst ruin your day."

I turned to face him. "Logan has never asked me that before now. He had to have heard us talking last night, which is what is prompting this now. We never really felt it was necessary to discuss with them because it never changed the fact that we were together. But when we split, it impacted Logan the most. He took it very hard."

Luke leaned down and kissed my forehead. "He was still a kid, right? That would be hard to process even at his current age. Give him time—he'll come around."

"Thank you. You always know what to say to help me feel better. I appreciate your help," I replied, as I wiped my tears once more.

We continued to clean up breakfast together before Luke took his place at the helm station to pull anchor and begin our ride to Savannah. The kids all sat on the flybridge together, while I stayed on the main deck beside Luke at the helm. The ride went by quickly, and I helped tie the yacht to the dock before we all disembarked.

We spent the day walking around the many shops, going in and out of each one. The kids all found some great things to buy. And because I had made such a big breakfast, no one wanted lunch, so we skipped it and continued on our walk.

Logan was walking by himself ahead of me, so I jogged to catch up. "I feel like I owe you an explanation and an apology. I'm sorry that was how you found out. When I was 16, I met Luke on Sanderling Pointe Island. Our families came here every summer for the next couple of years after that. We grew very close, and I was absolutely head over heels in love with him."

I gave him a chance to say something, and when he didn't, I continued. "Unfortunately, the year my dad left, we didn't make it back here that summer. To make matters worse, Mom and I had to sell the house and move, so I lost touch with Luke. It wasn't like it is today. We didn't have cell phones and social media."

I paused again to give him a chance to speak. "Did you love Dad?" he whispered.

I put my arm around his shoulders as a tear slid down my face. "With all that I could, I did. But Luke still held a very large piece of my heart. He was a long-lost love I grieved for a very long time. Your dad and I were content with never officially marrying. He always said that a piece of paper couldn't define who we were to each other."

Logan spoke up a bit more. "I just want everyone to be back together at the farmhouse," he said sadly.

I sighed. "It's really not that easy, I'm afraid. Your dad is now in a different state, I'm moving to Sanderling Pointe, and the farmhouse just sold. We are all headed in very different directions, even you and your brother are off at two different schools and will be for the next several years."

He looked up at me with a sad smile. "Yeah, I guess you're right. I kind of forgot that part. It's no big deal. Can we just drop this? I'm sorry for being mean."

With my arm still around his shoulders, I squeeze him closer to me. "Yes, we can drop it. Thank you for apologizing. I love you, and I hope you know how much you mean to me."

The day passed quickly, and with skipping lunch, the kids were complaining they were getting hungry, so we found a restaurant to tuck into for an early dinner. We all took turns relaying our orders to the waiter, who looked overwhelmed by the sheer number of people at our table and the chaos that came with it. I helped him as much as I could to ensure we would avoid any potential mishaps with the food.

While we waited for our food to come out, we went around the table to share whatever was on our hearts. One by one, the kids all mentioned how much fun this weekend was, but also aired their concerns about Luke and me rushing into dating. I listened to each of their concerns and held my response for my turn, which was coming up next.

Nervous, I smiled at everyone. "I am so grateful you all could join Luke and me this weekend. The memories made are ones I'll cherish for the rest of my life. With each of your points of concern with Luke and me, I just wanted to share a reminder that time is precious. We are not promised tomorrow. I made the mistake of walking away from Luke all those years ago—and I will not make the same mistake again. He has forever and always had my whole heart."

I turned to Luke as he spoke next. "I, too, am thankful you all could join Tess and me on the yacht this weekend. When we picked out the yacht, we chose this one with each of you in mind—and it is the perfect fit for us all together. I know that our relationship is new, and you all have your concerns, but I want to assure you that Tess and I have always been drawn to each other like two magnets unable to be stripped apart. Our chance to be together has come around once more, and we hope that you'll respect our decision to be together. It's not every day you are gifted with a second chance."

The food came just as Luke finished and was a welcomed break from the seriousness of the conversation. The kids all seemed at ease with what we both had to say, and everyone ate their food at record speed. Once we were finished with dinner, we made our way back to the yacht to pick up the kids' bags and call a rideshare to get them to the airport.

Saying goodbye was difficult. More than I was prepared for, as I wiped the tears from my eyes as the boys got in the car and it pulled away. Though I was glad to begin a new chapter on my own, it was still difficult letting go. Soon, they'll both find women to share their lives with, and they won't need me anymore.

Luke's kids were the last to leave. I stood and watched as they said their goodbyes to each other, my heart full from the amount of love between them. Emily and Brandon gave me a hug goodbye before Jacob came and stood in front of me. Unsure of what to say, just as I was about to open my mouth to speak, Jacob reached out and gave me a strong hug before bounding away with a wave back.

Luke reached over and grabbed my hand. "Are you ready to get back to the island?"

I intertwined my fingers with his. "I thought you'd never ask. Let's go!"

On the ride back to the island, I sat on the bow. The wind whipped my hair around my face as I stared out into the water. Dolphins would come up next to the boat and jump in and out of the water as we pushed forward. The sun was just beginning to set as we turned into Laughing Gull Marina, casting a warm yellow glow over the water and ships in port.

Luke idled the boat as I got up to secure the yacht to the dock. After the boat was secured, I waited as he turned it off and went to retrieve our bags. As much as I loved being on the yacht, I was looking forward to being back at the condo on solid ground once more.

We both got into our vehicles and made the short drive back to the condo alone, which brought up a new question I hadn't thought of until now. Am I doing the right thing by dating Luke now? The echoes of concern filled my thoughts as they played on repeat. *If the kids were this concerned, should I be too?*

NINETEEN

MONDAY, JUNE 20, 2022

Lucas Miller

The weekend with the kids opened me up in ways I hadn't opened up in a long time. I have always viewed my kids as extremely intuitive with picking up on things, so listening to their concerns had me a little rattled. *What am I missing? Did they see something between Tess and me that I couldn't?*

I admitted to myself that I did not have my head in the game since running into Tess that first night. She had a way of turning my head and my attention to her, which meant I was behind with work and finding a place to live on Sanderling Pointe. Relief washed over me when Sheila, my new agent, texted me about meeting at William's house for sale. Since he told me about it, I've wanted to see this house—and I jumped at the chance.

I needed to clear my head before I left for the day. I put on my workout clothes and headed out to the beach for a run. Running has always been my way of keeping in check with my body and ensuring I stay in good health. It was also something I had had little time to do since arriving here on the island, so I was a little rusty. By the time I got back to the condo, my knee throbbed from its workout. I popped two over-the-counter pain relievers to help dull the pain and made my way to the shower.

As I stood looking at my body in the mirror, I noticed the extra food and indulgences in desserts were packing on a little extra weight. Maintaining good shape required me to be more diligent in my workout routine. I continued with my morning routine and walked out of the bathroom, fully dressed and ready for work.

On my way out, I greeted Tess in the kitchen. "I am headed out for the day. If you need anything, just text me—but just know I have several meetings, so it may take me a while to respond."

She stood to kiss me goodbye, her lips soft and warm on mine and tasting of coffee. "Don't miss me too much today," she said with an ornery grin.

"You know I will," I teased her back.

With a quick kiss on her forehead, I headed out to my car. I put the top down and punched in the address, maneuvering out of the lot and onto the road. It was a short drive from the condo.

Turning right, I drove down a road lined with legacy oak trees with Spanish moss hanging from the branches. The houses were secluded from the trees in the front and sat with their backs to the channel. I turned into the driveway as my GPS instructed and pulled up to the house.

I got out of the car and looked around. The road was just wide enough for two cars and there was one row of houses, totaling ten homes. This would be great, because it also came with the dock on the back of the house where I could keep the yacht, which would save on monthly rental costs of the slip at the marina.

The house was white and two stories high, with windows all around to capture the views. Sheila greeted me as I walked up to the porch. "Welcome to 151 Heron Road. I'm Sheila."

I extended my hand. "Thanks for meeting me here, Sheila. I'm Lucas, nice to meet you."

Sheila led me into the house, and I half-listened to her as she rambled about it. I had already done my homework and knew all I needed to know about it—but this was the first time I was laying my eyes on it. My goal was to take in as much as possible. The kitchen was massive. I could see Tess cooking her big family meals in here, and we would all sit at one long table together. There was definitely plenty of room for both of our families to be in this space together.

The bathrooms and bedrooms were all recently remodeled and felt more modern, which I appreciated. It was definitely very turnkey, and that was appealing to me the most right now. We went out back, where there was a large pool and two more buildings.

I pointed to the building on the left. "What is that building?" I asked Sheila.

She met my gaze. "Ah, yes, that one is a secondary house with three bedrooms and two baths, a full kitchen, and living space."

I don't recall seeing that on the original listing that William had given me. "Is it included in the price too, or is it extra?"

She flipped through her paperwork. "It appears both buildings are included in the original listing price of $1.75 million."

I nodded, trying to hide my surprise. "Not bad. Can we look through both buildings, too?"

I followed Sheila to the guest house. It would be perfect for Emily and Brandon to stay when they came to visit, especially with any children they might have. There was a little work needing to be done to update it, but overall, it wasn't in bad shape. Next, we crossed over to the second, smaller building—which by the looks of it was possibly a pool house.

I was pleasantly surprised when we walked in to find it wasn't a pool house at all—but more like a bonus recreational space. There were large floor to ceiling windows that allowed in a ton of natural light while also lending a view of the channel. The sun reflecting on the water caught my attention—I could see Tess using this space for her artwork. There was a small bathroom and an even smaller kitchenette in the space as well, which was nice.

As I was taking it all in, Sheila interrupted my thoughts. "What are your plans? You had mentioned the possibility of moving here?"

"My plan is to open and run a satellite office here. Slowing down, enjoying life, and needing a home go hand in hand for me."

She looked interested in what I had to say. "Is there someone special in your life?"

I replied, "Yes, although it's still very new for us. We are complete opposites when it comes to living. She is more free-spirited and messy, while I prefer things tidy and orderly. We've actually known each other since we were kids, and back then she used to be just as tidy as I am now. I think I picked that up from her actually, but I recently learned she's no longer that way. I'm just trying to figure out a way we can cohabitate and not cause each other frustration."

She looked at me questioningly. "Hmm, I'm sensing a bit of hesitation from you."

I thought for a moment before answering. "I don't know if it's hesitation or if I'm just processing out loud. She's an artist, and I think this building would be a space where she could be free to be herself, while also keeping it contained and out of the main house."

Realization hit her face. "Ah, okay, got it. So, having a space of her own for her art is important to you. If you look at other homes, I'll add that to my list of requirements."

We wrapped up our tour of the house before getting into our own vehicles to drive over to the commercial buildings. I couldn't help but replay what Sheila said about sensing hesitation from me. *Am I hesitant to move in with Tess?* Perhaps slowing down isn't a bad idea. We are moving at the speed of lightning right now.

I pulled up to the gallery and got out of my car, meeting Sheila at the front. We walked through the gallery more slowly this time, and I shared with Sheila how I envisioned staging it for offices. She asked great questions about privacy, which brought up a challenge I hadn't thought of. Some clients prefer to do business behind closed doors, and this open floor concept wouldn't work for that.

Discouraged, I took a step back to look at it again. "I guess I could close in these spaces and make offices out of them."

Sheila sensed my frustration. "Would you like to look next door? That space already has some offices established."

Nodding, I agreed and followed her to the other space. The first time I walked through this space, I remembered how closed off it felt compared to the gallery. But, seeing it today, I noticed that there were offices lined on both sides. I counted six small offices, one large office which would work for me, and a large conference room in the back.

We could use the space in the middle of the building for a receptionist's desk and seating while clients waited, and we could even put in a coffee and water bar for guests because of its size. It definitely needed sprucing up a bit, but it would be less work than building out offices in the gallery space. Something really to think about.

My phone chimed as I received a text from Tess.

> Can you bring dinner home? Maybe some pizza tonight?

I looked to see what the time was. We had been touring these spaces all day. I texted her back.

> You got it. Will wrap up here soon.

I turned to Sheila. "I have taken up far too much of your time today, and I apologize for that. Thank you for showing me the three spaces."

She smiled warmly at me. "It was my pleasure, really. What do you feel your best options are with the three spaces?"

I pondered this question for a short moment before saying, "I am going to need more time to consider that and will have to get back to you. Can I have until the end of the week?"

She nodded. "Sure, take all the time you need. I'm just a phone call away."

She locked the door behind us, and I headed back to my car. I drove one street over to the pizza restaurant and called in my order from the driver's seat. They gave me a 30-minute wait time for pickup. This felt like a good opportunity to grab my journal and make a list of the pros and cons of both spaces for the offices.

Ultimately, I still struggled with which one to pick because they both offered something different. The second space needs more work, but is substantially lower in price, which leaves room in the budget for remodeling it to my specifications. This also meant that more work had to be done, which would delay my opening.

The gallery was practically move-in ready. There was a small office in the back of the gallery where we could hold private meetings with clients who preferred the closed door approach, but I really liked the idea of an open office feel. No work needed to be done at the gallery, which held the most appeal.

What are the odds that I just found my new home and office building today in one fell swoop? I didn't want to tell Tess until it was official, for fear of jinxing something and losing out on it altogether. For the first time since arriving on the island, I finally feel like I'm ready to move here and begin rebuilding my life and business. I just hope that includes Tess by my side.

TWENTY

MONDAY, JUNE 20, 2022

Spending time on the water with family gave me inspiration for my new collection. I spent the morning rough sketching out my ideas while Luke was getting ready. It would be completely different from any previous pieces that I have done before. But if all goes well, I could unveil it—and my identity—at the same time during my grand opening. It would be the perfect time for a shift in style and focus.

After Luke left this morning, I decided today would be a great day to work on my new collection. I dressed in my painting overalls and tee shirt, pulled my hair into a messy bun on the top of my head, and grabbed a drop cloth to prep the floor.

Grabbing my bag, I pulled out all of my paint supplies to determine which medium would make this collection come to life, and settled on watercolors. I set up my vintage travel easel and faced it out of the patio window to overlook the beach. Painting inside the condo would be in a more temperature-controlled environment, and would keep everything wet longer without the heat from the outside drying it up quickly.

I set my cup of water and brushes on the end table next to the sofa and picked up the first canvas to begin my work. After three hours, I stepped back to admire my painting. I decided it was ready to go just as it was, and immediately had an idea for another painting. Grabbing an apple for lunch, I went back to work on the second painting. I was in the zone, making quick progress as the colors glided effortlessly across the canvas, combining with each other in swirls of blue and gray.

Another three hours had passed, and I stepped back to take in the state of the current painting, determining that it, too, was ready. I picked up my cellphone and saw that it was getting late in the day. I texted Luke.

> Can you bring dinner home? Maybe some pizza tonight?

Not waiting for his reply, I moved the second painting to the table next to the first one and grabbed a third blank canvas. I felt real momentum for the first time in years. I have never painted this quickly and freely before, and I desperately wanted to finish the three pieces before I lost this rush of creativity. The sun was setting and the room was growing darker, so I wrapped up my third piece and finished with the final swipe of my brush.

I stepped back to look at all I had done today, and felt very accomplished. I have never painted so many paintings in one day. After I surveyed my surroundings, I realized I had gotten a little too carried away, and knew I needed to clean it up before Luke got home. He would not be happy to see it in this state.

No sooner had I stepped back, Luke came home with food in tow. He stood in the doorway looking at me, and then around the condo. "Hi honey, I am so sorry. Let me clear a space real quick. I completely lost track of time."

The look of sheer panic was visible across his tired face as he tried to take in what lay before him. I knew it looked bad. I rushed to collect all the paint tubes, palettes, and cups of water with brushes. With my hands too full, I reached for a cup and knocked it over, sending paint water onto the blanket on the sofa.

Luke set the food down on the only clean surface—the table by the door. He rushed over to pick up the blanket and frantically wiped at it. "What have you done?! You've ruined it," he yelled.

Confused, I replied calmly, "It's just water, so it will come out easily—besides why are you so worked up over the condo blanket?"

He refused to let me take the blanket from him and retreated with it into the kitchen, where he began cleaning it in the kitchen sink. Setting down my painting supplies, I stood to face him. Luke wouldn't look at me. I have never seen him this angry before.

He wrung out the blanket and delicately laid it across the washer and dryer before walking over to the stack of supplies I had set on the counter. Luke picked up my vintage palette, another gift from my grandmother, and tossed it into the trash can while shouting, "Clean up this mess!"

Stunned, I did the only thing I knew to do. I held up my paint-coated hand in his face. "Just stop! Why don't you head outside for a breather while I clean this up? Once it's all cleaned up and we can eat, I will let you know."

Luke stormed out the front door, slamming it behind him— and sending shivers down my spine as tears filled my eyes. It took a moment to collect myself before I walked over to the trash can to retrieve my grandmother's palette. I cleaned up the whole condo in silence, rinsing, stacking, and drying as I went.

I packed everything up into the bins I had brought in and returned them to my room. I carried the paintings one by one, being careful not to smudge anything, and laid them on the floor of the closet.

With the last painting in place, I stood back and looked at them next to the one I had done earlier. They all went so well together. Though I should be proud of my hard work, my emotions got the better of me as I stood and wept. I felt heartbroken that Luke thought my paintings were nothing but a big mess, and even more so that he so carelessly tossed a cherished heirloom of mine into the garbage as if it were nothing.

I pulled myself together long enough to go into the bathroom to wash the tear-stained paint from my face and hands. Facing my reflection in the mirror, I looked like a mess. It's no wonder Luke said what he did. I had paint all over me and in my hair. I cleaned up the best I could. The rest would have to wait until I showered later.

I headed out the front door and told Luke it was safe to come in for dinner. Not waiting for him to come in, I grabbed the food and carried it over to the table and began setting our places. He came in silently and sat down. I took my seat next to him, where we ate together in a silence as thick as the cold pizza cheese.

After we finished eating, I cleaned up the remnants of the food. "Thank you, Luke, for bringing dinner."

He stared at me. Nothing came out of his open mouth, so he simply nodded.

I wanted to remedy this situation, but I was worried I would only make it worse. "I'm really sorry that I lost track of time. It won't happen again."

Through clenched teeth, he muttered. "It's fine."

It didn't feel fine, in fact, it felt pretty awful to me. It was clear I would get nowhere with him in this state, so I decided it would be better to retreat for the evening. "I'm going to shower and head to bed early. See you in the morning."

I walked past him, and my hand brushed his. Luke flinched, and he jerked his hand away from me. My heart sank as I fought back the tears stinging my eyes. I made it to my room and grabbed my clothes before heading into the bathroom to allow my sobbing to be hidden among the sounds of the shower.

If Luke cannot accept me for who I am—messy and all—I don't know if we will work out. I have spent most of my life cleaning up after everyone else. When my mom couldn't get out of bed for weeks after the divorce, I was the one who took care of her and the house.

When I had Aiden, I was the one who tended to the home and his needs, and the same with Logan. I would spend birthday parties and holiday gatherings in the kitchen cleaning up after everyone and missed spending precious time with those I loved.

Now that no one else needed me to wait on them hand and foot, I allowed myself the freedom to be messy when creating, so as not to stop the gentle flow of creativity. Cleaning as I went felt rigid, and often I would obsess over making sure each brush was completely cleaned off in between uses. In doing so, my paint would dry and the painting would be ruined.

Before turning off the shower, I splashed the warm water on my face one last time. With the shower off, I stepped out of the shower, dried off, and got dressed. I applied moisturizer to my face and put my hair up in a towel to help it dry quicker. Haphazardly, I picked up all of my clothes and carried them from the bathroom to my bedroom, shutting the door behind me a little harder than I intended.

With my dirty clothes in the basket, I picked up my book and climbed into bed. I tried to read the same chapter three times, but I just couldn't get into the book. I set it down and lay in the dark room. The only sounds were the ticking of the clock next to the bed and the soft sound of the TV coming from the living room.

Luke was just on the other side of this door, and I desperately wanted to run to him and throw myself into his arms, and make this all better. Truth is, I was tired of always making things better. *When will someone choose me for me and prove that I am worth staying around for?*

TWENTY ONE

Lucas Miller

Sneaking out of the condo before Tess came out felt like the coward's way out, but I had to clear my head today. I scribbled a note for her and left it by the coffee pot, where I knew she'd see it first thing. I grabbed my things and headed out to Laughing Gull Marina to board my yacht and set up a temporary office. It would be good to have a place to work and entertain prospects, even if temporarily.

I got to the marina quickly since there wasn't much traffic this early in the morning. I still had some provisions on the boat left over from our weekend trip, so the first thing I did was brew a pot of coffee. While I waited for it to finish, I started unpacking a few of the things I brought with me and froze when I pulled out the blanket.

I felt badly about how I reacted yesterday, losing it with how messy Tess was with her painting. It was so overwhelming to me. Every surface was covered with paint, water, or canvases. There were even paint splatters on the floor, the walls—not to mention all over her from head to toe.

The worst part was that I had gotten so relaxed staying there with Tess that I forgot to put my blanket neatly away in my suitcase to keep it protected. It was the first time I had done that, and seeing Tess spill paint water on Lisa's blanket really sent me over the edge.

It's silly, really, that I cling to this blanket as if Lisa is still here—but it's the one thing I have that reminds me of her presence. Any time I miss her, I wrap myself in it and try to remember what it was like to hold her in my arms.

The beep of the coffee maker prompted me to set the blanket carefully across the sofa next to where I would work. Being impatient, I took a big gulp of steaming coffee and burned my tongue before setting the cup down on the table. I pulled out my laptop and fired it up. The fan kicking in was the only sound apart from the lapping water as the boats swayed in the waves.

While looking into some of the investment portfolios of my new clients, I watched the sun rise. I made my list of things to do for each of the clients, then called my main office to check in on how things were going there in my absence.

My morning flew by because my call to the office took a little longer than I had expected. They were doing okay, but still needed me for a few things, and one client was upset that I had left his portfolio in charge with my junior advisor. I knew I could smooth him over because the advisor I picked for his account is exactly who needs to be in it.

After hanging up with the office, I checked my phone to see if I had any missed messages or calls from Tess. Nothing at all, which isn't like her. I knew I had hurt her feelings and really needed to make it up to her somehow.

When we used to come here as kids on Tuesday nights, there were fireworks at The Pointe. This memory made me wonder if they still did it now. An idea sparked, so I did a few searches on my laptop and confirmed that they do indeed still have fireworks Tuesdays in the same place at the same time.

Excited, I picked up my phone and sent Tess a text.

> Do you have any evening plans?

I waited a minute or two, and despite seeing that she *read* my message, she never responded. Frustrated, I put my phone upside down on the table and walked back over to the blanket on the sofa. I picked it up and wrapped it around myself.

It was as good as new, with no stains or ruined spots at all, just as Tess had promised. I carried it with me to the flybridge as I climbed up and sat down at the front of the yacht. It was a beautiful day, and as I looked out ahead at the open water, boats were moving about slowly through the marina to head out onto the open water.

I breathed in the blanket, hoping for just a moment that I could still smell her, but disappointment filled me when her scent was no longer there. Tears filled my eyes, blurring my vision as I tried to blink them away. "Oh, Lisa, I don't know what I'm doing. I'm so mad you left me here all alone. Dating is super hard. I told you I wouldn't like it. Maybe I am better off alone forever."

As I reached up to wipe a tear from my cheek, a laughing gull came and landed on the seat next to me. It had a unique characteristic that caught my eye: a small gray heart in the white space just above its wing.

Moving my hands toward it, I tried to shoo it away. The bird retaliated by cackling loudly at me. I laughed at the situation and took that as a sign from Lisa that I'm being ridiculous and need to snap out of it.

For a short while longer, I sat there before heading back down. I picked up my phone and texted Tess again.

Dinner out at 8:00 pm. I'll pick you up at 7:45.

She replied almost instantly this time.

Sounds great, see you then.

I spent the next hour making a plan for a romantic evening that I hoped made up for my outburst yesterday. I knew I had to make it right and apologize, and this was the way I knew how. Hopefully she would understand that I'm not perfect, and I am trying.

At 6:30, I wrapped up my workday, which gave me time to head to the store to pick up items for a picnic dinner. I got lucky and could even get a blanket and a picnic basket that I remembered seeing when Tess and I came here for party supplies.

With everything packed and ready to go, I drove to the condo to pick up Tess and arrived at exactly 7:45. I grabbed the bouquet of flowers I had picked up for her and carried them to the door, where I stood and knocked.

She opened the door and chuckled. "You know the code, why didn't you just come in?"

She looked absolutely breathtaking in a pair of white linen pants and a beige and white striped sleeveless blouse. "I wanted this to be a proper date. These are for you, madame," I said as I handed the flowers to her.

She took the flowers from me with a big smile on her face. "These are stunning. Let me put them in water before we head out."

I went in with her to help with the flowers. "I'm really sorry about yesterday, Tess. I was out of line."

She quietly replied, "Thank you for that. I'm sorry for not having cleaned up before you got back. I was in the zone yesterday, which rarely happens, and I got carried away and lost track of time. It won't happen again."

I reached out for her and pulled her into an embrace. Her warm body against mine instantly zapped my heart back into action. I looked down at her, and she moved her face towards mine, where we spent just a quick moment making up for lost time.

She pulled away first. "Okay then, are we ready to head out?"

I laughed. "Yes, we'd better get going. Don't want to be late!"

We made our way back to the car, where I drove us to The Pointe and tried to watch her expression as I turned into the parking lot. "Do you remember this place?" I asked her.

She scooted forward in her chair. "Ooooh, The Pointe! I remember this place. Wait, is it Tuesday?!?! Do you think they'll have fireworks tonight?"

I pulled into a parking spot and turned to face her. "Chances are pretty good. Just look at this crowd!"

We got out of the car, and I grabbed the blanket and picnic basket from the trunk and reached for her hand with my one free hand. We made our way to the clearing, where people were quickly gathering to prepare for the fireworks. They would begin as soon as the sky went dark, which should be within half an hour.

I set the picnic basket down so I could spread the blanket out on the ledge where our legs could dangle over. "Somehow we had great luck today and could get our exact same spot," I said to her as I set up the picnic.

She reached into the basket and helped me with the food. "What are the odds of that?"

I was pleasantly surprised that she remembered the ending phrase that we used to always say. It has sort of stuck with me all these years, chance, odds, luck… "You remembered."

She looked shyly away as pink flooded her cheeks. "It goes with numbers and who you are. It reminds me of the day our paths crossed for the first time. Do you remember what you said?"

I don't know that I could ever forget what I said. "It was a one in a million chance that you and I had somehow ended up in condos next door to each other with a shared pool. Once we discovered we had defied those odds, it turned into a one in a thousand chance our families would become friends. When that happened, it became a one in a hundred chance we would last." My voice trailed off on the last part as I got choked up.

She looked at me, tears filling her eyes. "Well, we can still beat those last odds. There's still time."

We sat and ate our dinner while watching the sun set slowly until darkness crept in. We chatted in short bursts about how we used to do this as kids and how much fun it always was because our families would all be there too. Our favorite memory was how we would sneak away from them to come here because it was away from the crowds.

It was in this very place that I first realized I was in love with Tess, but I had been far too afraid to tell her how I felt back then. Looking back, I wish I had told her because it was the last year I had seen her until now.

A loud boom startled me as fireworks erupted overhead, lighting up the dark sky. The crowd roared at the start of the show. I leaned over and whispered in Tess's ear, "Tess, I'm really sorry. I overreacted. Forgive me, please?"

Tess softly replied, "It's fine."

Her tone slightly took me aback, as it definitely didn't sound *fine*. We sat together on the blanket, but it felt more like we were worlds apart with how much distance was between us.

I wasn't sure what else I could do to make things better between us. Clearly, there was something about the situation that I had completely missed. Another problem for another day, I suppose. I had forgotten how fragile relationships can be.

TWENTY TWO

Teresa Wright

For the second day in a row, I slept in and woke up to find Luke already gone for the day. He had been leaving early—likely to avoid me—to work on the yacht. Ever since our fight on Monday, I have felt as if I'm walking on eggshells around him, unsure how to act. I should have told him how much he hurt me with his crass response and his carelessness with my art supplies, but I just haven't been able to find the words.

Luke doesn't know that to me, art is more than just a hobby. It's my lifeline, my career, and my passion all in one. My inability to share with others exactly who I am as an artist comes from the fear of judgment. Truth is, I didn't realize that I would gain so much popularity among the elite.

When my first painting sold, I was ecstatic! So I kept painting. Eventually, I increased my prices—and my paintings continued to sell out quickly online. In my first year of selling, I made over a million dollars. I couldn't believe it. I have never shared my success with anyone. I have always kept the money in the bank to save up for my gallery and studio someday. Perhaps today could be that day.

Slowly, I moved through the condo after getting ready for the day, and as I sat down to pour my first cup of coffee, my phone rang. "Hello, this is Tess," I answered and waited.

"Hi Tess, this is Janine with Sanderling Realty. You stopped by the office last week and requested some listings. I sent those over to you but hadn't heard from you and just wanted to follow up," she replied.

With everything going on, I completely forgot to reply to her email. "Hi Janine, thank you for your call. I apologize for my delay in getting back to you. After reviewing the listings, I would like a walkthrough of the gallery space, if you are available."

She replied quickly, "I have some time today and could meet you there in an hour if that's not too soon?"

I was relieved. "An hour is perfect. I'll meet you there. Thank you!"

Ending the call, I hung up and suddenly found the energy to move at a more rapid speed as I started gathering everything I would need to take with me. I filled my tote bag with paperwork I knew could help speed up the process, as well as my notebook to jot down any notes I didn't want to forget.

As I went through the listings Janine had sent me last week, I ate a yogurt and some fruit, and had my second cup of coffee. My goal was to make sure I was choosing the correct properties for walkthroughs while finding a home. There were two promising ones, but they were definitely on the higher end of my budget.

I practically skipped to my SUV, eager to walk through the gallery with Janine. This felt like one step closer to making my dream come true. It must have been my lucky day—I didn't catch a single red light and made it there quicker than I expected, which gave me time to sit and look at the building from the outside a bit more.

The gallery was really charming, yet modern with its faux shiplap exterior. The black accents and signage really made the entire front of the building come to life. But, I couldn't help but feel it could use some pops of gold and brown wood woven in there to elevate it a bit more. I jotted down some notes in my notebook about potential curb appeal enhancements.

Another car pulled up beside me, and I checked the time. It was likely Janine. I got out of my car, grabbed my tote bag, and cautiously approached the petite woman. She wore a linen pantsuit in a light beige color with a white blouse underneath her matching blazer. She had brown hair cut to her chin and wore big black sunglasses and a light berry-colored lipstick.

Cautiously, I approached her. "Janine? Hi, I'm Tess," I said, with my hand extended.

The woman grabbed my hand and returned the handshake. "Hi Tess, yes, I'm Janine. Nice to meet you. Shall we?"

I followed Janine to the front door and waited for her to open it. Suddenly, I was very nervous, despite having already been here a few times before. I tried to look at the space with a fresh perspective—as if I had never stepped foot inside—to see if anything would jump out at me this time. Janine chatted about all the property stats, which I already knew and didn't have an interest in at the moment.

Our tour ended, and Janine turned to face me. "So, what do you think?"

I looked at her confidently. "I'm very interested in putting down an offer. However, I am also in need of finding a home. The home you sent me that is tied in with this property is way out of my budget and bigger than what I was considering. I have been debating renting instead of owning to allow myself time to build up this space for my gallery and studio grand opening—and then maybe looking for a home to buy in a year. Would you have any rental properties you could show me?"

She didn't seem fazed by my proposal. "I actually have six rentals available right now, and they are available for showings today if you have more time and would like to see them?"

I had nothing else to do today, and I really wanted to get a space where I could separate my art from my living space for now to help with the current living situation. I couldn't help but feel that if I could move my painting out, it would help keep Luke happy in a much tidier space. A compromise, if you will.

Janine handed me a list of addresses, and I followed her out to the first condo. It was unbelievably small for the price and simply wouldn't work for me. We spent the whole day touring the remaining on the list, and as I walked through the final condo, my stomach growled, reminding me I had skipped lunch. On the way over, I passed by an old favorite restaurant that I couldn't believe was still here, and now it was all I could think about.

I picked up my phone and texted Luke.

> I'm starving. Would you like to meet me for dinner at The Gentlemen Pirate?

He immediately responded.

LOL, is that place still in existence? I thought for sure it would be out of business by now. I can meet you there in ten minutes. A burger sounds wonderful.

Laughing at his text, I chuckled and responded.

It's a date! See you soon!

I turned to Janine. "Thanks Janine, you've given me much to consider. Let me think about it, and I'll get back to you soon."

I left the condo and headed over to The Gentlemen Pirate to meet Luke. He pulled in right behind me, and I found two spots beside each other and pulled into one, leaving the other for him. I checked myself in the car mirror to make sure I looked decent, considering I'd been running all day. Luke greeted me with a quick kiss after I got out of the car.

He extended his hand for me to grab. "You look lovely. Did you have a good day today?"

"I had a good day today. How about you?" I asked him.

He opened the door to the restaurant for me. "Not bad, very productive for sure."

We walked through the line to place our orders at the counter. I paid for both meals, picked up our drinks, and took our numbers to find a table while we waited for our food. We scanned the restaurant to find the perfect spot. Finding an old familiar table that was available, we quickly sat down at it. I slid the napkin holder to the center of the table to reveal our initials still carved on the edge of the table.

"Oh wow, look at that," Luke said as he ran his fingers across the carving.

"It's hard to believe it's still here after all these years. Some things clearly haven't changed here," I said, looking around the restaurant.

Our food arrived, and we picked up the burger baskets to take to the bar to load them up with nacho cheese and toppings. I, of course, loaded mine with a mound of pickles on the side. One can never have too many pickles. We made our way back to the table and ate in silence, both of us too engrossed in our food to be bothered to stop long enough to speak.

Wiping his mouth, Luke spoke first. "Fate brought us back together after all these years, during the same time we met as kids. This place is just as good as I remember it being. They have the best burgers to be found anywhere."

I chuckled. "They really are the best burgers and shakes money can buy."

We chatted longer about the restaurant before switching gears to a more present-day conversation. For the last couple of days, we have both been in our own worlds, and I wondered if he had made similar progress to mine on the home front.

I looked at him across the table. "Have you decided whether you are going to live on the island or head back home at the end of the month?"

He cleared his throat as if he were going to speak, but then pressed his lips firmly together. "This is all happening so fast, isn't it? We just found each other again, and now, here we are talking about moving to the island. It's all…a lot." He looked down at his hands.

I could tell he was struggling. "Perhaps, but it has always been my plan to move here, so that hasn't changed for me. I am still planning on moving ahead with that."

He looked up at me, hesitation in his voice. "Can you afford to do that?"

I was stunned by the way he implied I couldn't. I know we had never had a talk about finances before, but I also didn't realize he thought I couldn't hold my own. "Yes, of course I can. Why on earth would you think I couldn't?"

He fiddled with his thumbs. "I don't know how much an artist makes, but I can't imagine it's enough for the cost of living on this island. I just wanted to make sure you weren't setting yourself up for a potentially bad situation later."

My blood immediately boiled at the stereotypical response. He has done nothing but insult my work from the beginning—and hasn't even taken the time to ask me before coming to his own conclusions. Fighting tears, I stood up and calmly said, "No need to worry, I can handle myself."

I stormed out of the restaurant, leaving him there at our table, unable to look back at him. He seemed to view me as a charity case or a damsel in distress. In reality, Luke was in distress and in need of a place to stay—not me. I've done nothing but try to help him out, I've paid for my fair share of things for both of us, and I've never accepted a handout from him.

After I drove back to the condo, I went straight to my room, and wrestled with my thoughts. Anger consumed me; I had allowed myself to get wrapped up in the misguiding of Lucas Miller once again.

Here I was, willing to put my dream on hold to parade around the island like some lovesick puppy dog. I am a strong and independent woman and am more than capable of handling everything on my own. Tomorrow I can take control of the situation. But tonight, I'll allow myself the space to be in my feelings.

It had been a long while since I had a heart to heart with God. After pouring my heart out in prayer, I cried myself to sleep as I let go of the hope of a relationship between Luke and me once and for all.

TWENTY THREE

Lucas Miller

When I got back to the condo last night, it was dark, and Tess had gone to bed. I tossed and turned, unable to sleep all night. Our conversation played on repeat in my mind, and my back ached from the uncomfortable sofa bed. Waking up before Tess has become my new normal, which only made my decision to pack up all my items in my luggage easier. With the last item safely packed, I placed everything by the door and went to the kitchen to brew a pot of coffee.

Impatient, I poured a cup while it was still dripping out slowly, replaced the pot, and sat down to drink my coffee. I heard Tess come out of the bathroom after her shower and watched her as she looked at the luggage by the door and then turned to look at me with a puzzled look.

Nervous, I ran my hand through my hair. "I think it's best I give you your space back. You've been so gracious in letting me stay here with you, but I have the yacht now and have been working there long hours. It will be easier for me to sleep there, too."

Tess simply replied, "If that's what you want, I can't stop you."

She poured herself a cup of coffee and took it outside to the patio, where she sat with her hair wrapped up in a towel, still wet from her shower. She sat her coffee down on the table next to her and picked up her book to read, unbothered by my sitting inside watching her. The coldness in her actions confirmed my choice to move onto the yacht was the space we both needed right now as we collected our thoughts and determined the course of our relationship.

Not wanting to bother her, I cleaned my cup and put it away before quietly slipping out of the front door with my luggage in tow. When I reached my car, I turned to look back at the condo one last time. My heart felt pulled in an entirely different direction, but my head told me this was for our own good.

I loaded up my luggage and jumped behind the wheel to start up the convertible. I put the top down and took the long route to the marina to clear my head. What I needed to do today was spend time with a friend. When I got to the marina, I parked the car and, before getting out, texted William.

> Could use a friend today, you free? Can you meet me at the marina? I'm on my yacht.

Before I could even put my phone in my pocket, it chimed with William's response.

> William: *Sure man, on my way.*

I carried my luggage on board and took it down to the master cabin, putting everything away. It felt good not to be living out of suitcases and to have all my clothes in drawers and a closet for the first time since I've been here. Instantly, I felt as if I could think more clearly with everything in place as my anxiety receded.

I headed back up to the main deck just as William boarded. "Hey, man, thanks for coming out," I said while clasping his hand in a combined gesture of a handshake and a high five.

William nodded. "Man, this yacht is nice! Can you show me around?"

I led William through the yacht, showing him all the bells and whistles before firing it up and untying it from the dock for a quick ride out on the open water. I took him around all the local channels, showing him the sights while we chatted a bit about work.

"Have there been any bids on either of the commercial properties or the house?" I asked William.

He shook his head. "No, nothing substantial yet—but I know there have been several showings with the promise of a potential bid soon—I'm just not sure on which building. What have you decided?"

I maneuvered the boat to a great spot and dropped anchor so I could talk with William for a bit. "I am not sure, if I'm being honest," I said.

"Do you care to elaborate, or are you going to leave me guessing?" William replied.

I stood up and motioned to the stairs leading up to the flybridge. An incredible view would improve this conversation. I led him over to my favorite place to sit and relax while I prepared myself for the level of confession I knew I needed to have.

"Losing Lisa was the hardest thing I have ever gone through. Each day, I wrestle with whether what I'm doing would make her love me more or love me less. When this situation with Tess happened, it spun me in a completely different direction. For the first time in a very long and agonizing time, I felt alive again."

William nodded in understanding. "Do you remember how crazy about Tess you were in college? You were crushed about losing your shot in college ball that summer after your injury during spring training, but you were also excited to see her that summer. But she didn't come—and you came back to school, devastated because of how much you loved her."

I thought back to that moment in time. "I loved her, and I thought no one could compare to that amount of love—then I met Lisa. She filled that void for me, then left me here with it all over again. We didn't get a divorce; she died. I feel like I'm crossing a line here."

William replied, "There is no line, Luke. Lisa is gone. It's okay to move on. She would want you to. Do you feel ready to move on, or are you still not quite there yet?"

"My heart feels like I am, but my brain tells me I'm not," I admitted.

William was silent for a moment as he recognized my need to determine what it was I was trying to say. "When I'm with Tess, I lead more from my heart and less from my head. She gets me so jumbled up sometimes. I think I need a few days to really clear my mind. A break from us would do both of us good. I don't want to break up with her, but I need some time and space to figure this out."

William looked me dead in the eye. "Then you need to be honest with her and tell her that. There's nothing wrong with taking time to work through your emotions and feelings surrounding the loss of your wife. There also isn't a need to rush into anything with Tess. See what naturally progresses. Take time to actually date each other instead of rushing into living with each other like you had to."

This was exactly what I needed to hear. "You're right! In this whole situation of being forced to live with each other, we forgot the most crucial step in building a relationship—dating."

William added to that sentiment. "Exactly, so to help soften the blow, be sure you tell Tess that you'd like to take this time apart to date her, while also spending time on your own. You also need to speed up progress on these investments. There are some things I'd like to get wrapped up by Saturday."

I nodded in agreement. "I hope she'll be okay with our first date being on Sunday, since it sounds like I need to get work done."

We both laughed and spent another hour relaxing and chatting about him and his life before he had to get back to the office. We headed back down to the main deck, and I pulled the anchor and took us back into the marina. Once the boat was secure and William was gone, I pulled my phone from my pocket to text Tess.

I'm sorry for leaving without saying goodbye. You looked like you needed your space.

Thanks for giving me space. I just needed some time to process everything.

Understandable. Look, I am behind on work and need to get caught up. I need to work longer hours for the next few days.

I think some time on our own may do us some good, but can we plan on dinner Sunday night?

Of course, we have spent most of our time together, and I'm behind on a few things too. I'll try not to bother you over the next few days, but I'll miss you.

I wasn't sure how she would take the news, and I felt like a coward for sending it in a text, and not speaking to her directly. She answered pretty quickly, which put my mind at ease. Before I responded to her last text, a new one came through.

Don't forget to enjoy your time here too. I look forward to seeing you on Sunday.

I will, I promise. Enjoy your evening.

I checked the kitchen for food and realized I needed to order something to eat because there was nothing left here. I pulled up the food delivery app on my phone and placed an order for a pizza, which was promised to be here in under 15 minutes. That gave me enough time to pull out my laptop and get to work on building a makeshift workstation in the parlor.

I stepped back to enjoy my hard work. Not bad. I think this could work in the long term, and the connections were stable. Hearing a commotion coming from the docks, I headed out to see my pizza was there to be delivered. Perfect timing. I grabbed the box and headed back inside to toss it on the table and pick up a couple of slices to put on a plate.

I settled in at my workstation and opened my laptop. Before I could begin working on William's project, I needed to ease my mind. Between bites, I researched the potential of living on the island. Not knowing if opening a second location on the island would be worth the investment was stopping me from making a decision.

There were lucrative options that William and his colleagues were considering. The one investment they were all trying to convince me to jump on board with was the resort. The cost of repairs were so substantial that I had told William he shouldn't consider it without the backing of other investors. He now had Shawn, Alexander, and, more recently, Mike on board, but it still wasn't quite enough. It was risky, but if we could also get Josh or Matt on board, I could come in as the sixth investor. The return would help keep the satellite office here going while I built my clientele here.

I started a new presentation that would outline what I was thinking and how it could benefit all of us with a profit. It would require a lot of upfront costs on our part to remodel, staff, and reopen, but once it got going, it would pay back tenfold within the first three years. We could save on costs if we did some of the work ourselves. I felt like we were all a pretty handy bunch and had the stamina to do some remodeling. It would be a significant and fulfilling project for us all to work on together and see it come to life.

I tried to imagine what life would look like here on the island if I chose to stay permanently. Would Tess be patient with me as I tried to rebuild and open my heart back up again? I tried not to let my heart steer the direction of my presentation. This presentation was one that needed to convince the others that investing in the resort was the best bet for us all. Setting my emotions aside, I forced my brain to do the work.

It was 2:00 am when I finally stopped working on my presentation—I couldn't stay awake any longer. Satisfied, I closed my laptop and headed down to the main cabin to sleep. Exhausted, I fell asleep before my head even hit the pillow.

TWENTY FOUR

Teresa Wright

The condo feels cold and empty despite the warm sun shining through the patio door. As I sit at the kitchen table with my coffee cup in hand, I look sorrowfully around the empty living room. Not having Luke here now feels like a reminder of how bleak my life was before I came to Sanderling Pointe. Perhaps Luke was right, and some time apart would do us both good as we determine what we want in our lives and relationship now.

I downed the remaining coffee, set the cup on the table, and watched as a drop of coffee slowly dripped down to the table below it. I sat, staring at the drop of coffee as it pooled on the table for a short time before finally mustering enough strength to get up and clean up the remnants of this morning's breakfast.

"Now what?" I said aloud, gazing around the empty condo.

With no one there to answer me, I grabbed my phone and texted Beth.

> Hey friend! Hope you are doing well, was just thinking of you.

After hitting send, I remembered she was on the road today and likely wouldn't be able to respond for a while. Really needing to talk to someone, I opened a new message to send to Lynn.

> How are things going there?

Within seconds of sending Lynn's text, my phone rang. "You always know," I said when I answered.

"Do you want to talk about it?" Lynn asked me cautiously.

"I honestly don't know exactly what happened. One minute we were fine, and the next minute he was moving out and onto the yacht." I answered, tears pooling in my eyes.

"The last time we spoke, you said you spilled something on a blanket and he got upset," Lynn said. "Did more happen?"

"We had a few awkward encounters after that, but the most notable was over dinner at The Gentlemen's Pirate the other night. It was like having the money talk—without really having the money talk," I replied.

Lynn groaned. "Oof. How did that go?"

"Honestly, it didn't. He insinuated that as an artist, I couldn't possibly make enough money to afford to live here. I got mad— and I left. We haven't discussed it since," I admitted.

Lynn was quiet for a moment before responding, "I'm sure it is all part of the whole "starving artist" generalization. We both know that if you needed to pick up work to afford to live there, you would. That is your choice to do that though, and not really up to him."

I knew I had to be very careful about what I said next. No one knows who I am as an artist because I have kept that a secret.

I haven't even told my best friends. They would probably think I was crazy for doing this.

I took a deep breath in. "Lynn, can I tell you something I've never told anyone else? And I need you to promise you won't tell a soul."

Lynn didn't hesitate. "You know you can trust me, Tess. It will never leave this conversation."

I exhaled, mustering the courage to continue. "I won't need to pick up work here to afford a house. If I wanted to, I could pay for it with cash." There was no turning back now.

Lynn sounded confused. "What do you mean?"

"I am actually a highly sought-after artist. In the last year, I have gained popularity under a pseudonym. Thanks to the sale of my paintings, I actually made over a million dollars again last year," I confided in her.

A squeal erupted from Lynn. "What?!?! Are you serious right now? That's incredible, Tess! Why haven't you shared this with me before?"

I felt relieved that she had taken the news so well. "I honestly thought you'd think I'd lost my marbles. It was such a far cry from what I had wanted to do, but I have just sort of found myself in my art. It has become far more than I ever imagined it would."

Lynn responded, "Tess, I know you. I know you would only do what you felt was right within your heart to do. If this is what you want to do with your life, I will not only support your decision, I will applaud you for being brave and giving yourself a shot."

I wiped a tear as it fell from my eye. "Thanks, Lynn. I was just so lost after the boys both moved out. They no longer needed me—and I had put my whole life on hold for them, you know? It was time for me to do something for myself for once."

"And you deserve to do that and more," Lynn gently reminded me.

We chatted for a short while longer about how life as a mystery artist has been for me, along with my promise to come out with this news so she didn't have to bear my secret for too long. I assured her I was working on the logistics of that now, and that my secret success as an artist would be shared soon.

After my talk with Lynn, I felt much better—as if a burden had been lifted. I decided it would be a great day to spend painting more of my newest collection since I now had this space all to myself. I went back into my bedroom and pulled out the drop cloth, taking it out to the space by the patio doors. This time, I carefully laid it down to ensure the floors were completely covered. I moved the furniture farther away from my drop cloth area so I could be absolutely certain I wouldn't spill anything on it again.

Before I got started, I grabbed my headphones and turned on my favorite playlist, settling in on the first painting. I made great progress as I finished with the last brushstroke just as my stomach growled. It was a great stopping point for a quick lunch.

As I was munching on my salad, I sent Luke a quick text.

> I hope you are having a good day. Just thinking of you…

I finished my salad and turned my music back up. I grabbed the next canvas and picked up my brush to begin again. As the music would speed up, I found myself painting in rhythm a piece that stemmed from a beautiful memory. Blues, greens, and yellows swirled about my canvas to create a beautiful waterscape. After I completed the painting, I set it to the side to pick up my third and final canvas of the day.

Throughout the afternoon and into the evening, I painted as I watched the sun setting on the horizon. I took a quick break, long enough to grab a protein bar and refill my water, both in my drinking cup and in my paintbrush glass.

As I devoured the protein bar, I gazed at my painting in its current state. I couldn't help but wonder if I could make Sanderling Pointe my home without Luke—or would it always remind me of him?

One of my favorite memories is of our second year on the island. Luke took me to The Pointe one evening just before sunset. We walked down the pier out to its farthest point, where we sat with our legs dangling over the edge as we were suspended high above the water. It was the first time Luke told me he loved me.

Back then, I couldn't imagine a world without Luke in it. All these years later, now that we've been reunited, I don't think I can go through another heartbreak with him. I don't know what it is like to lose a spouse—but if I learned one thing, it was that grief has a way of showing up when you least expect it to.

Would Luke ever fully be ready to love someone again, to love *me* again? If he isn't ready to move here, I certainly don't want to push him into it. But I also believe that our love is worth fighting for. I gave up on it too quickly once—and I will not make that same mistake again.

I picked up my phone and called Janine. "Hi Janine, do you know if the gallery is still available?"

"Hi, Tess, yes, it is still available," she replied.

I was ready. "I'd like to make an offer at the asking price."

"Excellent, I will get that submitted for you. Have you decided where you'd like to live?" she asked.

I sighed. That was still a huge question. "No, not yet. The places you showed me just won't work for me and my family. I need to make sure I have plenty of space for my boys to come stay with me."

"There is still the house that can be packaged with the gallery. You said it was out of your budget, but I really think you'd love the house," she said.

I thought for a moment. "I'm just not sure."

"If you'd like to tour it on Monday, I can send you details to your email about the home," she replied.

"Can I consider it and let you know on Monday morning? In the meantime, if you have any other options that may fit my budget, please send them my way. I'm happy to look them over as well."

"Of course," she said, promising to follow up early in the week.

After hanging up with Janine, I jumped back into my painting, determined now more than ever to finish this collection for its debut in the gallery space at my grand opening. This collection was not like my others. It was more personal. I wasn't sure how it would be received, but it was something I felt I had to do. It would be a great way to step out from behind the pseudonym and make my debut.

I could picture how the gallery space would look once I got in there. I would set down roots here on the island and open it up to invite the community in. Teaching art was something I have always wanted to do, and this space would make that dream a reality for me. The only missing piece was Luke.

I was too afraid to admit it before, but I can't deny I have fallen in love with Luke all over again. The thought terrifies me, but it also fills me with a warmth that radiates from head to toe. I knew from the first time we met that I could see the potential for a life with him.

We were so young, though, that I knew the odds of us making it to marriage were extremely low. With the time that has passed, surely now our odds had to be greater. *Second chances like this don't just fall in your lap.*

TWENTY FIVE

SATURDAY, JUNE 25, 2022

Lucas Miller

Yesterday's excitement made it difficult for me to sleep last night. After presenting my pitch to the guys, a resounding yes echoed around the room as one by one, each of them were on board for the resort. In the end, I won over Josh as the fifth investor, which gave me the confidence to come in as the sixth.

Everyone was buzzing after the meeting, and to my surprise, Josh approached me, pulling me aside for a chat. We shook on a deal for me to manage his portfolio, finally landing him as a client. During our brief conversation, he explained that he also had ten people he wanted to connect with me as potential clients. Their business hinged on today's presentation, which meant their referrals were as good as done.

Despite it being a Saturday, I had a meet and greet set for them on the yacht this morning, and they could begin arriving any minute now. After a quick walkthrough to make sure I had snacks and drinks aboard for everyone, I made my way up to stand on the dock and await their arrival.

Josh led the pack down the dock toward my boat, and I could tell I was in for a treat. They looked like a fun bunch.

"Josh, welcome, gentlemen, thanks for joining me today," I said as I extended my hand to shake each of theirs as Josh introduced us.

After the introductions, we boarded the vessel, and I made haste in setting off. Once I found a place to drop anchor so we could get down to business, I could relax a little more. In all the conversations we had, I realized Josh was the spokesperson for this group, and they all looked to him to lead.

Our time was nearing the end, and I hadn't yet landed a single deal. Josh stood up to speak. "On behalf of everyone, I wanted to say thank you, Lucas, for bringing us out here for a great morning. I have spoken with each of the gentlemen here and assured them you are the right person to handle their accounts. They would all like to get locked in with you, so you can draft up the paperwork and send it their way."

This windfall was completely unexpected. I had hoped to land at least half of them as new clients, but knowing I had the commitment of all ten was huge for my business. This was exactly what I needed to show me that moving here is the right choice.

It was my turn to address the group. "Thanks, Josh, and thanks, guys, for trusting me with your portfolios. I'll have my office draft up the paperwork and get it over to you next week so we can get started."

After another round of handshakes, I fired up the yacht to head back to the docks. Once the yacht was secured and the last person had disembarked, I returned to my workstation to notify my office of what needed to be done next. It was the weekend, but I wanted to make sure all ten emails were waiting for my assistant when she arrived at the office on Monday.

The guys had all filled out my intake forms and left them for me on the table in the salon. Quickly, I scanned each one with my phone and saved it on my laptop to send to my assistant for processing. Wanting to get a good head start on their accounts, I spent extra time on each individual client to include in the email my recommendations for their accounts.

With the last email sent, I picked up my phone to call Sheila. "Hi Sheila, this is Lucas Miller. I want to put in an offer for the gallery space at $25,000 below the asking price."

"Hi Lucas, I'll be happy to pass along your bid. I'll keep in touch via text once I hear back," Sheila responded.

After hanging up the phone, I took a deep breath in and slowly let it out. The stress from this week was weighing on me, and my chest felt tighter than it had in a while. It was more noticeable when I was alone, which made me realize Tess kept me calm and grounded. Without her here, I spent every waking hour working— likely contributing to my stress.

As much fun as it has been working on the yacht, there wasn't enough room here for me to do my work productively. It also felt a bit relaxed compared to how I traditionally run business meetings, and the sooner I could get back to an office, the better. Ideally, finding a house to sleep in a normal bed would also do me some good.

To keep my mind off my pending bid on the gallery space, I grabbed a bite to eat and went through the listings for homes that Sheila sent me. Disappointed in all of them, my thoughts kept going back to William's house. It was perfect for Tess and me, and I knew finding another one that matched what it offered would be difficult.

About half an hour had passed before I received a text back from Sheila with an update.

> I'm so sorry. Someone else put in a bid slightly higher than yours. Can you go up on your offer?

> Lucas: Sure. Let's go up to $25,000 over asking.

> Okay, I'm on it. Will keep you posted.

An hour passed before I heard from Sheila again.

> You've been outbid again. What would you like to do?

This was frustrating. The gallery space is the perfect space for the offices, with its natural light and the large area upstairs. If I had to go with the space next door, it would take more work to make it how I wanted it to be. Doing the math in my head quickly, I came up with a number I estimated it would take to convert.

My phone rang, disrupting my calculations. "This is Lucas," I answered without looking at the screen.

"Lucas, it's Sheila. The other bidder isn't backing down and has increased now quite a bit. You will need to come up to outbid them," she stated.

This was something I hadn't calculated in my plans. Normally, I would walk away or ask to spend more time to decide. But I knew in situations like this, waiting could cause me to lose out on the gallery space. My stress level rose as I worried my plans might be derailed completely.

"My max for the gallery space is $2.5 million. Increase at $25,000 increments until we land it," I responded.

"Great, I will see what I can do and keep in touch. Keep your phone nearby. I have a feeling we'll get this taken care of today," she replied.

Nervous, I headed up to the flybridge to work out the energy building up inside of me. As I paced the perimeter, I questioned my decision. If the offer goes in at my max price, I don't think I can also get the house because of the investment I just made at the resort. That means I would have to live on the yacht for a while until things leveled out and some returns came in.

This is what can make or break an investment. I have to be smart here. The risk in purchasing the space means I'll be staying here on Sanderling Pointe, which is where Tess will be too. In the few days we've been apart, I've realized how much I need her in my life. Ultimately, that tells me all I need to know—the risk is worth it.

But maybe the challenge in purchasing the gallery space means I shouldn't move here. It's been two days since Tess and I have even spoken to each other. How do I know she still feels the same way about me? If I step back and reconsider, that may be smarter.

A loud ha-ha-ha-ha from my new friend, the laughing gull, stopped my pacing.

"Hello there, friend. What do you think? Am I making the right decision?" I asked the bird with a unique tiny gray heart shape in the white area above its wing.

Silence followed. Not a single peep. So much for that. This bird wasn't helpful after all. I shook my head and turned around, pacing again, when my phone chimed with a text from Sheila.

Congratulations! The other bidder withdrew, so the space is yours for $2.25 million!

Excellent work, Sheila, thank you! Let's set up a time to complete the sale.

After sending the text, I noticed the sun had set, and it was getting dark. Another day has come and almost gone without me reaching out to Tess. This was a moment worth celebrating, and I wish she were here to share it. Wanting to hear from her, I sent her a text.

Sorry for not reaching out sooner. It's been crazy here. I am looking forward to seeing you tomorrow.

The text changed to *read* quickly, and I watched as the three dots would appear, and then disappear a few times. When she doesn't respond, it makes me wonder if I have upset her.

Have I completely messed things up with her by putting time and space between us? Guilt began to gnaw at me, and panic set in. I reached out to steady myself as my legs suddenly felt like jelly.

Remembering what I need to do, I focus and point out the things I can see closest to me to calm the panic attack before it sets in.

Once I've calmed myself down, I sit in the captain's chair and stare off into the darkness. I counted the seconds it took before the light from the lighthouse reached my line of sight again. It had been a really long time since I had last prayed. While I am still not happy with God for taking Lisa from me, I thought I'd give it a shot.

"God, it's me, Lucas. Been a while, hasn't it? I may have found myself in a pickle and I sure could use your help. And though I know I am the least deserving person, I would be grateful. If there is any way you can keep Tess in my life, it would mean the world to me. I'm sorry for taking our relationship for granted. Amen."

If our relationship ends, will I be able to live here on Sanderling Pointe Island without Tess in my life? This wasn't a thought I had considered before now. All I could do was trust that everything would work out as it should.

TWENTY SIX

Teresa Wright

My heart ached for Luke, and the more I tried to stop thinking about him, the harder it got. Today, I needed a distraction, which is exactly why I rented a bicycle for the day. When I was here the last time, I spent most of my time on the trails, winding through the trees from one area to another.

My curiosity got the better of me as I started off in the direction I knew I shouldn't—Laughing Gull Marina. Something pulled me there, like an invisible force with a strength I couldn't fight. It was one of my favorite places on the island. But knowing Luke was there may have been part of it, too.

I wanted to respect his request for time apart, which is why I was carefully riding in areas out of sight from his boat slip. Once I made my way to the lighthouse, I dismounted my bike and locked it to the rack. After paying for a ticket, I began my climb to the top.

Despite practically knowing it by heart, as I wound my way up the stairs, I would pause for a moment to read the history behind the lighthouse. Halfway up, there was a single chair on a small landing that provided a moment of rest if you needed it. When I reached the chair, I took a moment to sit in it as memories of this very chair flooded my mind.

Luke and I often climbed the lighthouse together, usually after riding our bicycles here. He would always pull me onto his lap as we sat here to pass time. Tears filled my eyes, blurring the photographs around me. I wiped them away as they fell and tried to pull myself together.

My phone rang, which was a welcomed distraction. "Beth!" I exclaimed after seeing it was she who was calling. "How are you? Did you make it to the campground?"

She chuckled at my enthusiasm. "Yes, we made it yesterday. I'm so sorry I missed your call. It was a hectic ride in. I would have called you sooner, but we had a hard time getting set up."

"Well, I'm glad you made it in safely, that is the most important thing," I replied.

Sensing my hesitation, she guided me. "Do you want to talk about it?"

"Talk about what?" I asked as I tried to deflect.

Beth sighed loudly. "Come on, Tess, out with it. I can tell something is on your mind."

"Everything is just not going according to plan. When I first came here, I thought I knew exactly what I wanted, but then— there was Luke. He has turned my world upside down again." I paused after sharing.

"He has, but in a good way. You have often wondered what would happen if the two of you were reunited. Now's your chance to find out," Beth answered.

"I had thought so too, but that was before he needed time alone. We haven't spoken to each other in a couple of days, and I won't see him again until tomorrow," I breathed.

"How does that make you feel?" Beth asked softly.

I tried to open my mouth, but words escaped me. I wasn't entirely sure how to answer Beth's question. My feelings were hurt the last time we were together, and I feel like he ran away from our conflict instead of working through it together. It made me wonder if he would always choose something else—or worse yet someone else over me when times got tough.

Beth cleared her throat to get my attention. "What's going on in that beautiful brain of yours, Tess?"

"I just don't know, Beth. That's part of the issue. Maybe I'm overthinking things, but I feel like he's run away from me instead of being with me," I replied as tears fell down my face.

"Let me ask you this, Tess: do you still love him?" Beth asked.

In my heart, I knew the answer to this, but saying it out loud makes it more real. "Yes. I never stopped loving him," I admitted.

"And now that you know this, what is stopping you from allowing yourself to be happy?" she asked.

I took a deep breath in and slowly let it out before responding to her. "The odds are..."

"Forget about the odds, Tess. I'm going to ask you again, what is stopping you from allowing yourself to be happy?" Beth interrupted me before I could get out my last thought.

"I'm afraid, Beth. That I won't be able to keep him happy enough to want to remain with me. I'm worried that when things get hard, he'll turn away from me and turn into the arms of someone else," I confessed.

Beth let out a deep sigh. "Tess, remember that Luke isn't your father. Not all men make the choice to upend their families."

Her words hit me like a sack of bricks. Beth was absolutely right. I don't even know why I am worried that Luke would be just like my dad. They are polar opposites!

"Thanks, Beth. You always know what to say to help me see things more clearly," I said.

Not holding back, my friend had one more lesson for me. "Let me also remind you that God is there with you. You are not alone in this. Lean on Him when you cannot reach me. He will fill you with peace. And when you are ready, extend forgiveness to your father, just as our Father forgives us."

After hanging up with Beth, her words hung in the air around me. She was right, of course. Forgiving my dad is something I have tried to do before, but my anger always stops me from fully letting go. Now, I could see how holding onto the hurt my dad caused me is stopping me from allowing others to fully love me.

I stood up and continued my climb to the top of the lighthouse. Once there, I stared out onto the water and watched the boats coming in and out of the harbor. Beth's words replayed in my mind, so I closed my eyes in prayer, whispering, "Lord, I forgive my dad."

As I stood there with my eyes closed, the only sounds I could hear were the seagulls laughing all around. This brought a smile to my face, and I joined in with them by laughing so hard, tears came to my eyes once more.

Feeling lighter, I made my way back down the stairs of the lighthouse to retrieve my bike. I rode it down the docks to Luke's slip, but disappointment filled me when I arrived to find it empty. He must be spending time on his yacht with clients today.

It was getting late in the afternoon, and I had skipped lunch, so I made my way back to the condo on the bike trails. After heating up an early dinner, my phone chimed with an incoming text.

Hello, Teresa. I'm sorry to inform you that another bidder has outbid you on the gallery space. What would you like to do?

Do you know the number their bid is at?

It looks like they are at $1.75 million.

Let's go to $1.8 million. I have to get this space, Janine.

Okay, let me pass along the news.

Panic consumed me instantly as I felt I hadn't gone up enough in price to win the space. I didn't have a backup plan and needed to make sure I got this space. It's all I've worked toward for the last year. Not wanting to miss the mark, I quickly texted Janine again.

My max is $2 million all in. Let them know that is the number. I'll pay in full with cash.

Are you sure you want to do that?

I have no choice but to do this. All in, $2 million cash.

I felt like I needed to throw up. This was really risky considering $2 million was the max I could go. It would practically drain my business account.

Unsure of what I would do if the deal went through, I opened my laptop to go through my bank accounts and assets list I had created when I put my belongings in storage. It was a risky investment at this price. I would need to sell more paintings quickly to cover any additional costs that may come up with the building.

Nauseated, I shoved the plate of food away. I spent the next couple of hours coming up with a plan to create and sell new pieces to some of my biggest repeat clients. Satisfied with my efforts, I was feeling like I could make this work when my phone chimed.

Teresa, I'm so sorry. You were outbid again. They have gone over your max cap.

Thanks for trying. I appreciate your help.

Do you want me to send you listings for other potential spaces?

Not right now. Let me process this, and I'll be in touch on Monday.

My heart felt like it had broken into a million pieces. Devastated, I got up from the table and walked outside to the beach. My legs wouldn't carry me any longer, and I collapsed onto the sand beneath me. I didn't move from that spot as I cried until there were no tears left to fall.

My phone chimed in my pocket. The distraction caused me to look up, and I realized the sun had given way to evening setting in. I did not know how long I had sat on the beach, but knew I needed to make my way back inside. Before going in, I pulled my phone out of my pocket to read my text.

Sorry for not reaching out sooner. It's been crazy here. I am looking forward to seeing you tomorrow.

At first, I started a message to Luke that felt too desperate, so I deleted it. Then I tried another message, but it felt too bland, so I deleted it too. Unable to respond, I shoved my phone back into my pocket as I walked inside. Losing out on the gallery weighed heavily on my mind. I thought maybe a hot shower would help, but all it did was make me cry even more.

Once I was dressed for bed, I made my way into my bedroom and climbed in under the covers before turning off the light. What will I do now that I don't have the gallery? Things with Luke have not been going well, so maybe it was best for me to head back home. Only just as I thought that—I remembered I had sold my home to move here.

Not only couldn't I open my gallery and studio, I was homeless! My rental agreement would be up in a week, which meant I needed to find somewhere to go. This wasn't at all how I envisioned this trip back here. Not knowing what else to do, I cried myself to sleep.

TWENTY SEVEN

Lucas Miller

This morning I woke up nervous about tonight's dinner with Tess. To ease my mind, I laced up my tennis shoes and took a run around the harbor. It was already a hot June morning, and the humidity was causing my shorts to stick to my legs.

As I ran, I thought about how excited she would be to learn that I am moving here after all. Of course, I don't quite know where I'd be moving to just yet, but that would come when it was time. Distracted by my thoughts, I nearly toppled over a young boy who had bent over to tie his shoe.

"Sorry about that," I yelled as I quickly recovered and kept going on my way.

By the end of my run, I arrived back at the yacht drenched in sweat, my hair matted to my face. After a shower, I was feeling the strain of the run after being more lax in my routine for far too long. The best way to combat sore muscles was to keep moving as much as possible, and so I grabbed my cleaning supplies and began cleaning up the yacht.

My phone rang, and a quick glance showed me it was Emily.

"Hey kiddo, how are you doing?" I said energetically.

"Doing great, Dad, just wanted to check in on you. We haven't heard from you for a little while. Everything okay?" She questioned.

It really warmed my heart that she was always thinking of me. "Everything is going well. I've just been busy with work and trying to get new clients while I'm here."

"Have you had any success with that? I know you were hinging your bets on new clients for the decision to move there," she said.

Before now, I hadn't really considered when I would talk to them about my decision to move here. Not wanting to hold back from her, I replied, "Yes, actually, I'm up to 15 new clients now—which has me right where I need to be to open up shop here."

Emily cheered loudly for me. "Dad! That is incredible! You have to stay now, they need you there. Are you excited about the possibility of moving there?"

"Yeah, I think so, Em. It is a little hard. I don't want to be too far away from you and your brother. But I could use a fresh start, and this place has always been a second home to me."

We spent the rest of the phone call catching up. Instead of feeling sad when I hung up with her, I actually felt excited for what was to come next. Emily really eased my mind about my decision to move here, which took the pressure off it.

After checking my watch, I decided it was time to get ready for dinner with Tess, though I realized I had never told her what time to meet me. With my phone still in my hand from my call with Emily, I sent her a text.

> Let's meet at Souper Grouper in about an hour. We can come back to the yacht afterwards.

Okay, sounds good. I'll see you then.

The hour before we were to meet went way quicker than I was prepared for. Wanting to look my best for Tess, I spent extra time getting ready and even picked out the shirt she liked so much. She always says the color of the shirt brightens up my hazel eyes.

When I walked up to the door, Tess was there waiting for me. Seeing her again brought back feelings of excitement. "Hey stranger," I said with a quick peck on the cheek.

"Hi, it's good to see you," she said as she followed my lead inside.

We walked up to the hostess stand to get a table. "Table for two, please," I requested.

"Right this way," the hostess replied.

We followed our hostess to the table, where I quickly pulled out Tess's chair for her to sit in. After taking my seat, the hostess handed us our menus and then left us.

"So, how have things been for you?" Tess asked cautiously.

Smiling up at her, I replied, "Really well, actually. Things are finally moving in the right direction. Emily called me today too, which was great to catch up with her."

"Nice. That's great, I'm happy for you," she replied, without looking up from her menu.

Something felt off about Tess tonight. She wasn't her usual chipper and bubbly self. I couldn't quite put my finger on it, but something was definitely bothering her.

Her right hand was resting on the table while she held her menu in her left hand. I reached across the table and put my hand on top of hers. "What have you been doing the last few days? Did you get more painting done?" I asked with genuine interest.

"Yeah, I was able to get more done. Not that it matters now," she said, a hint of sadness in her voice.

Something is *definitely* bothering her. "Are you okay, Tess?" I asked cautiously.

Clearly annoyed, Tess slammed the menu onto the table and looked at me. "Do I look okay to you?" she snapped at me.

"Well, I have some news that will hopefully cheer you up. I gained several new clients this week and need to open offices here long term. Because of that, I have decided to move here, and I will go tomorrow to secure my new office space where the gallery is," I told her excitedly.

I watched her closely, as I wanted to see her go from sad to happy, but instead, I got quite a different reaction. Her jaw dropped, and her eyes narrowed as she zeroed in on me with a look that revealed she was angry.

"You are going in where?!" she asked a bit louder than she should have.

After looking around to make sure we weren't causing a scene, I looked back at her before I cautiously answered her question. "In the space where the gallery is. My friend William owns the building, and yesterday, after an insane bidding war, the other person finally came to their senses and dropped out—so I won it! Isn't that great?!"

Tess grew silent as the waiter came to the table to take our order. Grateful for the interruption, we both put in our orders for our meals and drinks. After the waiter left, I returned my gaze to her to get a read on what she was feeling. Disappointment filled me when I realized she looked anything but happy about my announcement.

This moment reminded me of another argument we had gotten into the last time we were here in 1996. We had gone out for ice cream, and she couldn't make up her mind about what flavor she wanted, so I ordered mine first and stood at the end of the row eating it while waiting for her.

When she finally got her ice cream, she took one look at me and started crying. When I finally got her calmed down, she told me I had taken the last of the flavor she had wanted, and she got stuck with something she didn't want.

She didn't understand how I could be so inconsiderate of her needs. It was completely irrational, and it wasn't like I did it on purpose. She waited a long time before deciding. How was I supposed to know the flavor I picked was what she wanted and was also the last scoop?

In the end, the argument was more about my lack of patience in making sure she had what she needed while going ahead of her to take care of myself. What that taught me about her is that she enjoys being made a priority in our relationship. Her feelings are important to her, and as such, I can learn from that moment and apply it now. The only problem was, I had no idea what she was mad about.

The only rational thing I could think of was to break the silence. "I thought you'd be happier," I said logically. However it came out sounding more accusatory than logical.

Tears trickled down Tess's face as she looked up at me. "I'm just trying to wrap my head around all of this."

Still not understanding, I had to know what this really was. "Do you not want me to move here any longer?"

My last question was met with silence, as I watched her pick at the salad on her plate. Watching her push a cherry tomato around and around only added to my frustration. *How could I fix this if I didn't know what broke it?*

We finished our meals in silence, avoiding the tension. At the end of our meal, I paid the bill, and we headed outside to the parking lot. Standing beside her car, neither of us spoke. The tension between us was palpable.

I had given her as much time as I could, and she still hasn't answered my last question. The longer I stood there waiting, the more I felt like an idiot. My annoyance grew by the minute.

Frustrated, I was the one to break the silence. "I don't know why you are so upset about this. I really thought this was what you wanted."

Unable to hold it in any longer, Tess burst into tears and turned away from me. When I reached out to pull her close to me, she flinched and pulled away. I really don't understand what is happening. Why is she so upset with me?

TWENTY EIGHT

SUNDAY, JUNE 26, 2022

Teresa Wright

My face burned from the heat seething throughout my body. Anger consumed me from head to toe as I replayed on repeat Luke's admission of buying the gallery out from under me. He was the other bidder?! How could he do this to me? He knew that was the space I wanted for my gallery.

To make matters worse, his plan to take a building that was rich with culture and history from this location and convert it into office space was too much to bear. My heart broke for all the local artists who would soon lose a space to showcase their artwork.

The last thing Luke said to me was, "I don't know why you are so upset about this. I really thought this was what you wanted."

His words only fueled my anger, and when he touched me, it felt intrusive. After turning my back on him, I spun back around to face him head-on. "How could you possibly know what I wanted since you haven't even spoken to me since Wednesday night?" I spewed.

Luke opened his mouth to say something, but I cut him off. "Do you even remember me telling you I wanted to open an art studio and that I found the perfect place?"

He thought for a moment before speaking. "Yeah, but I figured once you saw the price of the commercial real estate on the island, it would change your mind. You would be stretched thin on your artist's salary." He said dismissively.

The sounds of cars driving by and children laughing muffled as my vision darkened. I have never been angrier in my life. Anger was consuming me to the point that the only sound I heard was the rapid beat of my heart.

There was one of two things I could do now: I could lash out at him and really tell him how I felt, or I could calm down and speak reasonably with him. The air around us felt thick and heavy. My breathing felt labored, as if someone were sitting on my chest.

Bracing myself against my SUV, I took a deep breath and slowly exhaled. I repeated this a couple of times before my heart rate slowed down and I could again hear the sounds around us.

Curious about his statement, I had to know why he thought this. "What is that supposed to mean?" I asked Luke. "I make plenty of money on my artist salary and have more than enough for the space I wanted."

The look on his face told me that my statement shocked him. "Sorry, Tess, that's not what I meant. It didn't come out quite as I had wanted it to. I just know how expensive everything is here on the island because I've been spending the last several weeks looking at the numbers for my clients. It was wrong of me to assume you didn't have capital to invest."

Tears fell down my face without my permission. I had tried so hard to keep it bottled inside, but I couldn't fight them anymore. Part of the disconnect was that Luke didn't know what I knew, and I had to tell him.

I looked Luke in the eye as I spoke quietly. "I was the second bidder on the gallery. That was the space I wanted so I could help preserve its history in the art community. If you have done your research on that space, you will have learned it has been in the art community for decades. To see it turned into office space is disheartening."

The color drained from Luke's face, and before he could say anything to me, I cut in once more. "This conversation is getting us nowhere. I am going to go back to my condo to digest everything. We need some more space and time to process everything and to allow me the chance to regroup."

Not waiting for a reply, I unlocked my SUV and climbed in behind the wheel. After starting my SUV, I looked in the rear-view mirror and watched as he crossed over to his convertible. With Luke no longer in my way, I backed out of my parking space and headed to the main road.

Unable to go back to my empty condo, I made a left turn onto Harbour Way instead of continuing straight to get back to the main road that leads back to my condo. The road also just happened to be the road the gallery was on.

As I approached the entrance to the gallery, I slowed down and turned on my turn signal to turn into the lot. Once parked, I sat looking at the exterior of the building. Tears came full force as I wailed loudly. The pain of losing this space was difficult to navigate.

Never in my life had I ever been so certain of wanting to open my studio in a space. If it wasn't here, then where would it be? My anger made me question whether I would even want to remain on the island if I couldn't fulfill this desire. A part of me knew I would never be able to fully support Luke and his decision to turn the gallery into office space.

A soft knock on the window startled me. I looked up and saw Eloise on the other side. "Are you okay, dear?" She yelled through the closed window.

I held up one finger as I yelled back, "Give me just one minute, please. I'll be out in a minute."

Eloise took one step back and waited patiently as I grabbed a tissue to wipe my face. Eloise looked at me with kindness in her eyes. "Why don't we go inside and sit for a moment?" she asked.

"I really don't want to impose. I'm sure you were headed home for the day," I replied hesitantly.

"There's not a lot waiting for me there. I've got plenty of time to sit and chat with you," she said lovingly.

Eloise led me to the front door of the gallery, which she unlocked and opened for us to enter. The space looked bigger. Most of the artwork was already gone thanks to the sale she had been running for the last several weeks. There were tables and chairs set up in the space, which reminded me that the farewell party was coming up.

Unable to stop the flow of tears once more, I freely let them fall as I took a long, lingering look at the space. Eloise set her purse on a table close to where I stood and disappeared towards the back, where the kitchen area was. She returned with a bottle of water and a box of tissues. Following her lead, we sat down at the table.

"Now, Teresa, do you want to share what is on your heart?" Eloise asked curiously.

"Oh, Eloise, I have lost it. This space, my dream, all of it. There was a bidding war on the gallery, and the other person outbid me.

I tried so hard to get it, I maxed out at my highest point, and it still wasn't enough," I sobbed.

"Can I ask what you would have done with the space if you had won?" Eloise asked cautiously.

A smile crept across my face as I answered her. "You've inspired me so much, Eloise. My plans included the preservation of the history of the gallery and continuing to have a space for local artists to showcase their work. For the upstairs area, I planned on turning it into a learning studio with a stage at the front and easels set up for students to work."

Eloise reached across the table and patted my hand. "This old building doesn't hold the heart of the artists. It lies within them and is waiting to be discovered by a teacher who believes in them. A teacher, like you."

Her words comforted me in a way that felt like a hug from a friend. "Thank you, Eloise. I just wish I had a place where I could teach them." I said.

"Don't give up the search, Teresa. There are plenty of spaces available on the island, and with your creativity, you can create a new space for us all to love. I'll even help you find one if you'd like?" she asked optimistically.

"I would like that, thank you," I replied. "It is getting late, though, and I have kept you here long enough."

We both stood and gathered our belongings before heading outside to our vehicles. Eloise gave me a hug before turning and walking towards her car.

As I slid behind the wheel of my SUV to head back to the condo, I took one more lingering look at the gallery. The idea of trying to find a place as perfect as this one felt insurmountable. Can I find the perfect place now that this one is gone? Another question surfaced: what will become of my relationship with Luke now?

These questions will remain unanswered until another day. For now, I'll head back to the condo and get some rest. With a fresh perspective, I realized that tomorrow is a new day with a new chance to chase my dreams.

TWENTY NINE

Lucas Miller

Sadness consumed me like a weighted vest, threatening to pull me underwater. This feeling was all too familiar. Somewhere along the way, I had heard things get better with time, but I think that's something they say to keep you from dwelling on your situation.

After Tess abandoned me on our date last night, I wrestled all night, wondering if I was making the right decisions. She clouds my judgment. Her very presence makes me throw all reason out the window as I stumble around—doing what I think will not only make her happy but also make her want to stay with me.

Of course, I feel horrible for having hurt her so badly with the bidding war. In my attempt to do what I felt she wanted me to do, I did the opposite. Tess was right to question how I would know what she wanted when I hadn't spoken to her in three days. I was so caught up in my life that I failed to consider her dreams alongside mine.

Now, the day for me to close on the gallery space has arrived, and I don't think I can go through with it. The uncertainty of our relationship makes me second guess whether I should move to the island. Despite this uncertainty, I wanted to approach this with a level head. The logical thing to do is reach out to Sheila and reschedule.

Good morning, Sheila. I know we said we'd get together today for the closing on the gallery. I need to reschedule. Can we move it to Friday?

I just need to get with the seller to confirm. Do you have a particular time in mind?

Anytime that morning would be great. Thanks Sheila.

No problem. I'll keep you posted.

Relieved to have the extra time, I decided to take the day off to work through everything. After emailing my assistant to let her know I would not be available today, I prepped the yacht. Some time on the water would help me clear my mind.

I've found the perfect spot to anchor the yacht. It feels secluded and has minimal traffic because it is close to the shore. Once I reached that spot, I dropped anchor to keep from drifting. Just as the anchor was in place, my phone rang.

A quick glance at the screen showed me it was Jacob. "Hey son, good morning," I greeted him.

"Hey Dad. I wanted to check in with you because I haven't really heard from you for a while and wanted to make sure everything was going okay," he said, with a hint of worry in his voice.

Unsure of how I wanted to approach this, I decided it was likely best to try to just play it cool. "Well, I appreciate you checking in. All is well here. I've just been really busy with new clients," I replied. "What's been going on in your world?"

Hesitantly, Jacob replied, "Nothing new, really. Just spending the summer with friends in between shifts. Next month, I think a couple of guys and I are going to head down to Florida for a week."

"That sounds like a good time. Are you going to fly in or drive?" I asked curiously.

"It sounds like the guys want to fly in so we'll be there quicker. I was trying to convince them to drive so we could stop by Sanderling Pointe on the way home, but I was outvoted," he said sadly.

"Well, you know you are always welcome here, son. Anytime you want to come and bring friends, just let me know," I offered.

"Thanks, Dad. Are you sure you're okay? You don't sound like yourself," Jacob pressed.

"Yeah, I'm fine. Just a little tired from sleeping on the boat. It's not the most comfortable bed," I tried to convince him.

"How's things with Tess? Is everything okay there?" Jacob probed.

Just the sound of her name stirred the sadness up even more. "She's been really busy. We haven't been able to spend much time together this past week. Hopefully that changes soon, though," I said, feeling regret.

"Do you love her, Dad?" Jacob asked quietly.

His question made me wince. "Yeah, bud, I do. I just don't know if…" my words trailed as I decided to stop myself before I went too far. "Anyway, enough about me. Have you made your plans to return to school in the fall?"

Jacob and I continued our conversation about his school plans, avoiding any further talk about my relationship status. After hanging up with him, I felt guilty for lying. Sometimes, as a parent, you have to do what is right by your kids. And in this situation, keeping my romantic life private was the right call.

At 19, Jacob is fairly perceptive, though I always tried to shield him from problems his mother and I had. Tess was so new to my family, I didn't want to paint a negative picture of her as I worked through my feelings.

Tess has a way of walking out when things get tough. She abandoned me before, and I was crazy to think she wouldn't do it again. I was mad at myself for letting my guard down and not protecting my heart more. I knew better.

The stress of the situation caused the tightness in my chest to return—a warning sign that I needed to work on a way to relax. I walked into the kitchen and grabbed a bottle of water from the fridge before heading up to the flybridge.

I settled into one of my favorite spots to relax and put my feet up on the chaise. Leaning back, I closed my eyes and listened to the waves lapping against the boat as it lightly rocked. The peace I felt when I was alone on the yacht was something new.

I had finally found something that helped keep my anxiety at bay when it was building. There's something about being out on the water with no one around for miles. It's so peaceful, yet I felt grounded and safe.

As the tightness in my chest subsided, a sudden noise close to me startled my eyes open. Face to face with my new friend, the laughing gull's call echoed under the canopy.

"We've got to stop meeting like this," I said to the bird as I noticed the gray heart.

"Ha-ha-ha-ha!" the bird replied to me in response.

"Since we keep running into each other, it's only right that you get a name. Shall I call you Sandy?" I asked the bird.

"Ha-ha-ha-ha!" the bird replied in agreement.

"Okay, Sandy it is then. Named after the island you come from," I said.

The bird stayed perched on the rail next to where I sat, unfazed by my existence. Lost in thought, I confessed my feelings out loud to my friend.

"Do you want to know what's not so funny, Sandy? I feel horrible for not taking Tess's art seriously and for being the one to cause her to lose out on her dream space. Looking back, I realize we never really talked about our finances, and I just automatically assumed she didn't have the means to purchase commercial space," I said out loud.

Pausing, I wondered if perhaps it wasn't that she abandoned me, but that I actually pushed her away by my actions. Remorse filled me as I realized what I had done.

"Oh, Lord, I have messed up," I confessed out loud.

It's been such a long time since I spent time in prayer. After losing Lisa, I blamed God for such a long time. I couldn't understand how He could be silent as Lisa suffered and died. In the wake of her death, resentment and bitterness filled my heart as I walked away from God.

Suddenly, a flood of memories came over me as my worlds with both Tess and Lisa collided. There was a conversation Lisa and I had the week before she passed away, where she told me after she leaves I had to promise her I would try to find love again. She knew my history with Tess and made a point of bringing her name up in that conversation.

Through tears, I promised her I would try when I was ready, if our paths ever crossed again. Lisa told me I deserve happiness and to be loved for the rest of my life. "Never stop fighting for love when you get your second chance," were her exact words.

Burying my face in my hands, I wept. "Oh, Lisa," I cried. "I hope it isn't too late with Tess. I'll fight for her. I promise I'll do whatever it takes to get her back."

An overwhelming feeling of the need to take this matter to prayer flooded my heart. Instinctively, I responded by praying.

Lord, it's me, Luke. Of course, you already knew that, but it's been a while. Please forgive me for turning my back on you when I needed you most. Life got difficult. Now, it is difficult once more. I have a second chance at love, and I don't want to mess this up. Please give me the wisdom to know what I need to do to make things right with Tess. I'll do anything. Amen.

After my prayer, I took a deep breath in and slowly released it as an idea popped into my head.

"Sandy, I have to go back to the docks now. I've got to make things right!" I said to the bird as I stood.

"Ha-ha-ha-ha-ha!" the bird gave a cackling cry, like sweet laughter, as it began flapping its wings before it flew away.

The ride back to the dock felt like it took an eternity. Once the yacht was secured, I changed into my workout clothes, grabbing a bag with a fresh change of clothes and my water bottle. I made my way to the convertible to drive over to the gym on Sanderling Drive, just up the road from Tess's condo.

Mondays are usually leg day in my workout routine, but I canceled my workout with William this morning to head out onto the water. With a quick glance at my watch, I saw it was getting late in the afternoon and soon would be time for dinner. It was as good a time as any to go for a run on the beach.

After a warm-up stretch, I made my way down closer to the water where the sand was flat from the waves. After starting a workout session on my watch, I began my run toward Tess's condo.

Admittedly, I didn't have a plan. The only thought I had was to run towards her and take it as it comes. As I approached her condo, I could see her sitting on the patio. Her head was in her hands, causing her blond hair to fall around her face. She appeared to be crying.

Suddenly, this didn't seem like a good idea, so I immediately turned around and headed back a little way so she couldn't see me, but I could still see her. It pained me that I had caused so much hurt in her life. My heart ached for her, and all I wanted to do was run up to her and hold her in my arms.

Time stood as still as I watched her. The realization of my feelings for her hit me like a ton of bricks. I loved Teresa. There was no denying it now. Guilt gnawed at me again as I felt horrible for what I'd done to her.

A new idea surfaced, and so I ran back to the gym, showered, and got ready to head out to pick up my favorite dinner at The British Isles Pub. With my dinner next to me on the passenger seat, I headed back to the yacht to do something I've never done before—search for Teresa on the internet.

In a rush, I scooped up my bag and food as I hastily made my way from the parking lot back to my yacht. Once aboard, I tossed my bag haphazardly on the floor and walked to my office setup.

I set up my food next to the laptop, waiting impatiently for the screen to come to life as I took a huge bite of my fish and chips. As soon as the computer came on, I set my fork back in the container and began my search.

Stumped. I was confused when nothing came up for her except her social media page. When I went to it, I saw a photo of her I had taken just two weeks ago. She looked stunning with the sunlight creating a halo effect around her. Unable to stop myself, over the next several hours, I scrolled through and looked at all the photos she had shared.

My big idea was a bust that led me to a dead end. Instead of learning more about her artwork, I ended up missing her immensely. It was getting late, and I was getting tired. After shutting down the laptop, I cleaned up my mess from dinner, grabbed my bag, and headed down to my cabin. After a quick shower, I climbed into bed, where the last thought I had before falling asleep was—how do I make this right?

THIRTY

Teresa Wright

The sunlight spilled across the room and landed on my face. Groggy from sleep, I put my hand up to shield my eyes and looked at the time on the clock. It was 8:30 in the morning, and I was going to be late. Panicked, I jumped out of bed and rushed to collect my clothes for the day before taking a quick shower, brushing my teeth, and getting dressed.

To be honest, I had completely forgotten I'd scheduled a walk through of this house before I lost the gallery bid. When Janine texted me a reminder yesterday afternoon, I debated canceling, but didn't. I figured I had already lost the gallery space, which meant I had more money to invest in a long-term residence—although I had a feeling this place would be far too big for just myself.

With no time to waste, I skipped my morning coffee as I rushed out the door to make it on time for my meeting with the realtor at 9:00. Once I was behind the wheel of my SUV, I punched the address into my GPS and headed out of the condo lot.

As I drove down the road to the house, I couldn't help but think about yesterday. When I was on the patio, I swear I saw Lucas on the beach, standing behind the bushes. But it was hard for me to tell if it truly was him or just my imagination playing tricks on me.

I missed him fiercely. Being away from him made me feel like I was on shaky ground. In a way, he anchored me. The more I thought about it, the more I realized that life without him in it wasn't the life I wanted. Unfortunately, I wasn't sure we could work out our differences in our life decisions.

If I had to choose between the gallery and Luke, something told me that Luke was the only choice for me. Still, I was very heartbroken to once again have to give up on my dream to be with someone I loved. It made me wonder why I couldn't have both the man I loved and the business my heart desired.

My drive to the house was short, and I arrived quicker than I thought I would. Janine was already waiting for me when I pulled into the driveway. I scolded myself for not paying attention on the drive in. Lost in my thoughts the whole way here, I missed out on seeing what the area brought.

I got out of my SUV as I took a good look at what was before me. The house was white and two stories high, and windows all around to capture the views. It appeared there were maybe ten houses in total on this street, which wasn't too many.

Janine greeted me as I walked onto the porch. "Hello Teresa! Welcome to 151 Heron Road. Are you ready to go inside?"

"Good morning, Janine. Thank you. Yes, let's go inside," I replied enthusiastically.

Following Janine inside, she pointed out all the features on the main floor. The kitchen was a space where I could see myself cooking meals for both families—Luke's and mine. There was plenty of space to put a long table where we could all gather and eat together.

As we toured the rooms upstairs, I worried about how much this house would cost. Everything appeared to have been recently remodeled and looked expensive. Though I had remembered seeing it was out of budget, I couldn't remember the price. Still, I didn't want to spoil it until after I had seen everything.

Janine took me out the back door onto the patio, where the pool was. There were two buildings just beyond the pool, one on either side. We walked through the guest house on the left first. It was a smaller house that would be great when either my kids or Luke's kids had a family of their own. They could stay there and have privacy.

Trying not to get my hopes up, I cautiously followed Janine across the patio, where I stood in front of a building with glass all the way around. She opened the door, and my breath caught as I took in the 360-degree view of a lifetime. This space would be perfect for me to sit and paint in front of the windows. Prior to this moment, I had never thought of having a home studio to work and teach in.

"Janine," I asked softly, "how much did you say this property was again?"

She shuffled through the papers she was holding before answering me. "It looks like the asking price is $2.25 million unless you purchase one of the two commercial spaces, then it is $1.75 million."

"What two commercial spaces are you referring to?" I asked to refresh my memory.

"The gallery or the office space next door to it," she replied.

"Oh, I said while looking down at my feet. Well, the gallery has already sold, so I lost out on that. How much was the office space next door?" I asked despite knowing I couldn't afford both.

"The office space is $1.25 million, but would need some work done to it," she answered.

Doing the math in my head, I knew it would be roughly $3 million for both spaces. There was no way I could do that, and even $2.25 million for just this house was outside of what I was comfortable with. It wouldn't leave much room for me to progress my business in the direction I had envisioned.

"Well, thank you, Janine. It really is lovely. I'll have to do some thinking and check my finances to see what wiggle room I've got. Can I think about it and get back to you in about a week?" I asked.

"Sure, take all the time you need. I don't believe any formal offers have been made on the place yet," she replied.

After getting back behind the wheel of my SUV, I took another glance at the house. This time, as I drove back towards the condo, I noticed the road was lined with legacy oak trees with Spanish moss hanging from the branches. There was also a channel behind the house with a dock that would be perfect for Luke's yacht. It really had everything we'd need.

When I parked my SUV back at the condo, I couldn't help but wonder if maybe Luke was right. There was no way I could afford the real estate here on my own. Everything was just way overpriced. Had I come a year or two prior, I likely could have gotten it at a much lower price point, with all the damage that occurred. But now that repairs and upgrades had been made, everything went up in price.

Unsure of what to do next, I sat out on the beach for a while with my sketchbook. As I was drawing, several sanderling birds found their way near the water's edge. This was their home, and what this island was named after. They had become my favorite birds on the island. As I sketched, I included them just as I had seen them.

Happy with my sketch, I closed my sketchbook and thought about what I should do now. The idea of moving back home surfaced, and I debated the pros and cons of staying or leaving. One huge con of going back home was that I no longer had a house there.

This island was starting to feel cursed, and I felt defeated. Tears filled my eyes as I continued to wrestle with what to do. Out of nowhere, a laughing gull sailed down right in front of me, landing right next to me. It gave off a sharp sound that mimicked laughter.

Startled, I took a closer look at it and noticed a tiny gray heart shape in the white space just above its wing. What an interesting thing to see on a bird! I had to capture it, and so I grabbed my sketchbook and began drawing as it stood in place, almost as if it wanted me to draw it.

"Well, you're such a pretty bird," I said to the laughing gull as I finished her portrait.

"Ha-ha-ha-ha-ha," it called before flapping its wings and flying away.

The sight of the bird in flight brought a smile to my face. There was something in how that interaction went that made me feel lighter, more hopeful even. I made my way back inside the condo to eat dinner and check in on my best friends.

I opened our group chat and sent a message.

Ladies, I need help. I lost the gallery space, and I'm hitting dead ends on finding a place to live. Do I stay and keep trying, or do I admit defeat and head back home to Ohio?

Beth Reed

What does your heart say to do?

My heart says it's confused.

Lynn Taylor

You have to stay and keep trying!

Beth Reed

I agree with Lynn. You've come this far,—you owe it to yourself to try to see it through.

I suppose you are both right. Thanks for reminding me.

Not really wanting a full meal, I grabbed a tub of ice cream from the freezer and ate the remains. If I stayed and kept trying, that meant I needed to work things out with Luke, too. I wondered if he would even be open to working things out with me. He seems pretty set in life and isn't dependent on the need for a partner.

Perhaps love could change things for us both. If we love each other, it is important for us to keep trying to make this relationship work. But the one thing I know is that love never lasts. My dad proved that to me when he left Mom.

No sooner had I thought about Dad leaving—it hit me. I realized I was no better than he was. I was mortified—and immediately felt remorse for running from Luke on Sunday night at the restaurant. At that moment, I had to get away from him because I was angry. But now that two days have passed, I have yet to reach out to him and apologize for my actions.

I picked up my phone and went through my photos of us over the last month. Tears fell down my face, emotions overtaking me. There was no denying how much I loved Luke, but I couldn't deny how poorly my actions showed him how much he meant to me.

Not able to go to sleep another night without trying to make things right, I picked up my phone and sent Luke text messages.

> I'm really sorry for leaving like I did. I was so angry. I was afraid that if I didn't get out of there, I would say something I regretted.

> It has only been a couple of days, and I still need some time to process everything. Let's connect soon, though, okay?

The screen showed my text had been delivered, and I sat and watched to see if he read it. When the screen didn't change to show he had, I turned the phone off and set it aside. There was no sense in staring at my phone, waiting for something to happen. Of course, even that didn't stop me from overthinking the situation.

What if it was too late? What if Luke couldn't forgive me for leaving like I did? I wouldn't blame him at all—it was wrong of me to treat him that poorly. Though I didn't know where to go from here, I knew that making it up to him was the only way forward.

THIRTY ONE

Lucas Miller

Having a routine that worked like a well-oiled machine was important to me. Admittedly, when I first arrived on the island earlier this month, I became too lax. It's no coincidence that in my lack of routine, I gained weight. This week, however, I had committed to getting back to working out three days a week again.

Because I skipped leg day with William on Monday, I doubled down on Wednesday weights. I arrived at the gym at dawn, just as the sun was casting its warm glow across the water. Few others were at the gym this early, so I got a parking spot under the shade of a loblolly pine tree to keep the convertible cool in the hot southern sun.

Not wanting to waste any time, I made my way over to the weights to begin the leg reps I skipped out on Monday. Determined to complete them before William and Jason arrived, I pushed myself as fast as I could. With the last leg rep complete, I moved into setup for arms.

Momentum was good as I began my first set. I was so lost in the moment that I didn't see William and Jason come in until they were standing right in front of me. I sat the dumbbells down as I greeted the men. "William! Jason! Good to see you both."

"Good morning, Luke," William said. "How are you holding up?"

"Minute by minute, I suppose. I feel horrible about hurting Tess the way I did. Pushing her away was the last thing I wanted to do," I replied.

"That's rough, man," Jason chimed in.

"Why do you think you pushed her away?" William asked.

"At first, I thought maybe she was overreacting. After a couple of days of thinking about it, I realized how judgmental I was. It wasn't my intention to come across that way, and I feel awful about it. I understand why she got mad and left," I explained.

Jason looked confused. "What were you judgmental about?"

Nervous, I ran my hand through my hair. My reputation is everything, and I didn't want to go too far into it with someone I barely knew. "It was more of an incorrect assumption without clarification. Not giving her the benefit of the doubt and trusting that she knows what she is doing," I answered vaguely.

William jumped in to rescue me, understanding my hesitation. "The good news is, you learned something valuable about yourself—and about Tess. Have you spoken to her since?"

"She texted me late last night, but I didn't see it until this morning. It's too early to text her. I don't want to wake her. I'll likely respond to her when I leave here," I answered.

"Sounds like you'll be able to clear it up, then," Jason quipped.

Having gotten the memo, I clapped Jason on his shoulder in understanding. "I suppose I will. Anything else we need to talk about before we get started?"

William had a guilty look on his face that made it too difficult to pass up. "William, what's on your mind?" I asked him curiously.

Red flushed across his face, something I have rarely seen happen. "Well, I'm sorta seeing someone. It's new, and it's also long-distance, which is proving difficult."

Both Jason and I looked directly at William, shocked. He had sworn off women for the past three years, proudly telling us he was happy being a lone wolf. I knew that whoever she was, she must be an incredible woman to earn his affection.

"Are you going to tell us more or leave us guessing? Who is she?" I asked William.

Hesitantly, he spoke, "She's funny, extremely thoughtful, and smart. Our conversations flow so naturally because she is on a similar intellectual level to me, and I really like that. Of course, she's gorgeous with dark hair and eyes, and she has a smile that lights up the room."

"Do I know her?" Jason asked William.

After thinking for a moment, a look of realization crossed his face. "I do believe you have met her. It's not likely that you know her though, but Luke, you do."

"She's someone I know? How do I know her?" I asked him.

"She's a good friend of Tess's. We met at the party you both hosted on the beach," William replied.

Thinking back to that night, I had deduced it could only have been one of two women. Both of them had brown hair and brown eyes. The only difference between the two of them was their age, which pointed me in the direction I think he was.

"William," I started, "are you telling me you are dating Lynn?"

"Oh, thank goodness," Jason chimed in. "I was worried you were going to say Louise there for a moment. She caught my attention, and I have been chatting with her."

William tilted his head back and laughed. "Louise is a bit too young for me, but she's the perfect age for you. Lynn is the girl I'm seeing."

"What are the odds of that? We should get her to come back and visit so the four of us can go out," I suggested.

William walked over and picked up a set of weights and began lifting them. "How about we get on with what we came to do and figure out the logistics later," he instructed.

We completed our workout in just under an hour. After packing up our sweaty towels and gear, we stood around in the foyer. Jason didn't stick around, waving goodbye to us as he bolted out the front door.

Alone with William, he cut right to the chase. "What are you going to do to fix things with Tess? Do you have any ideas at all?"

"I have some ideas. Did you confirm with the realtor about our meeting Friday morning?" I asked him.

"Yes, I confirmed with her yesterday. Are you ready to close on the gallery?" he probed.

"Something like that," I said as I clapped him on the back.

William looked intrigued. "Saving the details for Friday, I see. I can respect that. Before I head out, do you want to grab some breakfast?"

There was no way I was going to a restaurant without showering first. A double workout meant I was in no shape to be in public. "Can I get a rain check? There are a few things I need to take care of before our meeting on Friday."

"Sure. You smell pretty ripe anyway, but I didn't want to be rude," William said between bouts of laughter.

We said our goodbyes as we walked out to the parking lot. I sat down behind the wheel-and immediately understood what William was laughing about. The smell of sweat and body odor was so strong I had to put the top down.

Luckily, the drive back to the yacht wasn't far. The best part about this island is that it's only 13 miles long. Everything you need is close by, no matter where you are on the island.

Once I was back on the yacht, I took a shower and got dressed before heading to my desk. To make things right with Tess, I believe the first step would be to acknowledge her text from yesterday.

Good morning, beautiful. I hope you slept well last night. Thank you for telling me how you felt.

Please know that I am very sorry for hurting you. I would love the chance to make it up to you when you are ready.

Thank you for apologizing. That means a lot.

I promise I'll do better.

> You already are.

Though I was grateful she responded, it wasn't in the normal way she would text me. Picking up on her hurt, I didn't want to push too much with this first interaction and ended the text with one last thing:

> When you are ready, you know where to find me. Your cardigan is here, waiting with me.

Part of me was disappointed for not having told her what I really wanted to. Saying those three words out loud makes it real. Of course, saying them for the first time would land better in person instead of through a text. I believed this was a reason for not going there just yet.

For the first time in a very long time, I felt hopeful. There is no doubt in my mind about how strongly I feel about Tess. Losing her is not an option. And I know that to win her back, I will have to open my heart fully. And therein lies the challenge.

I opened my laptop and saw the photograph we took together the day I bought the yacht. Happiness was shown on both our faces, our smiles beaming. We really looked like we belonged together.

A new thought popped into my head. We really *do* belong together—and there was a way I could make sure that happened. The odds may be against us once more, but I may have just figured out a way to stack the deck in our favor.

THIRTY TWO

Teresa Wright

Our voices echoed across the gallery space now that it was almost completely empty. Eloise had thrown a farewell brunch to say goodbye to the space many artists had called home over the years. After a lot of consideration, I had agreed to speak at today's farewell brunch, but as myself, without mention of who I am as an artist. It just didn't quite feel like the right time to reveal everything.

My talk was brief, but filled with appreciation for all the hard work that Eloise did to keep the gallery going for as long as possible. I left the artists with one final thought, a reminder that just because these doors were closing, that didn't mean that the doors were closing on them and their work. It was my hope that all the artists would continue to create pieces that celebrate the rich culture and diversity here on Sanderling Pointe Island.

After saying our final goodbyes, it was down to just Eloise and me. I had promised to help her clean up and remove everything from the gallery space and take it to her storage unit. As I wiped down the tables, she was folding the chairs and leaning them against the wall.

Eloise was the first to speak as we worked quietly. "How have things been going? Have you had any luck finding other options for your gallery?"

Sadness overcame me as I replied. "No, not yet. The ones you sent my way turned out to be spaces that needed more work than the listing led on. I feel just awful that I couldn't get this building and help save the gallery for the community. It's going to be difficult to find another place as good as this one."

"What is meant to be will always find a way, dear. Have hope that you'll find the right place at the right time," Eloise said, with a hint of optimism I envied.

"I wish I were as optimistic as you are," I replied. "Right now everything is such a mess, I don't even know anymore if this is where I am supposed to be."

Eloise crossed the room to come closer to me. "Teresa, you are right where you are meant to be. If life were easy, we would miss out on the opportunities that present themselves during trials. What new opportunities have been presented to you since your arrival on the island?"

"Well, I met you, which gave me a new friend. And I also bumped into Luke after all these years. Which was something I had always hoped to do, despite having given up on the idea a long time ago. So I suppose there has been some good to come out of my time here," I said trying to convince myself.

"That's the spirit," Eloise exclaimed. "You have so much to be grateful for. How are things with you and Luke?"

"Not great, if I'm being honest," I replied remorsefully. "We had a moment where I got angry and ran away from him. Just like my dad ran away from my mom and me suddenly. Luke didn't deserve that. I feel awful about how I treated him."

Eloise thought for a moment before responding. "You aren't your dad, Teresa. You are your own person."

Her words were comforting and perfectly timed. "Thank you, Eloise, for that reminder. I often forget that I am my own person. Before now, I used to think that love wouldn't last. But lately, all I can think about is how love is worth fighting for when you are fighting for the right person."

"And do you want to fight for love, Teresa?" Eloise asked.

"Yes, I believe I do. Our relationship is worth fighting for," I answered.

Eloise and I carried everything out to our vehicles after she locked the gallery doors for the very last time. Tears filled both of our eyes as we hugged in front of the building. I drove behind her to the storage unit and helped her unload everything.

With the last box placed, we hugged once more and went our separate ways. As I sat behind the wheel of my SUV, I drove in silence as I considered how I would fight for my relationship with Luke.

The collection I had been painting was to be unveiled at the opening of my gallery and studio. But now that I don't have a place to do that, I wasn't sure when it would be unveiled. Something told me I should still complete the series as a new idea popped up for me to paint.

Once I was back at the condo, I pulled out my painting supplies and the last two canvases I had remaining. One of them was the smallest size, which always challenged me to come up with just the perfect thing to put on it. Remembering my time out on the beach the other day, I grabbed my sketchbook to look back at what I had drawn.

The laughing gull stood out to me the most, with that cute little gray heart it had in the middle of all those white feathers. Initially, I had wanted to paint the sanderling birds on this smaller canvas, but now I know the laughing gull is the perfect companion to the rest of the collection.

It didn't take long to finish the painting because of its small size. After setting it aside to dry, I loaded up my last canvas. For a moment, I faced a creativity block so fierce that I felt lost. The stark white canvas mocked me as I paced back and forth in front of it.

"Think, Tess, think," I said out loud.

This piece has to be special. It's the final piece of the collection and needs to tie it all together if possible. Looking out the patio doors to the ocean, I allowed my mind to wander. A memory I had forgotten about popped into my mind. It was so vivid, I could see it as if I were standing there today.

Not wanting to waste a moment, I grabbed my brush and palette and began painting the scene entirely from memory. Hours went by as I continued to pour every ounce of my heart and soul into this painting. With the final swish of the brush, I stepped back to admire my work.

Tears flooded my eyes, and a smile crept across my face. It was perfect. Looking at it took me right back to that moment in time all those years ago. A lone tear spilled out of my eye and rolled down my cheek. In that moment, I finally knew what the name of this collection should be—*A Lasting Love Without Reservations*.

After cleaning up my supplies, I carefully set the paintings in the closet to dry. Luke was heavy on my mind, so I texted him.

Just thinking of you today. I hope you had a productive day.

It was a productive day. I was just closing up for the evening. Have you had dinner yet?

No, not yet. I just finished my collection. All the pieces are finished. I'm glad they are done, but I am starving.

Would you like to go out for dinner, or would you like me to bring something over?

You know what I could go for right now? Pizza! If you are up for an evening here, I would love to spend some time with you and a couple slices.

Consider it done. I'll call and place our order now and be over as soon as it's ready. Do you want your usual?

Is there any other option?

> Fair enough. I'll see you soon.

> Thank you, Luke.

> You're welcome.

After ending our conversation, I cleaned up and changed out of my painting clothes. Butterflies swarmed in my stomach as I knew he would be close to being here by now. I wasn't sure why I was so nervous.

There was a soft knock on the door, and I practically ran to open it. "Hi!" I said a little too eagerly. "Thanks again for bringing dinner over. Please come on in."

Luke brought the boxes inside and sat them on the table. I gathered plates, silverware, and napkins while he grabbed drinks from the fridge. Luke opened the boxes to reveal that he had picked up all of my favorites.

We loaded our plates with pizza, breadsticks, and boneless barbecue wings. As I took a bite of pizza, I did a happy dance in my chair as sauce dripped from my slice and trailed down my chin. Luke reached over with his napkin to dab the sauce away, never taking his eyes off mine.

"It's so good to see you happy. Your pizza must be good," Luke teased.

I swallowed my bite and wiped my mouth before speaking. "This is the best pizza. I used to dream about it all the time. I can't believe we haven't had it very much since being back here. Do you remember when…"

"We would sit on the beach and eat this every day? How could I forget?" Luke finished my sentence.

The memory made me laugh. "You would get so mad when sand would get in the pizza, which was practically all the time since we ate sitting on a beach towel."

Luke held up a slice for me to see. "At least now we are smarter and eating indoors. See, no sand. The pizza is so much better without it."

We both laughed effortlessly. Even though we had spent some time apart, coming back together tonight—it was as if there had been no change between us. That was always my favorite thing about the two of us. Months would pass before we'd see each other again. But the moment we were together again, it was as if all time stood still and we were the only two in the world.

Luke's brown eyes sparkled when he laughed. Pure joy and happiness radiated from him. It looked like he hadn't shaved for a few days because his once clean-shaven face was now filled with stubble that had grown in. I think I preferred this version of Luke. He seemed more relaxed than usual.

Caught in the act of staring, Luke looked at me with both eyebrows raised. "What's going on in that mind of yours, Tess?"

"I've missed you, Luke. I'm so sorry for leaving things the way I did," I said with sincerity.

Luke leaned in closer. "I'm sorry, too. It was wrong of me to judge you the way I did. Had I known that was the location you wanted, I never would have bid on it."

Unable to control my impulses, I grabbed his face with my hands and pressed my lips against his. We shared a kiss filled with longing and love. It was one that spoke louder than either of us could have. All those lost moments and difficult times faded away as they nestled in between new memories we've made together. In it, we found each other once more. And for the first time in my life, I couldn't wait to see what our lasting love would bring us.

When our kiss ended, I rested my forehead against his. Nose to nose, I simply whispered, "I love you."

Luke placed his hand on my chin and lifted my mouth to his once more. When we finished our kiss, we pulled apart and looked at each other. I was nervous about Luke's feelings about my declaration.

A smile broke across his face. "I love you too, Tess."

My heart soared. Knowing he felt the same was all I needed to know—whatever came next would be okay. Even if I couldn't show him my new collection in the gallery space, I knew that someday I would be able to present him with the pieces he inspired me to create.

Luke is the only man who has ever shown me that love could be lasting. My love for him had never left me for a single moment since we last saw each other 26 years ago. Though the odds of us getting a second chance at love were against us, together, we beat them.

THIRTY THREE

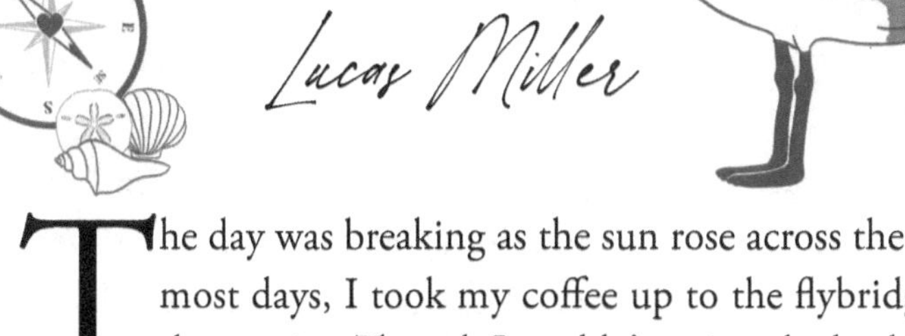

Lucas Miller

The day was breaking as the sun rose across the water. Like most days, I took my coffee up to the flybridge to watch the sunrise. Though I couldn't wait to be back in a house, I really enjoyed spending time on the water. It forced me to slow down more and pay attention to things I otherwise would have missed.

As I polished off the cup of coffee in my hand, my friend, the laughing gull, landed on its usual perch next to me. Interestingly enough, this time she was silent.

"You know, Sandy, life's short. I need to stop being so serious all the time and start allowing for some more spontaneity in my life."

In the silence, I allowed my mind to wander as I stared out across the water. I'd been waiting for my big ah-ha moment to arrive for a few days now. Every idea I had seemed like it wasn't big enough to make things right with Tess. There has to be something I am missing.

My thoughts went back to last night, when Tess told me she loved me. It felt incredible to hear her say that to me. I had been so hesitant to tell her how I felt. Somehow, her telling me first made it easier for me to reciprocate. I've only ever loved two women in my life. Lisa and Tess.

When I first arrived on the island, I wasn't sure if I would be able to move forward from Lisa. It felt like an impossible feat to open myself up to the possibility of love again. When you lose your spouse, your entire world turns upside down. There is an enormous void that occurs in the wake of their absence that seems impossible to fill.

With Lisa gone, I was left to pick up the pieces of all our broken hearts. The kids were my priority, and ensuring they were okay was the driving force behind all my decisions. Eventually, we all reached a point where we began living life again, and I felt it was time for me to make a change.

Initially, coming to Sanderling Pointe was going to be an extended vacation. Though I had given our home to Emily, I had originally planned on getting a condo back home and downsizing. The only problem with that plan was that there wouldn't be enough room for us all to gather over the holidays, and Emily would need to host at the house.

Knowing she wouldn't like that, I had to come up with a different plan. William had been trying to get me to move here for the last year. He finally convinced me to come for an extended visit and give it a shot. Who knew I would end up moving here?

The first day back on the island is one for the books. I'll never forget the way Tess looked after I ushered her friends out the door. She was the last person I expected to see.

With Tess back in my life again, I could feel myself losing control of my feelings. It wasn't until I let go of the need to control them and allowed things to happen naturally that I saw how much

I needed Tess in my life. If I were going to live on this island, I only wanted to do it with her by my side.

The question was…how? How do I pull off this insurmountable feat? Suddenly, it hit me. The idea I had been praying for was so clear, I knew exactly what needed to be done.

I glanced at my watch and realized that if I didn't leave now, I would be late for my meeting with William and our realtors. My sudden movement startled Sandy, and she flew off with a cry.

With my briefcase in hand, I rushed off the yacht and to the convertible as quickly as I could. Because I was running behind, I didn't have the extra time needed to put the top down. I drove faster than I should have to get to the office on time.

After putting the car in park and shutting it off, I grabbed my briefcase and headed in, where I greeted the receptionist. "Hello, Lucas Miller here for closing with William Jones."

"Welcome, Mr. Miller, please follow me," she replied as she stood.

I followed her to a small conference room where both Sheila and William were waiting for me. Though I had made it here quickly, I had arrived ten minutes late.

"It's about time you showed up," William teased. "I was worried you had changed your mind."

"Hello, Luke, I'm Jack, Williams' realtor. Please have a seat," he instructed as he stood to greet me.

Once we were all seated, Jack pulled out the documents for me to sign. "Jack, please hold off on that for a moment. I have something I wanted to say."

William groaned loudly. "I know that look all too well. Spill it, Luke."

Because William and I had been friends for so long, it was difficult to hide things from each other. He knew me better than anyone else. I shouldn't have been surprised when he could tell that I had changed my mind.

"Let me get right down to it," I began. "I no longer want the gallery space. You should give it to the other bidder at their first offer price. It wasn't fair of me to draw up the bids like I did."

Sheila cut in, "Luke, that's common in sales of this nature. You didn't do anything wrong, and you won the space fair and square."

"With a change in revenue like this, I will need time to discuss with my client," Jack stated.

"Before we get to that point, I believe I have come up with a way that will help everyone," I replied cautiously. "What I would like to do is purchase both the house and the second space next to the gallery for my offices. I would like to offer $3.5 million for both."

William let out a loud breath. "Luke, that is over the asking price. Are you sure?"

"Yes, I'm sure. It is coming in at what the asking for the house would have been on its own and the asking price for the commercial space. It should also get you your asking price for the gallery space with the other bidder. You will get everything you need out of this deal."

"William, do you accept Luke's offer?" Sheila asked.

William seemed to consider it for a moment before the realization sank in. "Yes, I accept Luke's offer. Jack, do you have the contact information for the other bidder on the gallery?"

Jack flipped through his manila folder. "Yes, I have the realtor's information here along with the initial bid."

"Great, let's draft up the new paperwork and get the house and the office space signed over to Luke, and then when we are done with that, you can reach out to them," William instructed.

Over the next hour, I signed the paperwork for both the house and the office space. Because they were both unoccupied, William handed the keys to me after everything was finalized.

"Welcome to Sanderling Pointe Island—officially," William said as he reached his hand out to shake mine. "I'm really glad you are moving here."

"Thanks, man, I'm glad too," I replied.

"Do you want to go and celebrate?" William offered.

"Not yet, there's still more for me to do," I replied as I gathered everything into my briefcase.

"I completely understand. When everything settles down, let's get together to celebrate," William said.

"You got it! I'll be in touch," I yelled over my shoulder as I rushed out the door to my car.

As I drove to Tess's condo, every red light threatened to slow me down. My impatience grew as I begged the lights to change to green so I could be back on my way. I had never noticed there were so many traffic lights on the island before.

All I could do was hope she would be there when I arrived and that I would get there before the call came in. I wanted to see the look on her face when they told her the gallery was hers.

This outcome was one I should have thought of sooner. It's a way for both of us to stay on the island, and Tess can fulfill her dream. With Tess in the gallery, my office would be next door to her studio. Having her next door during the day gave me something to look forward to.

Finally, I reached her condo and parked my car. As I got out of the car, a moment of panic hit me. What if it was too late? We didn't talk about it yesterday, and I did not know if she had found another place. This could have been a bit presumptuous of me.

"What are the odds she has already found another location?" I wondered aloud.

A quick calculation told me the odds were infinitesimal. So small, there was no way she would have had time to lock in another location. It was likely that I was overthinking it.

Not wanting to waste another minute, I walked up to her door, where I saw her suitcases standing outside. She didn't tell me she was leaving, yet it appeared she was moving out. Needing to get to her before it was too late, I threw the door open and ran inside to find her.

THIRTY FOUR

My month in the condo had come to an end, and I needed to make sure I had everything before locking up. After putting my last suitcase by the front door, I went back inside to do a final walk through. Despite not using every drawer, I still opened them all to make sure I hadn't put something in them and forgotten about it.

I was going to miss this place. There were so many great memories made in this condo that it felt like home to me. After one last glance at the bedroom, I turned and walked down the hall towards the front of the condo when I almost ran into Luke.

"I have to talk to you," Luke exclaimed excitedly.

Surprised to see him, I tried to stop him. "Luke, we have to…"

"Wait, before you say anything, please let me say something," Luke interrupted me. "Yesterday, we briefly touched on this, but I really am sorry for everything I did. For not taking your work seriously, for getting upset with how messy you sometimes are, and for not fighting for you when I should have."

My phone rang, and a quick glance showed me it was Janine. "It's my realtor." I said to Luke.

"Answer it," he said.

"Hello," I answered.

"Teresa, it's Janine. I have some good news for you. Do you have a moment?" she asked.

"Sure, what's the good news?" I asked curiously.

"The gallery is yours. The other bidder backed out of the space, and the seller is offering it to you at your original bid price. Do you still want it?" Janine explained.

Tears fell down my face as I looked up at Luke. "Thank you, Janine, yes. I do still want it."

"Great! Can you meet me at their office to complete everything this afternoon?" Janine asked.

"Yes, I can do that. Can you please text me the address? I am in the middle of moving out of the condo and don't have anything to write with at the moment," I asked her.

"Consider it done. I'll text you the details next. See you this afternoon," Janine replied before hanging up.

After I hung up the phone, I threw my arms around Luke's neck and hugged him. "Thank you, Luke, I can't believe you…"

Luke leaned in and kissed me in response. There was a hint of passion and longing behind the kiss I hadn't felt before. A shift had occurred between us, and its electricity could be felt.

The sound of someone clearing their throat interrupted us. I pulled away from Luke and saw the cleaning crew had arrived. "I'm so sorry. We are heading out now," I apologized to them as I grabbed Luke's hand, pulling him out the front door.

Flustered, I walked right past my suitcase as I pulled Luke out to the parking lot. When we got to the car, he held up my forgotten suitcase and smiled. "You may need this," he said with a big grin.

We both burst into laughter like we were teenagers who had just gotten caught by their parents doing something they shouldn't be doing. I was laughing so hard I doubled over while holding my stomach as tears streamed down my face. It felt so good to laugh this hard.

Once we calmed down, Luke was the first one to speak. "Where are you moving to?"

"Actually, I'm not sure. I was hoping I could get into a hotel for a few nights even without reservations," I answered him.

"Don't bother. You can stay with me on the yacht for a few days while we work together on furnishing our new home," he said confidently.

Unsure if I had just heard him correctly, I had to ask, "Oh, *our* new home?"

Luke smiled as he replied, "Yes! I bought a house today that will be perfect for us. There is even a space for you to set up a home studio to your liking. I promise I won't even go near it so you can be as messy as you need to be. Do you want to see it?"

"Yes! Do you want me to ride along with you or follow you there?" I asked while motioning towards my SUV.

"You can follow me. It's not too far from here and is on the way to the marina," he answered while putting my suitcase in my trunk.

Once I was alone behind the wheel of my SUV, I took a moment to regroup. The way I felt was surreal, as if I were dreaming. Not wanting to be left behind, I followed Luke out of the lot and down the street. When he turned onto Heron Road, the butterflies in my stomach grew.

He turned into the driveway and parked. I followed suit and parked behind him. After I got out of my SUV, I joined him in front of the house and looked up at the front porch.

"Tess, welcome home to…" Luke began.

"151 Heron Road," I whispered.

Luke turned to me with a puzzled look on his face. "How did you know the address?" he asked.

More tears fell down my face as I stood staring at the house in disbelief. "Because I was just here earlier this week. After not being able to get the gallery, I started expanding my search to different homes with room for a home studio. This is the one I wanted, but it was just too far out of my budget."

We walked up the stairs and to the front door, where Luke unlocked it and opened it for us to enter. Once inside, we went to the kitchen and stood looking out the patio doors at the water. The view from the kitchen was breathtaking. But then again, the view from anywhere within the house was gorgeous.

"Do you want to explore it a bit more now that it's all ours?" Luke asked, as if reading my mind.

"Yes, I have been dying to get back inside here since I walked through it the first time," I answered.

Together we walked through the entire house and talked about our plans for each room, which child we would assign to which space. It felt incredible to be making long-term plans with Luke as we discussed ways to combine our families together for the holidays.

After our tour of the main house, we went out back to the guest house. It was a little dated and would need to be upgraded, but mostly everything was move-in ready. As we were standing inside the guest house, Luke's phone rang.

"It's Emily," he said.

"Answer it," I replied.

Luke answered the phone on speaker, "Hey Emily, you're on speaker and I've got Tess here with me."

"Hi Dad, hi Tess," Emily said. "I'm glad I was able to catch both of you. I have something I wanted to share with you."

"Oh," Luke replied, "what's that?"

"I'm pregnant! You're going to be a grandpa!" Emily cooed.

With congratulations excitedly given, Luke hung up the phone and turned to me. "Looks like getting this house was perfect timing," he said, motioning to the living room of the guest house.

"It will be perfect for Emily's growing family when they come to visit. They can stay here and keep a crib for the baby so they don't have to travel with one each time," I offered.

We walked back outside and locked up the guest house before making our way over to the second building. Excitement bubbled up inside me to have a space dedicated to creativity without bounds. Luke opened the door and motioned for me to step inside ahead of him.

"Your studio awaits," he said softly.

We walked to the middle of the space and stood looking out the windows as the sun sparkled across the water. Luke stepped in behind me and wrapped his arms around me, pulling me closer to him.

"I think we'll be very happy here, don't you?" he asked.

"Yes, very," I agreed, with tears threatening to form.

"I know this feels like a lot all at once," Luke started. "We can take our time moving in here together. I can stay on the yacht just out there on the dock, and you can sleep in the main house."

Luke had said once before how difficult it was to move on after losing Lisa. I didn't want to push him too fast into anything either. "We don't have to rush anything. I want you to be comfortable. But I think we could get you set up in the guest house and off that boat if you'd prefer."

Luke thought for a while before responding. "That's actually a great idea. I could work on the upgrades while staying in it. As much as I enjoy being on the yacht, I could really use a good night's sleep in a normal bed. It's been a month since I've been able to do that."

We stood in the space for a moment longer to allow ourselves the chance to make plans. Satisfied with the direction we had agreed to, we unloaded my SUV of most of its contents. I placed all the boxes of art supplies and wrapped paintings into the studio space and some of my belongings in the foyer of the main house.

We removed the remaining suitcases from the trunk of my SUV and placed them into the trunk of the convertible. Though temporary, I looked forward to spending time with Luke on his yacht for a few days.

My phone chimed, indicating a text had come in from Janine.

Shared a pin

This is the location where we will meet to finalize everything for the gallery. Can you come within the next thirty minutes?

Yes, I will get ready to head that way shortly. Thank you again.

See you soon.

"Luke, I need to head out to close on the gallery space. Do you want me to meet you back here or at the marina?" I asked.

"You can meet me at the marina. I'll take your luggage over now and set it up in one of the rooms down below for you," he answered.

"Sounds great, I'll see you again soon," I said, with a quick peck to his cheek.

The drive to the realtor's office was quick because every light was green. It felt like it was my lucky day today. The closing took about an hour to sign all the paperwork.

Afterward, William walked over to me. "Welcome to Sanderling Pointe Island. Congratulations on the gallery. I cannot wait to see what you do with it."

"Thanks, William," I said. "I'm looking forward to carrying on the tradition of having a dedicated space for local artists."

"They will be glad to hear it," William remarked.

After saying my goodbyes, I walked out to the lobby, where a familiar face was sitting and waiting. "Lynn? Is that you?" I asked, a bit puzzled.

Startled, Lynn blushed as she faced me. "Tess! I didn't know you'd be here. How are you?" she asked as she leaned in for a hug.

"I'm fine. What are you doing here?" I asked her, confused.

"Lynn, we are good to go…" William stopped mid-sentence as he saw the two of us standing there.

I looked at Lynn and then at William and back to Lynn again. "Wait, are you two…?"

Lynn nodded with a grin on her face. "Yes, we are. I am only here for a couple of days to spend with William. I meant to tell you, but I knew it would be a quick trip and you were busy."

"You don't have to explain anything to me. I'm happy for the two of you. I'll leave you to it, but Lynn, please call me after your trip," I instructed her.

As I walked out to my SUV, I felt lighter, happier even. It appeared things had worked themselves out in ways I never expected. Lynn and William were an added surprise I didn't see coming. I honestly don't know how it could get any better than this.

SIX MONTHS LATER

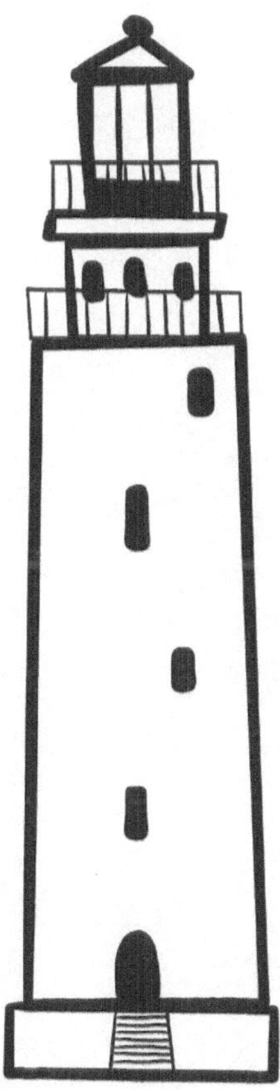

THIRTY FIVE

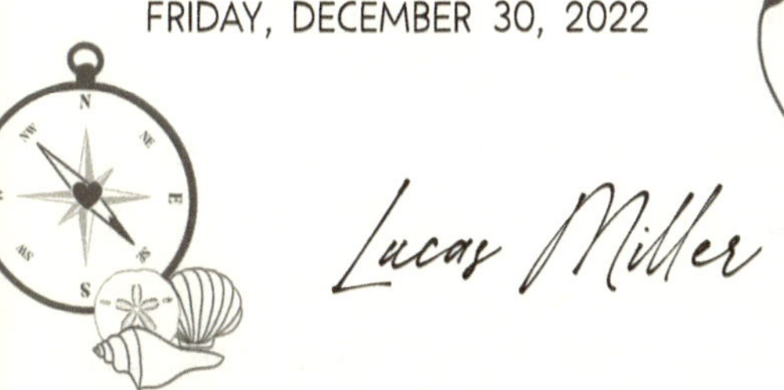

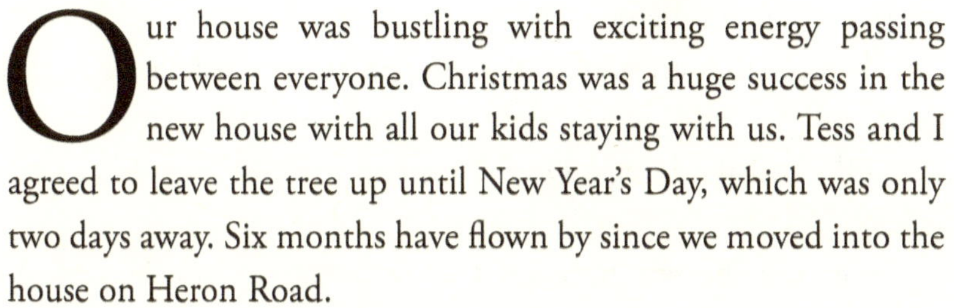

Lucas Miller

Our house was bustling with exciting energy passing between everyone. Christmas was a huge success in the new house with all our kids staying with us. Tess and I agreed to leave the tree up until New Year's Day, which was only two days away. Six months have flown by since we moved into the house on Heron Road.

The guest house upgrades were completed just in time for Emily and Brandon to stay in it. Even with the extra guests in the house, I could stay in one of the spare bedrooms. Admittedly, I was getting more comfortable around Tess, and as our relationship progressed, the idea of sharing a bed with her no longer frightened me.

I was finally reaching a place where I felt comfortable enough to enter this new chapter. I was grateful she agreed to go at my pace of comfort within our relationship. It was important to me that whatever I did, it honored the memory of my relationship with Lisa.

As I walked into the kitchen, the smell of freshly baked cinnamon rolls greeted me, along with the chatter among my kids. My day today was hectic with a tight schedule, and if I was going to get everything done, I would need to hit the road. To keep up my charade, I grabbed a cinnamon roll wrapped in foil as I reached Tess to say goodbye.

"I am going to head out now. I'll be back later this evening," I said to Tess with a quick peck on the cheek.

"Wait, do you have the list of things I need?" Tess asked.

I patted my shirt pocket with my free hand. "I have it right here."

"After you get everything on the list from the store, don't forget to pick up the flowers," she reminded me.

"I've got that on the list, too," I said as I inched closer to the door.

"Oh, and the linens! Don't forget the linens!" she exclaimed loudly.

Noticing she was nervous, I knew I had to ease her mind. "Tess, I promise I have it all under control. I have your list right here in my pocket with all the instructions. I'll get it all taken care of."

She relaxed a little as she softened toward me. "I just need everything to be perfect for tomorrow."

"I've got you, but I have to get going," I said with another quick peck on her cheek.

"Wait! What about…" Tess interjected once more before being cut off by the ringing of my phone.

"I really need to take this. It's my contractor. I promise, Tess, I've got this under control," I said as I walked out the front door.

After a quick call with my contractor, I learned that the renovations on my offices would be fully finished in one week. Finally, no more working out of my house. When I started the car, I saw I was already late for my first appointment. Setting the wrapped cinnamon roll on the front seat, I buckled in and headed to Sunny Side Up, where Tess's boys were waiting for me.

The lot was already full when I arrived, which made finding a spot to park tricky. Once I found one and parked, I rushed out of my car to the front of the restaurant where the boys were waiting.

"Aiden, Logan, thanks for meeting me here," I said, with a quick nod to both boys.

"We should be up next," Aiden said.

"Brown, party of three. Brown, party of three," the hostess called.

"That's us," Logan said to the hostess.

"Right this way, please," she said as she led the way to our table.

Once we were seated, we placed our order right away. Though I was certain the boys both had cinnamon rolls before they left the house, I knew they would still eat a full breakfast.

"Do you think Mom is ready for her big day tomorrow?" Logan asked me.

"Yeah, I think she's getting there. She's a bit stressed out, making sure everything is ready to go. But I think once she's in there, she'll relax a bit more," I answered.

"I'm really happy for her," Aiden said. "This has been her dream for a while now. It's great to see her go after what she wants."

"Speaking of that," I said hesitantly, "I know she's really happy that both of you are here to celebrate with her. She means so much to me, and I know she means the world to both of you. That is why I would like your blessing to marry her."

Logan grinned from ear to ear. "Yes! You have my blessing for sure. She is totally herself when she's around you, and I didn't know if I would ever get to see that side of her again."

Aiden looked unsure. "Will you actually have a wedding?"

I understood his hesitation, especially with Tess's history with their father. "Yes, I'd like to think we would have a wedding. Perhaps in June."

Aiden sat up straighter and smiled. "Then, in that case, yes. You have my blessing too."

Relief filled me now that I had both of their blessings. "Thank you, both of you. Please keep this under wraps. My plan is to surprise her tomorrow evening. After breakfast, you are supposed to pick up the suits for all the guys at the shop. They are in my name and already paid for. You can take those back to the house and help her set up the rest of the day."

"Looking forward to it all," Logan said.

We finished our breakfast and, after paying the bill, I walked down the street to The Black Pearl jewelry store to pick up Tess's ring. It was a three-stone emerald-cut ring. The two diamonds on the outside were each one carat, with a three-carat stone in the center.

As I was looking at the ring closer to inspect it, the shop door opened and I heard a group of women laughing as they came in. Too lost in my close inspection, I didn't notice who the women were until it was too late.

"Luke! What do you have there?" Lynn exclaimed loudly.

"Is that what I think it is?" Louise chimed in.

I quickly put the ring in the box and closed the lid. "Ladies, good to see you. Nothing to see here, just a small gift for Tess on her big day tomorrow."

"That looked like more than a small gift," Beth pointed out with a smile.

As I debated whether to tell them, I noticed there was someone new in the group. "Hi, I'm Luke. I don't believe we've met." I said as I extended my hand to the newcomer.

"Oh, hi Luke. I'm Melissa. I'm Tess's cousin," Melissa said as she shook my hand back.

"Nice try, Luke. Now that you know us all, it's time to show us what you're hiding," Lynn demanded.

Nervous, I ran my hand through my hair and decided it would be best to come clean. "Fine, ladies, you caught me in the act. If I show you, you all must promise not to spoil my surprise. I've almost nearly pulled this off, and I can't have it ruined."

"I promise!" said Beth.

"Me too!" said Lynn.

"Sure," said Melissa.

"Of course," said Louise.

"Now show us already!" Lynn exclaimed.

Slowly, I opened the box to reveal the ring nestled inside. "I chose a three-stone ring to show the merging of our two families into one. The smaller stones on the outside each represent our families individually, with the larger stone in the middle representing us all coming together. I plan on proposing tomorrow night."

A resounding series of "awwwwwwww" flooded my ears as each of the women gushed over the ring. I must've gotten it right. Each of them took the time to share in their excitement and asked me if I needed any help, to which I assured them I had this all under control.

With the ring picked up and safe in my pocket, I headed to the Driftwood Deli and Grocery to pick up everything on the list Tess requested. There was so much on the list, it took me several hours to get through it all. With the car full, I picked up the linens before heading back to the house.

I went over the list Tess had given me to ensure I didn't miss anything when I saw the florals were scheduled for pickup tomorrow morning. Everything else was accounted for, so I could finally head back home.

When I arrived home, I carried in as much as I could before yelling out for some help. "Hey guys, I'm home. Can anyone give me a hand unloading the car?"

Jacob, Aiden, Logan, and Brandon all came to my rescue and helped unload the car quickly. They were moving faster than I was, but with the last bag brought in, I put all the food in the extra refrigerator to keep cold until tomorrow.

By the time I had finished, I could hear laughter coming from the living room. Curious, I walked over and stood in the doorway, watching everyone interact. They were in the middle of playing a new game together. I leaned against the wall and watched as they played, taking it all in.

Tess came up next to me and linked her arm through mine. "It's so beautiful seeing them together like this, isn't it?"

"Hi, you," I said as I leaned down and kissed her forehead. "It sure is beautiful. How was your day?"

"Oh, you know, crazy busy," she said as she yawned. "It's been a really long day. It's almost dinner time, and I haven't even started cooking."

"How about we order pizza and have them deliver it tonight?" I suggested.

"Great idea. That gives me more time to put the finishing touches on the signs. They are currently drying out in the studio, but need another element added," she replied.

After Tess headed back out to her studio, I placed the order for dinner and then headed up to my room to put the ring in a safe place. When I pulled it out of my pocket, I couldn't help but open the box again to look at the ring.

We spoke briefly about getting married someday, but not wanting to give away my plans, I always downplayed the discussion. Now that the time had come, uncertainty made its way in again. *Am I making the right choice by proposing now? Will she even say yes?*

Normally, I would allow these types of questions to cause panic within me, but instead, all I felt was peace. That's how I knew I had made the right decision and that this was the right time. Tess fills my world with a joy that floods my heart.

The peace I am feeling now comes from knowing that God has brought me to this moment for a good reason. Even when I turned my back on Him, He never left me. He answered my prayer and gave me this second chance at love. Though I am far from perfect and still mess up, I am confident that I am right where I am supposed to be. That alone gives me great hope for the future Tess and I will create together.

THIRTY SIX

My heart pounded loudly in my ears as I stood alone in the exhibit room, looking at my collection. In about 15 minutes, my family and closest friends would come in for a mini-reveal before I opened the doors of the gallery to the public for the first time.

Holding on to the secret of who I am as an artist has been extremely difficult. After tonight, it will all be out in the open—no more secrets or hiding behind a name. Now was the time.

Honestly, I don't know why I wanted to reveal that I was the one behind the art. It has been extremely successful without my identity being known. I suppose I just reached a point where I was ready to accept every facet of who I am as an individual and celebrate all that I have accomplished.

Nervous energy flooded my body as I looked across the paintings. This collection was so different from my other pieces. Nobody has seen any of these paintings—not even Lucas. I've kept them covered over the last six months, and now, here they are on display for everyone to see. What if they don't like them?

My phone chimed, and as I looked at it, I realized I was running behind. They were all likely standing at the front door waiting for me to open up the gallery. After shutting the door to the exhibit room, I rushed up to the front of the building, where I saw the smiling faces of those who love me most.

I unlocked the front door and ushered everyone inside. "Welcome everyone. Thank you for coming, please right this way. I'd like to say something before we begin the tour," I said with a crack in my voice.

Everyone followed me to the middle of the gallery, where we stood with art from local artists all around us and a long row of tables set before us with food and drinks as we welcomed in the new year.

Luke cleared his throat loudly. "Can I say something first, Tess? Please?"

Nodding, I stepped to the side to allow Luke to speak first. His thoughtfulness warmed my heart and eased my nerves.

Luke grabbed my hands and pulled me closer to him. My heart began to beat faster as all eyes were now on both of us. "I just wanted to say you amaze me, Tess. Your hard work and dedication to the arts are inspiring not only to the community but to me as well. Thank you for sharing this space with all of us and all those who are yet to come. Congratulations on the opening of your gallery."

Tears filled my eyes, causing me to blink them away quickly. "Thank you, Luke. I am so honored to have you by my side today as I unveil my newest collection. But before we get into that, please grab something to drink and fix a plate to nibble as you take in the art throughout the main gallery space. I just ask that you keep to the open areas only, the rest will be revealed soon."

As everyone did as I instructed, I turned to Luke to thank him for saving me by speaking first. "Thanks for speaking first. I was so nervous I didn't know if I'd be able to talk. You really helped me there."

Luke squeezed my hands. "You're very welcome. I've got one more thing I wanted to share, but felt it was best to do so when it was just the two of us."

"Well, it looks like everyone has begun to wander around the space, so now is as good a time as any. What's up?" I asked curiously.

Luke turned to face me before starting. "Tess, you stole my heart the moment you threw a football in a perfect spiral to my brother, Daniel. When I lost you, I thought I had lost my whole world. But, as fate would have it, here we are being given a second chance to get it right this time." Luke kneeled down on one knee before continuing, "I have loved you for most of my life, and I hope to continue to love you till the end of it. Teresa Rosa Wright, will you marry me?"

Shocked, I smiled and cried as I happily announced, "Yes, absolutely I will marry you, Lucas Benjamin Miller!"

Luke stood up and kissed me, which led to an eruption of cheers throughout the gallery.

With everyone back in the same space again, it seemed now was as good a time as any. "Before we celebrate, I would love to share with you all my newest collection—*A Lasting Love Without Reservations*. Please follow me to the exhibit room."

Slowly, I opened the door to allow everyone inside to view the collection. There wasn't a dry eye in the room as they all looked at each painting, a moment in time captured through paint.

Luke turned to me with tears in his eyes. "I cannot believe you have done all of this. Here's one of the yacht, and another of all four of our kids sitting at the helm. I can tell it's them because their hair and the way they are sitting is just like that day."

I reached out and grabbed Luke's hand and squeezed it. "Come with me. I want to show you the final two pieces in the collection."

We turned the corner where we faced the last two canvases. I watched as Luke pulled his hand to his mouth in surprise. "I know this bird! That's Sandy! I would recognize her anywhere with that gray heart in her white feathers. But the big painting is...wow. Tess. It is us when we were younger, sitting on the beach wrapped up in a blanket as the sun is setting. I remember that night as if it were yesterday."

"It was the night you first told me you loved me and promised me you'd marry me someday," I said. "It feels like a lifetime ago, but it is a night I'll always remember. You kept your promise."

Luke leaned in to get a closer look at the painting and pointed at the name in the lower right-hand corner. "Wait a minute. Are you *THE* T. Bianchi? Everyone talks about the mysterious person behind the name."

The entire room flooded to where we stood, as we now had their attention again. "Yes, it's true. I am T. Bianchi. Only a few people knew it was me because of the name, but now I am ready to tell others."

We all made our way back out to the main gallery space, where we filled our glasses to prepare for the countdown to midnight. After the glasses had been poured, Luke clinked his glass to get everyone's attention again.

"I'd love to propose a toast before we ring in the New Year. To T. Bianchi, we love and know her as Teresa Wright. May your gallery be just the beginning of all your dreams coming true."

After the toast, I began the countdown. "10, 9, 8, 7, 6, 5, 4, 3, 2, 1—Happy New Year, everyone!"

Luke pulled me closer to him to welcome in 2023 with a kiss that meant so much more now. Life with him by my side was something I had dreamed about—and for the first time, I was excited to plan my wedding.

As the party ended, Luke and the kids helped me clean up the gallery. Watching everyone work together brought joy to my heart. I whispered, "Thank you, Lord," as I felt immense gratitude for everything I had.

For the longest time, I didn't believe that love could be lasting because not everyone was faithful and stayed with their spouses. With help from Beth, I realized I needed to forgive my dad and let go of the past. It was hard to believe that I was now just a little older than he had been when he left. This realization put things into perspective for me and helped me let go.

Everyone makes mistakes, but our mistakes don't define who we are for the rest of our lives. We have the power to learn and grow from them with a promise to do better. One thing I learned this summer was that life is short, and forgiveness is freeing.

Now that my secret was out in the open and I had forgiven my father, I felt like a huge weight had been lifted from my shoulders. As 2022 came to an end, with it went all those things I had carried for so many years.

The promise of a new year gave me so much hope and excitement to look forward to. There was only one thing left to do...set the wedding date.

EPILOGUE

SIX MONTHS LATER
SATURDAY, JUNE 3, 2023

Teresa Wright

Cars were honking as they drove past me. My guess is that I was a sight for sore eyes. Standing in the middle of the sidewalk with Melissa's arms up under my dress, literally sewing me in it right before I walk down the aisle. It wasn't her fault, though. The dress she designed for me was perfect in every way imaginable.

The problem happened when I got out of the car. I broke a seam, and it caused the train to come toppling down onto the ground. Despite the slight delay, I was still very happy. It was our wedding day, and it couldn't be more perfect.

Louise was my wedding director and handled putting together everything, including the decorations. Between my two cousins, I felt the two of them should go into business doing this for others. With both of them standing here with me, I decided to tell them as much.

"You know, Melissa, you really should go into business designing wedding dresses. You are amazing at it. And, Louise, you should go into business as a creative director for weddings because you knocked it out of the park!"

"Mom would never let me do that," Melissa said sadly. "Though I am considering a change."

"This is something I have wanted to do for a long time. I have been saving up money for the last few years to start my business," Louise said. "Maybe someday."

"Well, I could see you both in the wedding industry and working together. You'd be incredible!" I told them both.

"Mom, are you ready yet?" Logan asked as he and Aiden appeared to walk me down the aisle.

"You're all set," Melissa said as she lowered my dress and stepped back.

"Looks like I am," I said to Logan. "Are you boys ready to walk me down the aisle to Luke?"

Louise and Melissa went ahead of us to start the ceremony. The music grew louder as we approached the entrance to the beach. With Logan on my left and Aiden on my right, the three of us kicked off our shoes at the end of the boardwalk before walking barefoot in the sand down to the water's edge where Luke was waiting.

Beth's husband, David Reed, was our officiant. Getting right to it, he started as soon as we were in place. "Dearly beloved, we are gathered here today, in the sight of God and in the presence of family and friends to join Lucas and Teresa in holy matrimony, without reservations."

Everyone chuckled at the irony of the last part of the opening remarks. The rest of the wedding was beautiful and went off without a hitch. Afterwards, we all went to The Drunken Pirate, where we had reserved the game room for our reception.

Luke and I picked this as our location more for nostalgia than elegance. We knew it would likely be difficult to make it look like a wedding reception since it was a family restaurant. But Louise far surpassed all our expectations and decorated the room in a way that made it feel like an elegant wedding reception.

We all ate our meals and endured the toasts that seemed to go on forever. After that, it was time for us to have our first dance. We took to the makeshift dance floor, where I put one hand on Luke's shoulder and my other hand rested gently in his. We swayed to the music until the sound of silverware clinking against the glasses interrupted our song.

"I do believe that is code for kiss," Luke said before leaning down to kiss me.

The crowd erupted in cheers, satisfied that we had fulfilled the obligation to present them with a kiss. "Today has been incredible," I said to Luke. "I am so excited to finally be Mrs. Teresa Miller!"

Luke pulled me closer to him. "Mrs. Teresa Miller has a ring to it. I could get used to hearing you called that. Have I told you lately that you look stunning in your dress?"

"Only a thousand times," I said to him.

"Well, you look stunning in your dress. Consider it a thousand and one times," he said to me.

The song ended, and we made our way back to our guests. This was the time during receptions when the bride and groom always got split up and had to talk to those in attendance. Even as I made my rounds, I found myself looking for Luke, to anchor myself in his presence.

Louise was standing off to the side, checking everything. Grabbing my purse, I took my chance to speak with her. "Everything is stunning, Louise. You really outdid yourself. You can't even tell that we are in the back party room of a family restaurant. I'm serious about you really needing to go into business doing this. You have an incredible gift."

Louise had a sparkle in her eye as she shared her plans with me. "I am considering it, but have even bigger plans of one day owning a venue to host ceremonies and receptions. The place I am considering is quite expensive, so I have been saving up as much as I can towards it."

Opening my purse, I grabbed an envelope and handed it to Louise. "Perhaps this can help a little."

Louise smiled shyly. "Thank you, Tess, you didn't have to do that."

"I know you said it was a gift for us, but we also wanted to give you a gift for all the hard work you did for us," I said.

"That is very kind of you both. Thank you," Louise replied.

"I'll let you get back to what you were doing and finish making my rounds. Please try to enjoy yourself. It is, after all, a party!" I encouraged Louise.

After leaving Louise, I made my way over to Melissa. "I just wanted to say thank you again for designing and making such a beautiful dress for me to wear. I'm so sorry you had to do the last minute alterations right before I walked down the aisle."

Melissa chuckled. "That was the funniest thing I think I've ever done. Everyone was honking as they drove by."

"I'm sure they didn't quite know what to think was going on when they saw us standing there like that," I joined her in laughter.

"You definitely make my dress look stunning. It suits you perfectly," she said sincerely.

"Melissa, you are really good at fashion design. How is your business coming along?" I asked her gently.

"It would be great if my mom would stay out of it," Melissa scoffed.

"Is it possible for you to get out from under her and do your own thing?" I asked, genuinely curious.

"Honestly, I am not sure. If I were to do that, I think I would have to start all over again with a whole new brand. It would involve a lot of work and money to do, but it would be worth it. Something to consider," she answered.

I reached into my purse and pulled out an envelope and handed it to her. "Well, perhaps this can help go towards starting your dream business."

"Oh, gosh, Tess, you didn't have to do that. I told you the dress was my gift to you," Melissa exclaimed.

"I know, but you went above and beyond the call of duty as my personal designer, and we wanted to give you a gift for helping make our day so special," I explained to her.

Melissa smiled at me, tears glistening in her eyes. "Thank you, Tess, honestly. I promise to put it towards my dream business."

Moving on to the next person, I made my way to where Lynn and Beth stood at the edge of the dance floor.

"Ladies, I hope you are having a lovely time," I said.

Beth reached out and hugged me. "The best of times. Thank you again for having us and for your generous love offering for David."

"We couldn't have gotten married without him," I assured her.

"Everything is stunning, Tess," Lynn said.

"Thank you, Lynn. I'm so glad you were able to make it. How are things going with you?" I asked.

"On target," she said cryptically. "Things with William are going extremely well despite the distance between us. If I had to guess, a big change is coming soon."

"I do hope that means you'll be joining us on the island soon enough," I encouraged her.

My favorite song began to play, and I scanned the room to find Luke. Our eyes locked, and we both began walking towards each other until we were out in the middle of the dance floor once again.

"Mrs. Miller, may I have this dance?" Luke asked as he held his hand out for mine.

"Of course, Mr. Miller." I replied as I joined him.

We swayed to the music, pausing only to kiss when the sound of silverware clinking against the glass returned. As the song ended, there was a sudden interruption as one game came to life. "Shoot your shot!" It called to us.

Luke dipped me backward and kissed me as the crowd cheered. After he lifted me back up, I grinned at him and said, "Now that's what I call a slam dunk!"

"How about we get out of here and make our way to the yacht? We have an early sendoff tomorrow morning for our honeymoon," Luke suggested.

"I am so excited to go up and down the coast for the next couple of weeks. I have always wanted to do that!" I said enthusiastically.

Luke smiled at me tenderly. "It will be perfect because we'll be together. I am really looking forward to it too."

"Did you remember to make the reservations for the slips we'll be docking in?" I asked Luke playfully.

"Nah, I figured we'd just show up and try to get in without reservations. How hard can it be to get a last minute reservation this time of year?" Luke joked with me.

"Life with you is going to be so much fun," I giggled.

Acknowledgements

Welcome to the Roadmap to Romance book series. Publishing this series has been a labor of love and a dream of mine for many years!

I am so very grateful for so many people who have supported and encouraged me along the way. Every time I write a new book, I seem to struggle with the exact words to express just how grateful I am, but I'll give it my best shot.

First and foremost, I want to express gratitude to Mike for always believing in me and being my biggest cheerleader. When I told you I had this idea for a seven book series, you immediately told me to go all in and make it happen. Part of me hoped you would have tried to talk me out of it—but looking back now, I'm so glad you didn't. That was the exact push I needed to stop dragging my feet and turn the impossible into possible. Mike, there are days I don't know how to express how much you mean to me, but I hope that in every story told, every knowing glance, and every pause in the kitchen wrapped up in your arms shows you how deep my love for you is. Marrying you on that island was nothing short of a dream come true. Thank you for being adventurous and going with me to scout potential locations to base my books on. The trips we've taken together have been incredibly fun, rejuvenating, inspiring, and best of all—they have drawn us closer to each other. *Our love story is my favorite.* Thank you for writing it with me. I love you, always and forever.

To my family, we are blessed. I don't say it enough, but I am so grateful for two parents who have been the greatest example of lasting love. Through good times and bad, the two of you have stood next to each other; unwavering, filled with love, and always moving forward together. Your love story has taught me what it takes to not only find lasting love, but to work hard to keep it going. Thank you for taking us all on family vacations where we had the freedom to be ourselves, ride bikes on the trails, and spend the afternoon in the lighthouse. That island became our second home because of the trips we took. Returning there with the whole family as adults was a full circle moment that I will cherish forever. Thank you for bringing joy and beauty to my life.

To Mike's family, thank you for your unwavering support and encouragement to keep writing. I am so grateful you were able to join Mike and me for our wedding on that island. The day was purely magical because of all the little touches you each put into it. I am so grateful for you all.

To Jamie, a big thank you for encouraging me to keep trying and not give up on this series. You have been a sounding board, an advisor, and the person to give me a fresh perspective when I needed it most. Thank you for allowing me to freely express myself when I am in your presence and still loving me when I am at my lowest.

To the girls—Carrie, Megan, and Tracy. Life is so much better with the three of you in it. Thank you for not thinking I'm crazy when I share with you my audacious ideas and dreams. Your encouragement and prayers keep me going. Thank you so much for being great supporters and keeping me laughing on days I'm stressed out about deadlines. I honestly don't know if I'd be where I am now without your support.

To Michelle, thank you for the weekly check-ins. They keep me grounded and focused, while also providing the exact level of encouragement I seem to need. Thank you for sharing from your heart and showing me it's okay to be vulnerable and real in the fiction we write. It has helped me create characters with more depth, feelings, and spiritual transformation. I am grateful for our friendship.

To Tami, my coach and friend. The spiritual growth you've helped me achieve is nothing short of a miracle. God brought us together, and for that—I'll be eternally grateful. Your spiritual guidance helps me look at the bigger picture, get out of my own way, and listen to what God is saying. You helped me find a way to be obedient to Him in all that I do, including my fictional writings. Thank you for praying for me, encouraging me—and not just listening to me, but actually hearing what I was saying. I'm so grateful for you, my friend.

To Niki, my editor and friend. Honestly, this book wouldn't be where it is without you. You are truly gifted as an editor, and I am so grateful for the hard work and help you put into making this book ready for publishing. Working with you is always insightful as I learn from you and see the Spirit leading. Your approach to editing is one that is in perfect alignment with me and my writing, and I am so grateful for your approach. Thank you for all the work you did and for your friendship, encouragement, grace, and support.

To all my friends, life would be oh-so-lonely without you in it. So many of you have played a major part in it, and while I wish I could shout you all out, please know you are on my heart right now as I am typing this.

A big thanks to the island and its residents for providing a safe place to grow up. Though this book takes place on a fictional island, I drew inspiration from a beautiful island that gave me a lifetime of memories there that will live within my heart for the rest of my life.

This book began on that island in 1994 when I was 16 and scribbled in my journal—*what if one day I wrote a story about love on this island? One with three brothers the same age as us?* All it takes is an idea for a story to get started. Finding that note in my journal in 2019 has turned out to be the best reminder of a goal I once had.

And to Jesus, to whom all things are possible. You have gifted me with an imagination that carries me to new heights. Thank you for helping me through the writing process by reminding me how capable I am. When I first said I was going to write romance books, I didn't know how I could do it and honor you in the stories. You showed me the way. I'll always be grateful for the blessings in life you've given me.

Shonda Ramsey is a friend, encourager, and leader. She has published two Christian Non-Fiction books: *Authentically Anchored*, and *Braver with Belief.* With a desire to teach, she published four Boldly Woven devotional magazines, an *Authentically Anchored Companion Workbook*, and a *Called to Serve* guided journal. Shonda is now publishing her seven book clean and wholesome romance series, *Roadmap to Romance.* Inspired by road trips and real-life experiences, this series invites readers to slow down and enjoy the ride.

As a multi-passionate entrepreneur and Christian author, after overcoming personal struggles, she discovered her passion for helping women fulfill their calling to create. Besides her writing, Shonda offers graphic design services for authors and entrepreneurs, specializing in book covers, branding, and book formatting. She also offers coaching, consulting, courses, resources, and workshops for the faith-driven woman who creates—whether that's a book, brand, product line, or all three.

Shonda lives in Ohio with her husband, Mike, and their Yorkie, Coco. When she's not writing, you'll likely find her lost in a creative project, camping with her husband, laughing with friends, or dancing in the rain.

Her goal is to write books that resonate deeply with her readers by covering real and challenging topics while ending on a positive and hopeful note through a deepening of faith. Through her writing and design work, she aims to inspire faith, authenticity, strength, and the courage to be one's true self.

Shonda encourages you to connect with her at
www.shondaramsey.com.